ANDROS

DRAWS THE LINE

Bruce Edwards

Lean
Press

Portland, Oregon

Editor: Michael Ryder, Portland, Oregon
Cover design and interior artwork: Nicole Schnell,
    Schnell Creative Group, LLC
Original cover art: Peter X O'Brien
Composition and page design: William H. Brunson,
    Typography Services, Portland, Oregon

ISBN: 1-932475-01-X

This Lean Press quality paperback was printed by
    Malloy Lithographers, U.S.A.

Lean Press
www.leanpress.com
1-503-708-4415

05 04 03   1 2 3

This is a work of fiction. Any similarity to actual persons, living or dead, or to actual events, is purely coincidental.

Midnight
at the Majestic

ONE

SEATTLE GREW FROM TOWN TO CITY in the mid-1960s, after people from the world over flocked to the World's Fair and discovered that there were a few good days between the rainy ones, and that those good days were more than good. They were glorious.

Aside from boosting the population and the economy, the World's Fair left behind a permanent civic center that still functions as part of the core of Seattle's cultural life. The Seattle Center, where the actual fair took place, remains on the north edge of the downtown center of office and government buildings, department stores, and hotels. The Space Needle, an elevated monorail, (constructed to bring the people to and from the fair), an opera house, a science museum, and a playhouse, were among the permanent bequests to the city from the event.

Despite the growth spurt and cultural benefits that the World's Fair gave to the city it was a while before the city could support big time professional sports. But it wasn't long before sports caught up with culture. In 1976 the Kingdome was completed and the Seahawks kicked off professional football. When the Mariners started playing there in 1977, Seattle had arrived.

The Kingdome's impact on its surrounding area was nowhere near as dramatic as the Seattle Center's. Built on the south end of the downtown area, it spurred a renovation of the historic business district of Pioneer Square adjacent to the dome. But the sprawling and venerable light industrial area south of the dome was largely uninfluenced by Seattle's metropolitization. There, large trucks were repaired; furniture, carpeting, and building products were wholesaled; and all sorts of jobbers, wholesalers, importers, exporters, and commercial middlemen hung their hats and warehoused the small inventories they liked to keep on hand or, for some reason, couldn't move.

And even after two years of baseball and three years of football there were only a few places to spend the night around the Kingdome. If you came in from out of town to see a game or attend a cultural event, you stayed in one of the new or remodeled hotels in the central business district. The Majestic Motel, built before the Kingdome was a glitter in the City Fathers' eyes, was the exception. Located three blocks south of the Kingdome and a block east, built on a whole city block when land was available for such extravagances, the two-story building was surrounded by surface parking. Its large red neon sign on the roof could be seen from the freeway to the east. But pity the poor unwitting traveler who saw that sign and had to figure out at freeway speed what exit to take, and then how the hell to get there.

With two stories on both its east and west wings, the Majestic Motel needed that parking lot. The rooms of the lower floors of each wing had sliding glass doors that opened right onto the parking stalls, providing easy access for the tired traveler who could load and unload without having to use the interior hallway. For other more wary transients, the sliding glass door provided the means for a quick exit.

In one such room on the ground floor of the west wing, on the alley side, Irene "Reeney" Johnson had her reasons to be comforted by the sliding glass door. Reeney never liked to be crowded and she liked to be ready for anything. That evening, to ready herself for the evening's festivities, her lithe, tawny body lay naked on the floor of the motel room. She had been stretching and exercising for about a half-hour as she waited for the evening to begin. Her white dressing gown was under her, protecting her back from the grimy rug. She put her arms over her head and stretched, extending from her toes to her fingers.

3

Then she pulled up her knees while drawing up her arms, slowly pivoting at her waist. When her elbows reached her knees, she slowly moved back to the full stretch position. Her light brown skin was moist with perspiration.

A soft knock at the hallway door.

"Yes?" she called. "Be right there."

She picked up the gown off the floor and slipped it on smoothly.

"Who is it?" she said in a friendly voice.

"Tangerine, honey?" A deep voice, speaking close to the door.

As Irene turned the doorknob, the door exploded open, knocking her to the floor.

Quickly she was on her feet, moving away from a husky black man as he pushed into the room, but her dressing gown encumbered her movements.

The man deliberately closed the door behind him. She watched him, catlike and wary. He wore a beige velveteen shirt with matching pants. A white velvet cap with a purple flower-patterned edge was cocked jauntily just above his left eyebrow. Something was terribly wrong. This was not some john sent to her motel room by Terry.

He stepped suddenly toward her, and she kicked out at his crotch—a mistake. Lightning-quick, he clutched her foot and twisted upwards. She went down again. She tried to crawl toward a large purse lying on the bed. The man knelt on top of her, one knee across the top of her body. He got a firm hold on her right wrist. He squeezed hard and at the same time got to his feet, yanking her up and pulling her towards him.

With her right arm behind her, he moved to a half nelson on her right arm. She was now fully restrained. She stopped struggling.

"Good, good, that's real good," he said quietly into her ear.

She relaxed at his soft words. "What you want coming in here like that? You scare me, honey," she said.

"Let me jes look at you, mama. You really some woman."

4

As his grip loosened she turned to him, staying close to his body. She looked up at him challengingly, her dark eyes wide. Her black hair fell softly over the satin robe.

He appeared to relax. He put his left hand on her shoulder, drawing her to him. She yielded and put her left arm around him. He moved his left hand gently behind her neck and tilted her head toward him. Then he struck the flat of his open right palm against her mouth. He held onto her neck with his left hand and struck again. There was no sound except the claps of his hand and a guttural escape of air from the woman as if she were trying to release the pain.

She did not struggle, but defiance sharpened her eyes, as if she were searching for an opening to strike back at her tormentor. He allowed her no opening. He dragged her into the bathroom, took a towel, and ran cold water over it. He took her back into the room and handed her the towel.

"Here now, Tangerine-baby. I think you gonna have a sore mouth. That's too bad. I could start with your eyes next. You could be out of business for a long time."

She held the cold, wet towel to her mouth. Her eyes stared at him with a cold, hard fury.

"Now, I'm thinking the next thing I'm gonna do is go find me some more ass and jes put them out a business too," he said affably.

He stroked her straight black hair and spoke softly. "See, mama. You're workin' my ground. You ain't hurtin' me none, but what if I let every grab-ass hooker on the West Coast come up here and move in? *Could* hurt me.

"So now you jes listen," he said. "Get your outfit outta here. Tonight. Now. I'm leaving, but if I have to come back I'm bringing some people with me. Bad people. Whew, and I mean bad."

He jerked her hair. "Unnerstan' me?"

She said nothing, her dark eyes watching over the top of the towel she still held to her mouth. He pulled away the towel to observe his handiwork. She flinched.

5

"You can still work, mama. It'll hurt a little, but you can work. Only some place else. If all you ain't outta here in two hours, you're gonna see me again. Only next time, you people are gonna be hurt. Unnerstan' what I'm talkin' about? Really hurt."

Swiftly he released her and was out the door, closing it quietly behind him.

He turned and jogged down the hall, checking his watch. 9:20. He walked quickly across the mist-moistened parking lot to a white Cadillac convertible. The red leather seats glistened against the floor light as he opened the door. He started the car and flashed the headlights three times. Then he drove quickly out of the parking lot.

Three men nestled low in a 1970 Oldsmobile across the street watched him leave. They were drinking coffee and the driver had to wipe away the steam from the window to view the parking lot.

"Everything's OK. Beaman's done his part," said the driver. "You gonna be ready when old Whitey shows up, Sammy?"

"I guess," said the young man in the back seat. His hair was long at the sides, down to his neck, and parted in the middle. He wore a light blue golf shirt inside his jacket. He looked young, naive, and scared.

"Just relax, Sammy," said the man in the passenger seat. "We'll be with you when the time comes. If it screws up, it screws up. One time on a drug raid we had Foster here dressed up like a pizza deliveryman. Instead of opening the door, the guy opened a front window. And there was Foster here, getting directions where he's supposed to deliver some goddamn pizza. We had to go back and break down the door. Time we got in, the house was clean as a whistle. Hell, it either goes or it doesn't. We get paid the same."

"Nobody ever let me forget that bust, Sarge!" Foster mumbled. "Everybody calling me pizza boy, telling me just exactly where to deliver that friggin' pizza."

They sat silently for a while.

A purple Dodge van with a shiny metallic finish and one-way circular windows in the cargo area pulled into the parking lot.

"Here he comes now. Come on to mama, Whitey," said the sergeant.

The van pulled up to the curb at the loading zone near the motel's west wing. A slim young man with remarkably white dyed hair wearing a black shirt and pants and a gray sport coat got out of the van and ran into the building.

The men in the Oldsmobile got out without speaking. Sammy walked toward the outside entrance of the west wing. Foster trotted around the west end of the building to cover the sliding glass doors on the north side of the rooms. The sergeant walked into the motel through the lobby. A white Ford LTD with two other men and a woman drove into the parking lot and parked near the west wing. A patrol car pulled in behind it.

Sammy went ahead by himself and found Room 114. He stood for a moment outside the door. He could hear low, excited voices inside the room. He knocked softly.

The voices stopped.

"Yes?" he heard a feminine voice say.

"I'm looking for Tangerine," he said.

"Tangerine ain't here now," the voice said. "Go 'way."

"Hey, lady," he said loudly, his words slightly slurred. "Don't give me no shit. This is Room 114. I want Tangerine. I need Tangerine. I mean I ne-ee-eed Tangerine."

The door opened quickly. The man in the black shirt and gray sport jacket stood there. He had a Nordic mien, with high cheekbones and a muscular frame. His ash white hair was carefully styled. He grinned at Sammy.

"Hey, man, settle down," he said.

"You here, too? Looks like you beat me. You told me you been once tonight already."

"Yeah, yeah. I'm a real tomcat. Look it. I got old Tangerine here myself. Come on down the hall here," he said quietly.

He took Sammy by the arm and pulled him to the room next door. He knocked softly.

"Margie? It's me. Got a friend for you."

A female voice came from the other side of the door. "I got somebody, Terry."

"Oops, sorry." He grinned at Sammy. "Busy night, huh? That's ok. Come on, sailor. I'll get a room for you."

He led Sammy out of 114 and down the hall to Room 118. He knocked lightly.

"Shirley?"

The door opened. A blonde haired girl in blue jeans and a halter sweater stood in the door. She exposed a lean, muscular belly above the jeans and below her halter.

"Hi, Terry," she said. "Whatcha doing here?"

"Hey, Shirley. I was just helping my friend get a date. You available?"

She smiled. "You know it."

She took Sammy by the arm and led him into the room.

"See you, sailor," Terry said, closing the door.

The radio was playing a soft rock beat. The woman moved with the music. Her bare feet darted quickly on the beige carpet.

"Boy, that Terry. He knows all you girls."

"Mmm," she groaned softly.

It was no use to try to get anything out of her. She was high.

He moved stiffly, trying to dance with her, but her energy was frenetic.

She reached out and pulled him to her, her body slowing down but still moving. "Terry called you sailor" she said. "Are you a sailor-boy? I love sailor-boys."

"Yeah. I just got in."

She reached around him and stroked his buttocks. "I'll just bet you're ready for li'l Shirley. Ain't you, sailor-boy?"

She patted the billfold in his back pocket and pulled it out.

"Let's see what you got here, sailor-boy. For two hundred dollars I'll drive you crazy tonight."

Sammy jerked the billfold out of her hands. "Two hundred dollars? I ain't got that much."

She started dancing again, her head back. "Geez, I hate money hassles. Why don't you just tell me what you've got and I'll decide what we do?"

"I got twenty dollars," he said.

Her eyes flashed momentarily out of her torpor. She stopped dancing. "Listen. What is this? You don't even get inside that door for less than a hundred."

"Who says?"

"I says. Terry says. Reeney says. Don't you know nothin'?"

"Terry? You mean that guy who just opened the door?"

She nodded, her hands on her hips.

"What's he got to do with it?"

"Boy, are you out of it. Show me your wallet," she said. She reached to pull it back from him.

He hesitated.

"Come on. We're getting no where."

He released it.

"Look here," she said. "Eighty-five-six, seven, eight, nine. You're holding out on Miss Shirley, sailor-boy."

She smiled and hugged him. She stood back and removed the four marked twenties from his billfold. She gave the billfold back to him and put the money in the pocket of her jeans.

"What's Terry gonna say if you don't come up with a hundred? I'm sorry, Shirley, you saw it's all I got."

No reply. She started dancing again, her arms around him. She reached around in front of him and pulled his shirt out of his pants. She put her hand up underneath his shirt and began rubbing his stomach and chest.

"Oh," he moaned, moving with her hand.

"You're ready, aren't you, darlin'," she whispered.

"Uh huh," he said. "What are we gonna do?"

She pulled his ear to her lips and licked inside his ear. "I'm gonna fuck your brains out," she whispered.

Sammy tensed. "That would really be nice, ma'am, but later. Right now you're under arrest."

The girl stopped. "You kidding me?"

Sammy turned on his cop voice. "No ma'am. I want to advise you that I am a police officer and that I'm arresting you for prostitution. Just stay where you are. Keep listening to the music and dancing. I'll consider any resistance on your part to be obstruction of a public officer."

Sammy kept his eyes on her. She seemed hypnotized by him. He backed to the door and opened it quietly. Then he knocked loudly on the door and called out, "Room Service."

From the far corner of the hall came the sergeant and another man. The sergeant walked quickly down the hall to Sammy.

"Our boy is in 114," Sammy said. "They've got at least three of the rooms on this side of the hall."

At the other end of the hall three men and a woman appeared. One of the men was in police uniform.

"Jamieson, stay there. Price, go to the other end of the hall. You two come here," the sergeant said quietly.

The man and the woman joined Sammy and the sarge outside Room 118.

"Where's the money?" asked the sergeant.

"She put it in her jeans," Sammy said.

The Sergeant walked over to the woman and felt the pocket of her jeans. He removed the small roll of twenties from her right front pocket. He checked the numbers on one of the bills.

"Gimme cuffs," said the sergeant.

One of the men at the door walked into the room and handed him a set of cuffs. The sergeant kept his eyes on the girl.

She watched him put the cuffs on her in a detached way, as if her hands belonged to someone else. As they closed, the metallic snap woke her.

"Rape!" she yelled suddenly. "My God! Rape! Help me! Rape!"

The sergeant turned to the female officer. "Stay with her, Ryan. Come on, Sammy, let's hit 114 first. Come on, come on, come on," he said to the others.

The two men started down the hall. At the end of the hall, they saw Terry and Tangerine break from Room 114 and sprint toward the exit away from Sergeant Gordon and Sammy. Just outside, the uniformed police officer, a large man with a pronounced double chin, blocked their escape. Terry hunched his body low and tried to run into the officer's midsection with his shoulder. The officer side stepped and Terry went down. He tried to roll away, but the officer was on him, connecting with a rabbit punch to Terry's kidneys. Sammy sprinted around the fracas and caught up with Reeney and tackled her. Her large purse slipped from her grasp and fell to the ground.

Sergeant Gordon caught up. "Cuff them and put them in different cars. Did that man assault you, Price?" he asked of the uniformed officer.

The hefty officer lifted Terry to his feet by jerking up the cruelly tight cuffs. "Naw, sarge. He's just a little playful. I think we've reached an understanding."

Just then, Foster appeared and motioned to the sergeant. "You better come in here, Sarge."

The sergeant followed Foster to the door of Room 116. Sammy followed and peered inside over the sergeant's shoulder. The sliding door in the back of the room was open. A man stood in the middle of the room, shirt unbuttoned, holding a suit coat. He was in his late forties, dark-haired with flecks of gray at the temples. A young-looking girl, wearing a flimsy red dress, sat on the bed.

"I stopped him as he was going out the sliding glass door," Foster said, pointing at the man in the business suit.

The sergeant and the man looked at each other wordlessly. Finally, the man broke the tense silence.

"I suggest, Sergeant Gordon, that you don't ruin what might be an otherwise good bust by making an unlawful arrest," he said.

"Am I thinking of busting somebody here, sir? Why would I do that?" the sergeant asked.

"I don't know what you're thinking about doing. I was leaving through that glass door and this man stopped me. Unless you intend to arrest me, I shall leave through that door."

The sergeant looked toward the silent girl. "Is this guy a friend of yours, honey?"

The girl was silent.

"What were you doing in here with this man, honey?"

No answer.

The man smiled. "I'm leaving now. You know where you can reach me."

The man turned and walked slowly through the open sliding glass door. Foster glanced at the sergeant. Gordon shook his head silently.

"Whatever you say, sir," the sergeant called after the man. Suddenly, he ran to the door and called after the man. "Our report should make interesting reading for your deputies, sir. Who's gonna make the charging decisions?"

No answer. He turned to Foster. "Stay with her," he said. The sergeant went into the hall with Sammy.

"OK, we'll talk to the kid and see what we can get out of her. I'll get Ryan to drive her. She can make a deaf mute sing."

"What's this all about, Sarge? Who was that guy?" asked Sammy.

The sergeant laughed. "Shame on you, Sammy. Don't you recognize your superior officer? That man is Sherman Falkes. He's your duly elected prosecuting attorney, King County's chief law enforcement officer."

Jane's elegant seat

TWO

A BEAUTIFUL PUGET SOUND SATURDAY AFTERNOON, and Paul Andros was spending it mucking out manure from the horse barn. The light rain that had fallen the previous evening had dried up quickly, and now the air was stifling in the empty horse stalls. Dust clung to his sweat and swirled in the shafts of sunlight as he shoveled dung and old straw into a wheelbarrow.

His daughter, Beatrice, was in charge of cleaning up after the two horses, but she was at summer camp. Andros was taking advantage of her absence to give the barn a real cleaning, rather than her usual lick and a promise and out the door. The truth was he relished the opportunity to work on his property. He enjoyed using muscles other than those he normally used for sitting in conferences or shuffling papers at his desk. He was absorbed in creating order out of the dirty shambles left by the two healthy animals and a well-intentioned but slapdash eleven-year-old. This work yielded the kind of satisfaction Andros could never get out of dealing with the legal messes his clients made of their business and personal lives.

"Paul!" His wife Jane called out to let him know she was back from her early afternoon ride. From the barn door he watched her leading Candy into the corral. Although he did not really care for horses, Jane and Beatrice loved them. Both rode almost daily along the Seattle water transmission line right-of-way that bordered their farm. Over the years it had become one of King County's unofficial bridle paths.

A few minutes later Jane came in the barn to put away her saddle and pick up the grooming brush.

"Hey. You've made a lot of progress," she said. "My God, look at you! Where did you get that outfit?"

Andros looked down at his impromptu barn-cleaning clothes: gabardine pants from a discarded business suit and a white dress shirt, sleeves rolled up above his elbows.

"Whatta you mean?"

Andros was a medium-sized man. Well-coordinated, but developing the slight paunch of an out-of-condition athlete. His complexion was olive, and his thick black hair and brown eyes further evidenced his Greek ancestry. Even shoveling horse manure on a hot Saturday afternoon, he attacked the task with his characteristic intensity.

"Nothing. I guess it's alright to clean out a barn in your business suit."

Jane Andros, tall, rangy, with thin and straight dishwater blonde hair, wore a pair of bleached jeans and a baggy T-shirt with the faded graphics of a recent Bumbershoot Festival. A Mariner's ball cap kept her hair from falling in her eyes.

"Anytime you want to lend a hand is OK by me," Paul said.

"First gotta rub down Candy."

"How was the ride?" Paul asked, imagining Jane's elegant seat—military-erect at canter, and forward leaning at a gallop, as if whispering encouragement in the horse's ear.

"It was great. Marvin sends you his regards," she said sweetly. Marvin was a neighbor who frequently happened to be riding on the right-of-way when Jane came by.

"Marvin!" Andros grunted to himself.

"What, dear?" said Jane.

"I'm glad you had a nice ride."

"Thank you, Paul."

A bell on the south wall sounded. The telephone was rigged to ring in the barn, but there was no instrument there.

Paul nodded toward the house. "Would you answer that? If it's for me, I'll call back."

Jane hurried from the barn.

Paul carefully loaded every scrap of manure and shred of straw into the wheelbarrow to take to his fertilizer pile. He was methodically cutting out the thickets of alder around his property and creating a border of fruit trees: prune, plum, pear, apple, cherry, and peach. One day he planned to start making an acceptable fruit wine from his own orchard.

He had emptied the wheelbarrow and was returning to the barn when Jane called to him from the door. "It's Dad. He says you'd better come to the phone. Now."

Jane never questioned her father's requests. Paul always wondered whether she had been as respectful of her father as a child as she now was as an adult. It seemed to Paul that she viewed her father as akin to an extraterrestrial: remote, incomprehensible. Andros—who worked with him every day—saw his feet of clay. H. Scott Turnbull was charming, a formidable and brilliant attorney, but in the end a mere man after all, unpredictable, equivocal, and, most appalling in Andros' eyes, unorganized. Paul did not leap to respond to Scott's patriarchal demands.

He pushed the wheelbarrow outside the barn door. Jane remained, watching. He would return that evening to water down and sweep the barn floor. Tomorrow he would take the ripened manure from the pile and disburse nourishment to his hungry young trees.

Mona, Beatrice's filly, who was in foal, strolled lazily to the side of the corral where he was parking the wheelbarrow.

"She'll be back soon, girl." Andros told the horse as he walked unhurriedly to the house. He resented his father-in-law's intrusion on his home life. Their lovely old farmhouse on twenty-five acres meant more to him each passing year. But his early rising and late-to-come-home work habits kept him from enjoying what he and Jane had worked hard for.

He took his rubber boots off in the mudroom, went into the kitchen in his stocking feet. He could feel the texture of the gray slate floor as he padded over to the white wall phone by the breakfast booth.

"Yes, Scott. Still there?" he asked.

Instead of the burst of carefully enunciated, agitated profanity Paul expected, H. Scott Turnbull's voice was low and patient. "Paul," he paused. "We have a matter here that we've decided you may be the only man to handle."

Paul was immediately alert to Scott's bedside manner: the confident tone that meant the client was within hearing—and jumpy.

"What is it, Scott? Can't it wait 'til Monday?"

"Paul. I'm sorry to have to tell you this. Sherm Falkes is dead."

"Sherm? Can't be. My God, I just ran into him last Friday at lunch."

"No, it's true. He killed himself early this morning. Seattle police were raiding a whorehouse operation and caught him in bed with some underage bimbo. It looks like he couldn't face the scandal."

Paul sat down on the thin cushion that fit over the bench seat against the wall. The kitchen area had paneled windows on two walls to let in the brief winter light from the southwest. In the summer, it heated up unbearably. Paul slowly lowered the blinds over the breakfast booth as he absorbed the news.

"How did he do it?" he asked.

"Drove his car around a dead-end street barricade on the west side of Queen Anne. The car flew off an embankment, fell forty, fifty feet, and caught fire."

"Are they sure it's him?"

"Yes. It was his car, and they were able to check dental X-rays almost immediately."

Paul sat quietly absorbing the shock. "Thank you for letting me know," he said. "Glad I didn't hear it on TV."

"Don't hang up, Paul. We've got a problem here. Life has to go on. I'm down at the County Administration Building with Jim Ferranti and Elizabeth Newgate from the county council. We're discussing an interim successor to Sherm. The county council appoints the prosecutor until the next election. With a scandal and violent death to account for, plus other issues the county is currently facing, the choice has got to be very carefully made."

Andros looked out the window across the driveway to the corral. He could see Jane leading Candy to the shady overhang area between the barn and the corral where the horses were saddled, unsaddled, and groomed.

"What the hell are you doing down there with Jim Ferranti and Liz Newgate?"

"Axel Foreman asked me to come down and meet with the executive and a representative of the council."

Andros immediately grasped the connection. Axel, a long-time county Democrat, thought of himself as a kingmaker. His and Scott's paths had crossed over numerous public issues. The county council had a Democratic majority led by Mrs. Newgate, while Jim Ferranti, the county executive, was Republican. The council had to make a careful choice, one that Ferranti would not necessarily applaud but would not fight.

Scott continued, "I've suggested that an acceptable compromise would be someone apolitical. Someone who would agree not to run at the next election. By then some young Hessian, or Hessianess, will turn up from one side or the other who wants the goddamn job."

Paul collected himself. "Am I the acceptable compromise, Scott?"

"Your name came up and, although I don't want you away from the office for three or four months, I couldn't think of any one else."

Paul did not respond. Instead, he rearranged the napkin holder and salt-and-pepper shakers on the breakfast table. He tried to focus in his mind's eye on the craggy face of his father-in-law.

"Scott, let's think about this. We've been together six years now since I left the prosecutor's office," Paul started. "I'm running the office because you wanted out of the logistics. We now have six attorneys in the office, five secretaries with central word processing, a receptionist, a part-time bookkeeper. We have probably the worst possible law office size, but we're making it work and we're making money. Now you want me to abandon the office, my own caseload, and the private clientele I've built up to go play prosecutor for the rest of this year? Why should I do that? Why do you want to do that to us? We're partners. Remember? I don't think it's a good partnership decision."

Andros frequently had to remind Scott that they were partners. Scott let Paul manage the day-to-day matters, then frequently decided to do something or spend money without consulting Paul.

"Paul. You will be only an acting prosecuting attorney. And I'll take over your private cases."

"You'll take my caseload? What are you? Two people? You got no cases of your own? We'll have to bring in somebody or ship stuff out. Lose clients. And what about the job itself? I'd be playing a daily game of "Meet the Press" with reporters who will be screaming for background on whatever Sherm Falkes was up to. By the way, what the hell was he up to?"

"All we know is that Seattle PD raided a prostitution operation at the Majestic Motel south of the Kingdome and caught Sherm in a room with a fifteen-year-old girl who appeared to be part of the operation."

"Swell. In my spare time, I'll be trying to establish a semblance of respect from over two thousand sneering Seattle cops and all the other cops all over King County who by now have collectively concluded that corruption is running rampant in the prosecutor's office."

Paul paused for Scott to respond. Scott kept pointedly silent. Paul spoke. "So you guys concluded that I might be a logical choice from the prosecutors' alumni club? Avoid a credibility gap with the present prosecutor's staff by appointing an outsider?"

"That's the conclusion we came to," Scott answered.

"Why me? There are dozens of other suitable choices." Paul hated spur-of-the-moment decisions.

"Paul," Scott said. "I'm glad that you've decided. It's important to get the Falkes matter behind us."

Andros choked with anger at his partner and father-in-law's presumption that he could make commitments on Paul's behalf. Finally, he regained enough control to reply. "I suppose you've got everything worked out, asshole."

Scott answered precisely. While he left the formulation of details to Paul or his other associates, negotiations were H. Scott Turnbull's forte.

"Due to your limited tenure, it is understood that you will still consult on your private practice matters, but I will be handling them. We will withdraw from any potential conflict situations. You will have complete authority over the prosecutor's office, of course. And an upfront agreement to assign whoever you designate to investigate the Sherm Falkes matter with whatever emergency budget appropriation you need."

That was that. Scott was telling him that he had made the commitment and neither of them could back out. Scott being not only his partner, but family, Paul had to accept Scott's decision.

"That's a start," Paul said coldly. "I'll think about it over the weekend and see if I've got anything else going on. Listen, I've got to talk to Liz."

Paul knew Liz Newgate from his time as chief deputy prosecutor under Sherm Falkes. She had been a legislative and budget ally of the prosecutor's office. They had kept in contact after he left the office.

"By all means," said Scott, relieved to escape Paul's frosty tone. He moved the phone to the table, sat, dialed Newgate's number. Turning his back to Paul, he spoke briefly in a low voice, then passed the receiver to Paul.

"Hello, Paul. Liz Newgate here. I want to say that, if you accept, I will appreciate your personal sacrifice in taking on this mess. I'm sure the other council members will agree to appoint you."

Paul sighed. "If you come up with another candidate, I'd be just as glad if you forgot about me. But I can see that an outsider makes sense. Is Monday a council meeting day?"

"Yes. Every weekday's a meeting day from eight a.m. to eleven p.m."

"Ok. I'll be there at eight on Monday. I want the formalities over before the prosecutor's staff comes in at nine o'clock. I don't know all the other council members, so if you want to give them my number after you talk to them, I'll be glad to speak with them personally. But we shouldn't have any weekend meeting of more than two of them without notice to the press."

"I understand, Paul. I suspect they'll be glad to avoid this problem altogether."

"Besides," Paul said, "if the Republicans want to make a partisan fuss, you've got a Democrat majority to do what you want anyway. Since Sherm was a Republican, you could make it look like the Republicans were trying to cover up the Sherm Falkes scandal. Something like that."

"Paul, I never thought of that. You know how we try to avoid partisan politics on the King County council."

Paul laughed. "That's reassuring, Liz. I'm going to have a full plate in the prosecutor's office and I want to stay out of fun and games on your side of the street.

"I should say something to Jim Ferranti before I hang up, shouldn't I ?" he said abruptly.

"That's correct, Paul" she said.

"Ok, let me talk to him."

"Again, I want you to know I appreciate this Paul," she said. "Jim, he wants to talk to you."

After a brief delay a deep voice said, "Hello, Paul. This is Jim Ferranti. I think we've met before."

They had met, but only briefly. "Certainly have, Jim. I think Herb McAuliffe is Sherm's head of civil?"

"Yes," said Jim.

Paul knew that Herb was very much in Jim's camp and Jim would not want any change in how the prosecutor's office dealt with the county's bureaucracy.

"Well, Jim, if I'm appointed of course I'll have full authority, but I want you to know I would not plan any changes in civil, even though it was my pet when I was chief deputy."

"Good. Good, Paul. It appears that Sherm may have had some sort of tragic breakdown, and we need to do whatever we can to restore confidence in law and order."

Paul inwardly winced. So the party line on Sherm Falkes was going to be "tragic breakdown."

"Well, I certainly agree that restoring confidence will be one of our challenges."

"The executive's office will do what we can to help, Paul."

Yeah, thought Andros, until we need a budget increase or some support to settle a lawsuit.

"I think Scott wants to talk to you," Ferranti concluded.

"Yeah, Paul," Scott said. "I'll be by later to talk about the office."

"Make it tomorrow. Jane and I are going out tonight."

"Ok. I'll come by about noon for brunch."

"All right. But you can do one other thing while you're being the great Mr. Fix-it. I don't want the governor or the attorney general getting into this, but I'd like some outside investigative help. Use your contacts and call the governor. Ask him if he can free up Einar Torgeson in the Human Rights Commission for a few weeks."

"Your old nemesis."

"Yeah. This time I'll have him on my side."

Paul hung up.

Jane. Where was she? She had not come in while he was talking. Scott must have told her about Sherm's death before she came to get him. He wondered if Scott had mentioned that he was negotiating Paul's appointment as interim prosecutor.

He went over to the kitchen sink for a drink of water. It wasn't fair, him being dragged into this mess, he thought, but where did it say it'd be fair? It was certainly not a good business decision. He would insist on keeping his partnership status with Scott. That way Scott would share in the difference between his partnership income and the lesser amount of his temporary prosecutor's salary. He doubted that in all his wheeling and dealing Scott had thought of that.

He started to make some notes for Monday, but decided it could wait. First, a talk with Jane.

He went back outside to the barn. Jane was still inside hosing down the floor. She shut off the hose and watched him approach her.

"Scott told you about Sherm Falkes, didn't he?"

"Yes," she said, noncommittally. Jane's manner was slightly awkward and hesitant, but she was perceptive, and capable at everything she did. She and Paul had met when Paul was a law student. Paul was a close friend of Jane's older brother, Tom, who had gone into securities law after graduating and now lived and practiced in New York, probably, Paul always believed, because he could not stand living and working in the same town with his overbearing father.

"I've been thinking about it. What do you think happened with Sherm—I mean the girl . . . the hotel room?" she asked.

"I don't know. The hotel thing surprises me, really. It surprises me more than his death . . ."

"It's ok to die, but don't do anything kinky!"

Paul was surprised at her ironic tone. "Are you upset by Sherm's death? You never seemed to care for him."

"You know I avoided Sherm Falkes like a plague. His ex-wife even more so. Carol? Was that her name?"

"Yeah."

"It's just that I'm overwhelmed that someone we know did anything as human as to have sex with a prostitute. It's like I see Sherm in a new light. And why a prostitute? I thought he and

Carol got divorced because he was bedding down every other woman in Seattle."

"I didn't keep track of his girlfriends. But, you know, he never chased any of the women at the office. He said he learned his lesson about that before he got into law."

"Was he ever not a lawyer?"

"Oh yeah. He went into advertising during and after college. In San Francisco. He was an account executive and everything. But he left the firm after one of his office girlfriends married the boss and got his ass kicked out."

"Vengeance is mine."

"So sayeth. Yes. That's how he got up here. Got headhunted to be advertising manager for Pancroft-Wilby down in Auburn."

"The truck firm?"

"Yeah. He went to law school while he was working there. And then moved to the prosecutor's office after he graduated and passed the bar. Never left. He'd been there several years before I came."

"He was so . . . social. He and Carol were always at some play or art gallery opening."

"I always thought of him as the society page prosecutor. And with his advertising background he could walk the walk and talk the talk with the art crowd. He met Carol in his ad-manager days. She was in the art department of one of the agencies and then went to work for Norbusch. The talk at the office was that she made as much money as he did."

"What motivated him? Politics?"

"Yeah, I think so. Got the bug. That, and I think he liked being in a position where he could use his professional spin background with a bunch of amateurs. The rest of us were dufusses when it came to dealing with the press and public relations. When there was a problem in the office, old Bascom would trot down the hall and talk to Sherm. Pretty soon Sherm was the guy the press talked to. Sherm loved that shit. He'd talk about a case somebody else tried as if he won it. But I for one was always glad to let him do his thing."

"He always looked and sounded good," Jane agreed. "I wonder why he couldn't make the prosecutor being caught with a prostitute sound good?"

"Maybe he ran out of ideas."

"Does . . . does dad want you to get involved?"

"He signed me up without even consulting me. They needed an outsider, but someone who knows the ropes. Prosecutors alumni club . . . All that."

"Why did you ever leave, Paul? Didn't you hate going from chief civil deputy to flunky for my father?"

"Not really. Scott had a lot to teach me and I had a lot to learn about his world. Still do."

"What is his world? Little old ladies with more money than they know what to do with? Dealmaking? Political fundraising?"

"What is this? Are we fighting here? Maybe you could let me know what it's all about."

"I'm sorry. Better not say anything now. I'm going in and take a shower."

Andros' mind raced. He returned to the barn, methodically finished the washdown, and put away the tools. Then he headed to the house. He was seated at the kitchen table making notes when Jane came in wearing her bathrobe. She took a bottled iced tea from the refrigerator and stood at the sink.

"What are you going to do?" she asked matter-of-factly.

"Your father made the decision for me. I'm locked in. I guess I'll be filling in as prosecutor until the next election."

"I thought you'd do it. But I don't think it's just because Dad trapped you, which he did and which he shouldn't have. I think you want to do it. You always have to prove yourself."

"*Prove* myself? I don't have to prove myself."

"You could have stayed forever at the prosecutor's office. You liked it. But Dad beckoned with the challenge of private practice and you were gone."

"He said he needed help. Enos slowing down, swamped with cases."

25

"You thought you could fix things. That you could find an answer."

"Sure . . ."

"Paul. What are you getting yourself into here?"

"What do you mean?"

She looked at him carefully. A shrewd look he seldom saw on her usually contented, good-natured face.

"You know very well what I mean. You and dad don't have any notion of what you're getting yourselves into here. You know that I hate public life. Fundraisers. Banquets. Paul Andros' 'little wife.' Boring speeches. Smiling at nothing. Being pleasant to people who would take everything you had if they thought they could. It's so hypocritical."

"Politics is hypocrisy developed to an art form," Paul observed.

"That doesn't make it all right," Jane snapped.

Paul raised his hands over his head in a self-protective pose. "Don't take it out on me. I didn't create the world."

"But you always think you can change it. Charging off on a white horse . . ."

"You obviously don't think I should do this. It was your father's idea, not mine."

"Don't get me started on him. I think I liked him better when he was a lush. At least he stayed out of trouble. What's going to happen at the office?"

"Well, Enos can't step in and won't. Everyone else is essentially a hired hand. I'll have to worry it out."

"Dad must be getting older, " she mused.

"It isn't that, so much. He's still quite capable, but we've changed the practice from the way he worked all his life. When I came into practice with Enos and Scott, there was just us three lawyers and Mrs. Taylor. Then Mrs. Taylor retired. He and Enos sort of wandered around in a daze. I took over and we brought in more people. It didn't make sense to have all that business and the office not able to handle it. He and Enos would just send it down the street."

"Can't John Parsons take charge? He's been there a while."

"Yeah. John's the logical choice. We've got to restructure the partnership anyway. It's time to recognize how valuable he is to us."

Paul sensed that Jane really didn't want to talk about office re-organization. "Look," he said, "I'm sorry I talk like a lawyer, but I am a lawyer."

"It's not that. I'm just concerned about what you're getting into. I'll get dressed and we'll go get something to eat."

After she was gone, Paul sat back and looked at his notes for taking over the prosecutor's office. He had to focus on his objectives and not get lost in the details. He had that feeling he used to have at the start of a tennis match: like entering a long, dark tunnel. The only way to get out was to keep going forward. Soon you don't want to be there, but you're trapped in the contest and you've got to keep going to get out. It used to be that he loved the thrill of tennis tournaments, playing at a more competitive level. But he had reached the point where he no longer enjoyed it. Now Scott had signed him up for another kind of tournament. For another long, dark tunnel.

Showdown at the
OK Corral

THREE

To keep keg sales rolling on Sunday nights there was a pool tournament at the OK Corral. The seedy tavern was located in unincorporated King County, just north of the Seattle city limits. It was crowded and noisy. The only etiquette observed was to avoid pushing the shooter's cue while he or she was making a shot.

Terry Barnes had emerged from his room in the dingy motel next door and blended into the free-for-all atmosphere. Nursing sore kidneys from the arresting officer's rabbit punch, he moved slowly to a pay phone in an alcove that led to the smelly toilets. He dialed a number in the Queen Anne exchange.

"Hello," said one of the three female children of the household.

"Let me speak to your father, please," he directed.

Intense requests to summon her father were an everyday occurrence to the girl.

"Daddy," she called. "Phone."

A large, dark-complected man put down the paper he was reading in front of the living room TV. He took his time to amble across the hallway to the dining room and take the phone from the impatient girl.

"Thank you, Virginia," he said.

The girl left the room without acknowledgment. The man took a writing tablet from the top shelf of the china closet, which was exclusively devoted to his paperwork, and seated himself at the dining room table.

He spoke quietly into the receiver. "Yes?"

"You pig fuck!" Terry said angrily. "Where were you last night? The fucking bondsman cleaned me out and took my van.

I'd like to see your useless pig guts spilled out in front of you while you watched with your little pig-fuck eyes. Geez..." Terry was exhausted with his inability to express his frustration. His eyes were red and his face was drawn . He was edgy from lack of sleep and tension. The large man on the other end of the line did not move. He listened, his pen poised on the tablet.

"But this morning" Terry finally continued," when I read the paper I got to thinking that maybe that old pig fuck has ideas of his own. Things have very quickly gone to shit and I have this feeling things are gonna get worse."

The large man looked around the room, thinking to himself and saying nothing, his face passive. At last he spoke. "Our friend seems to have cut himself off from our arrangement."

"Jesus Christ! I can't believe it. You know, Sherm wasn't a bad guy but you are the asshole of the Universe!

"Look," Terry continued. "The party's over. Sherm's gone. I'm done. You're done. People are gonna start putting two and two together. When they do, I don't want any fingers pointed my way about Sherm's death. So you know what I did? I started asking myself some questions. Like how come I worked my ass off for protection I never got? I did your little chores for nothing. What do I get? Half the Seattle police force busts me and my girls and I get charged with everything in the book so's I can't even make fucking bail without some asshole bondsman takes my beautiful van with fourteen fucking coats of paint."

The large man spoke firmly. "I heard nothing until the backup was arranged. It was too late to do anything."

"Stick it up your ass. Just listen and shut up. Now I tell myself to hit the road. But then I read the papers about Sherm. 'Possible suicide.' That makes me think, if I'd like to kill the old kingpin asshole, what about him wanting to kill me? He sure don't want me around to sing if the cops catch up with me.

"So I write a letter, a long letter about me and Sherm and the girls. And I didn't leave you out. You and all those little errands I done for you. It's all down in writing with a lawyer.

One you don't know. If I get snuffed, he takes it to the press, the governor and the state patrol."

"What if this lawyer decides to browse through this letter?" asked the large man.

"He don't know nothing. I told him I was afraid a girlfriend's old man was out to snuff me and I was using the letter to keep him cool. He could care less as long as he's paid. He gets twenty-five bucks a month just so he knows I'm alive. No bread, he opens the letter and mails copies to all those people you wouldn't like to hear from.

"So what I want from you, Mr. Kingpin Asshole, is for you to do some voodoo to get my paperwork lost. Meanwhile, I'm gone. So long as I'm alive, you're alive. So long as I'm out, you're out."

Terry paused, reviewing in his mind everything he had wanted to say. He hung up without waiting for a response.

The large man carefully hung up the phone. He got up from the table and returned to his overstuffed chair in the living room. He picked up the paper and tried to read, but he found himself reading the same words over and over.

Soon the large man picked up the phone and dialed a number.

"Twenty minutes. Art's Drive-In," he said.

The bright lights and soft mist gave the cars parked at the drive-in a glossy look. The large man parked his, went inside, ordered a cup of coffee, and sat down at a corner table. Customers were coming and going, but only a few ate their burgers and shakes inside. The tables and chairs were a bright orange supported by chrome legs. The atmosphere was designed to be cheerful but uninviting to lingerers. The large man settled into the chair at the corner table as if he were prepared to sit there for hours.

A good-looking, gray-haired, uniformed policeman entered and ordered a burger.

"You're looking hot tonight, Annie. When are we going out, dear?"

"Oh, Sergeant Newsom, you'd just get me in trouble."

"Hey, now, I'm the po-lice. I'll save you from any trouble."

"Yeah, you will . . ."

The sergeant took his burger and coffee to the corner table and sat beside the large man. "What's up, Jake? Any word on what the hell happened with Sherm?"

"Been off this weekend. But I did get a call from our friend. He's got a problem."

"I'll bet he does."

"If homicide doesn't buy the suicide angle on Sherm's death, he thinks they're gonna make him a suspect."

"Ow. Well, who the hell knows. Maybe the fuck did it."

"What's the difference who did it. Terry Barnes is gonna look attractive as a suspect, and if he gets scared, which I can tell you he definitely is, no telling what kind of tales he's gonna want to tell."

Sergeant Newsom let out a soft whistle and put down his burger. "He's got a temper. Maybe he'll resist arrest."

"I never seen him carrying. Fact I made it a point to tell him not to or he was all done."

"There's always a first time."

"You and the others keep an eye out for him. It would be nice if we had first shot."

"So to speak. You know, Jake, Ventures Seven is due a payday. Last week you said Sherm was handling the money?"

"I'll be taking care of things. But we're stopping operations. I know you guys were due something, but I went to the Argo yesterday and couldn't find a goddamn thing."

"Sure, Jake."

"I'm not shitting you, Artie. I couldn't even find the fucking rent receipts."

"Don't shit a shitter, Jake."

"Look, you gotta settle down and you gotta settle your guys down. We can't afford a falling out. Things were good. Now they're fucked. I'll do something for you guys when I can, but we're just gonna have to button things down."

The girl brought over a coffeepot to their table. "You guys want a refill?"

"Bless your little heart. Now I can stay awake for our date."

She refilled their cups.

"Why do you think that prosecutor guy killed himself? Wasn't that awful?" she asked.

"It was. It was awful," said Sergeant Newsom soberly. "I guess the scandal was just too much for the guy."

"Yeah. I hope that'll teach you guys to behave yourselves."

"No way. Not when you're around, Annie-girl."

She laughed and went back behind the counter.

Newsom sipped his coffee. "Where the fuck did those guys come from, Jake? Gordo? What the hell was that stiff-neck doing working a vice deal?"

"Don't know. Find out Monday."

"Whyn't he just let Sherm go, for godsake?"

"That's Gordo. New wave cop. You-me we'd a let him walk."

"What an asshole."

Jake peered into his cup, neither confirming nor denying Sergeant Newsom's assessment.

The Maternal Order of Police

FOUR

"Do you solemnly swear that you shall enforce the Constitution of the United States of America and the constitution and laws of the State of Washington?"

"I do."

Judge Hormsby and Andros lowered their right hands and shook hands briefly. The judge nodded unsmilingly to the seven-member council seated at the long dais in the King County council's meeting room and sat down. Paul remained at the podium. He adjusted the microphone and looked down at the typewritten statement he had placed there before the swearing in.

"I have a brief statement I would like to make. I would like the press to understand that I will have nothing further to say except through the King County prosecutor's usual public information procedures.

"For most elected officials the occasion of being sworn into political office is a time of elation at having accomplished a long-sought and difficult goal. This is not the case for me today. I am here simply to fill a gap and to provide continuity to the office of prosecutor, which was suddenly vacated by the death of Sherman Falkes.

"The council, the public, and all members of the law enforcement community of King County should know that I was a friend and co-worker of Sherman Falkes for many years. The council, the public, and all members of the law enforcement community should also know that I will not involve myself or the office in any cover-up of the circumstances of Sherman Falkes' death. I intend that his death shall be fully and independently investigated. At the same time, I intend to see that the flow of other cases through the office will be maintained.

"I will serve as prosecutor for only a short time. This fall there will be an election to determine who will be the next King County prosecutor. I do not intend to run in that election, nor will I take part in it. I am simply here to hold down the fort until help arrives. I appreciate the council's confidence in me. I will do my best to justify your confidence. I began my legal career as a deputy prosecutor and am now honored to be asked to fill in while the electorate decides who should be the next elected prosecutor. Over the past six years, while I have been in private practice, I have worked on the judicial council and the legislative committee of the bar association to help provide laws and judicial rules for speedy and effective law enforcement. I have worked on United Way, Medic One, and numerous other community activities. I have done so because this is my home. I am here now for the same reason. This is my home, and I intend to see that my home will continue to be a place where the laws are equally and effectively enforced for the safety of all.

"Thank you."

"Thank you, Mr. Andros. On behalf of the council, I would like to extend our thanks and best wishes. Please let us know what the council may do to assist you," said Henry Tremaine, the council president. "That concludes the swearing-in ceremony. I suggest that the council recess and we will then convene with our regular agenda at nine a.m."

Paul picked up copies of his statement and headed for the door. Once outside in the wide hallway, several reporters closed in on him for special interviews. A TV cameraman stood beside a local TV news announcer who motioned to him. Paul stopped briefly.

"I have copies of my statement to council here if you didn't get here in time to hear it. Otherwise, I have nothing to say at this time. Please, no request for special interviews. Any new information we obtain will be available for all of you in due course through the prosecutor public information procedures."

"Come on, Paul. Nobody follows those," someone said.

"They do now," Paul said quietly and continued walking. He went through the fire door to the stairs in order to avoid waiting for an elevator. It was four flights down to street level.

"You can at least let me walk with you," a voice spoke behind him. It was Sam Havens, a reporter for *The Seattle Sentinel* and an acquaintance of many years.

"Off the record? I don't want to cut old friends, but I really don't like the habit some reporters have of wanting special interviews that end up changing the intent of a public statement."

"Sure, off the record. I got nothing else to do."

They started down the stairs with Paul in front.

"Well, well. Can't stay out of the public trough, huh, Paul?"

"I wasn't really eager to do it, pal, but hell, a few months from private practice will be a change," Paul said.

"What made you do it? Take on this mess?"

Andros thought again about the overbearing father-in-law who had thrust him into this situation. Still, his family and business relationships were not matters to discuss with Sam Havens. Besides, he had to admit to himself that, although he knew it hadn't been wise, Paul's ego was flattered by the quick and unanimous manner he was selected.

"Is this for print?"

"Not unless you say so."

"Well, between us and not for publication, the answer is hubris, Sam, good old commonplace hubris. The very same that has swollen the egos of political leaders and elected officers for time immemorial."

"You? Andros the taciturn technician? You wanted to be anointed? I can't believe it."

"Why not? If you prick me do I not bleed?"

"When were *you* ever pricked? You always took the high ground as legal liaison to the council. All these fireworks going on and there would be Paul Andros, summarizing points of view and trying to herd the politicos toward a compromise. I always hated the way you diffused things."

"That was my job. Doesn't mean I didn't have a point of view. But what good's a point of view if you can't get something to happen? We're talking policymaking, but the prosecutor is not a policymaker, just a technician. An elected technician."

"Anything you're going to do that you always wanted to do when you were in the office?"

"Not enough time to delve into office management. I'll go with what's there."

"Then Herb McAuliffe will still be running the office?"

Paul hesitated. "Sherm gave Herb a pretty free hand?"

"You can say that again."

"Let me ask you a question, Sam?"

"Sure."

"When was the last time you talked to Sherm and what did you talk about?"

"I saw him last Thursday morning outside county council. He had been over with one of the young civil deputies to talk with council about a settlement with a road contractor. I talked to him after."

"How did he look?"

"Huh?"

"Did he seem worried, relaxed, what?"

"Casual, political. Full of bullshit, as usual. He sent the young deputy on his way and we chatted. He mentioned he was going to Canada on vacation, taking his son and daughter for a week."

"Did he discuss business?"

"We joked about futuristic tax schemes."

"Yeah?"

"He said they've tried taxes on everything else. How about a tax on orgasms? He thought they could call it an 'ecstasy tax.' I said something about a new line guys could use like 'Hey baby, I'll pay your ecstasy tax.'"

"Sounds like Sherm. Did he talk about things going on in the office?"

"No. I talk to Herb and the criminal court staff about cases — so Sherm and I usually chatted about county business rather than the latest murders and maulings."

"Anyone else cover the courthouse for *The Sentinel* now?"

"Bill Perkins."

"Any gossip from Bill I should know?"

"I think the feeling with Bill and the others at *The Sentinel* was that after his election to a second term he sort of lost his edge. First time through the election grinder he was all bright-eyed and bushy tailed. He was Terrill Bascom's protégé, but nobody knew what that counted for. He gets elected. He's his own man. See any difference in the office? No. He's just another initiate to the old-boy network."

Paul's eyes narrowed. "What old-boy network?"

"You know, Paul. It's Seattle. Can't even get a job as a dock-worker unless your daddy or granddaddy dies and wills it to you."

"*The Sentinel*'s op-ed page is assigned reading for its reporters?"

"Yeah, I know, I know. The young Turks have been beating the drum for diversity in public and private employment. But you know they're right. They just piss you off 'cause they're such zealots. But remember what the sheriff's office was like before they made it civil service?"

"I wasn't there."

"Well, I can tell you. It was as in-bred as Easter Island. Everybody was related. And who cared about the low salaries when a deputy could vacuum the streets for all the spare change he needed?"

"Things are changing, Sam."

"Check Sherm's deputy roster. How many black, Chicano, Asian, and women are on the staff?"

"Geez, Sam. Give me a break. I'm only gonna be there for three or four months."

"I'm not on your case. I'm just saying maybe our op-ed boys and girls—oh, yeah we now have a woman editorial writer—maybe they're onto something."

"So what about Sherm. You got anything more than that he was one of the good old boys?"

"I'll ask around, but I haven't heard anything. I'm just a broke-down old political reporter."

Andros looked at Sam steadily as he opened the ground-floor door. It was true that Sam—gray-haired, middle-aged, in the baggy sport coat—wasn't an aggressive investigative reporter, but he recalled from his years as a prosecutor involved in the county's civil affairs that Sam understood political and legal complexities, and he was fair. While some other reporters loved to stick politicians with their fumbling articulation of issues, Andros knew of many instances where Havens had quoted what an elective officer meant to say, rather than what he or she had actually had said in an awkward or incomprehensible way.

"Give me a call if you hear anything."

"I will. Good luck to you, Paul."

Andros shook hands firmly with Havens and headed down the tunnel joining the County Administration Building to the courthouse.

He entered the office of the King County prosecuting attorney at 8:40 A.M. He had arranged for the swearing-in ceremony to occur well before 9:00 A.M., the usual starting time for the prosecutor's office. The waiting room was empty. Paul strode down the hall past the empty attorneys' offices to the corner office that had belonged to Sherman Falkes three days before. The windows overlooked the waters of Puget Sound, blue as the clear sky. A blessed rarity to be cherished.

Andros looked around Sherman Falkes' office. He and Sherm had formally said their good-byes six years ago, having worked together as deputy prosecutors for Terrill Bascom, the elected prosecuting attorney who had hired them. Bascom had appointed Paul as chief civil deputy a year before he retired, but it was Sherm who decided to go through the necessary political rites to be elected as the prosecuting attorney. Leaving the politics to Sherm was fine, but Andros did not want to run the office for him. When Scott Turnbull suggested that he needed help in his private practice, Andros decided he had a greater obligation to his father-in-law and to his family.

Oddly, considering their long friendship, Falkes had accepted Paul's decision to leave with a demonstrable lack of understanding and good will. Andros left the office within the week of his resignation and had never since been invited back. Sherman did not initiate lunches or social contacts which, on reflection, suited Paul. They only saw each other occasionally on the street and at bar functions over the past six years. After a few superficial pleasantries they would part and go to their separate lives.

Sherm's desk was clear. The office was a showpiece for the delegation management motif. If management is the art of getting things done through other people, Sherman Falkes was a manager. Andros always preferred a more hands-on, involved style, but he recognized the pitfalls of interference with assignments of work and delegations of authority. Although Paul pestered delegates about their assignments much more closely than Sherm, he was careful to instill responsibility in those who worked under him.

"Paul. I can't believe it."

Paul turned to see Mary Lynn Pierce, Sherm's secretary, standing in the doorway. She was a heavy woman in her early fifties. She wore a blue suit with a burgundy blouse. Her blue eyes were glassy as she looked expectantly at Paul. She looked about ready to break down. Paul wanted her working. He dismissed the idea of embracing her and spoke matter-of-factly.

"Mary Lynn. Thank heavens you're here. I have just been sworn in to replace Sherm and I need your help to get organized. I hope you will agree to stay on and help me."

She started to cry. "Oh, Paul. Of course I'll help. It's just, I don't understand. The paper said he committed suicide!"

"I don't understand either, but we'll be looking into it further. The thing is that now we've got to get the office under control, get the deputies to their trials. Make sure our part of the criminal justice system is running. Right, Mary Lynn?"

She nodded.

"Good. Let's go in your office."

Mary Lynn's office was next door. Paul led her there and she sat down.

"Type this memo and circulate it to all office personnel."

The memo, handwritten on a yellow, legal-sized pad was easily legible:

To: Staff—King Co. Pros. Atty's office
From: Paul Andros
Subject: Administrative Issues

This morning I was appointed prosecutor by the King County council. This is an interim appointment until the November election.

I am personally initiating an investigation into the death of Sherman Falkes. I hope that each of you will cooperate in whatever way you can with that investigation. Although you will be contacted individually, please let Mary Lynn Pierce know if you can provide any information of immediate use.

Unless you are discussing the Sherman Falkes' death with myself or one of the investigators working with me, I believe that no useful purpose will be served by discussing Sherman Falkes, or the circumstances preceding his death, outside this office. This means if someone offers you information, let me know, but try to refrain from gossip.

All members of this office are quasi-judicial officers or their assistants. We are the prime movers in the criminal justice administration system. Most importantly, we are an independent branch of that system. The police, the courts, the press, and the public will be scrutinizing each one of us in the coming months. I hope they will see a highly disciplined office of dedicated professionals performing their duty.

You may discuss with the press those cases to which you are assigned, within the guidelines. Statements concerning office policy, or management, or the Sherman Falkes case will be my responsibility solely.

I look forward to working again with my many old friends and colleagues in the office and to meeting and working with those of you who have joined the office since I left. Attached is a schedule for me to meet with each of you.

Paul stood by as she sat down to type out the memo. "I want to talk to everyone individually, Mary Lynn, so list everyone in fifteen-minute intervals in alphabetical order, two-thirty to four-thirty daily until we work through everyone. They can skip around to meet their other schedules, but make sure I don't have dead time. Got it?"

"Yes, Paul."

She began typing before he left the room. Herb McAuliffe was standing in the hall waiting for him. Looking a bit ruffled.

"So you're the new boss," Herb said in his low emotionless voice. A sort of legal automaton, spare with words and quick to reach conclusions, Herb was unshakable once his mind was made up. Paul looked into his blank, blue eyes and couldn't tell what he was thinking. He maybe resented Paul being appointed instead of him.

Paul willed himself to relax and smiled as he extended his hand to Herb.

"Herb. Well, Liz Newgate and Jim Ferranti called me on Saturday. They wanted an outside person to come in on an interim basis."

"I know. Jim called me and we discussed it. I told him you were the ideal solution," Herb said.

Paul was inwardly relieved that Herb McAuliffe was not going to be upset at his presence in the office after all. Now he only had to worry about the hours he would spend arguing with Herb over legal issues.

"Mary Lynn's typing a memo to the staff telling them to keep calm, don't gossip, and look good. Come on in the office and tell me who's who around here and who's doing what."

They walked into the corner office that had once belonged to Sherman Falkes to discuss personnel and office business. They were standing by the door, with a view down the hall to the reception room, when Paul suddenly called out.

"Mom!"

He hurried toward a handsome, black-haired woman peering down the hallway into the still empty office assistants' area. She wore a black worsted dress with white edging around the collar, down the front, and around the sleeves. With her black straw bolero hat, leather purse, and a folded newspaper, she looked formal and foreboding. As Paul hurried toward her, his arms extended. She arched her eyebrows and appeared to look through him.

She took a step back, but he grabbed her, pulled her to him, and gave her a hug.

"Mom, I'm sorry. I ..."

"In the newspaper," she interrupted. "I read in the newspaper Paul Andros is to be appointed prosecuting attorney. You are my son, Paul Andros? You are going to be appointed the prosecuting attorney? This is perhaps news a mother might be interested in? No. Not this mother. She doesn't care ..."

"Mom, I ..."

"The mother of Paul Andros doesn't care if her only son lives or dies. This is, of course, well known. So no one need bother to call. Maybe, if her son dies, she'll see the death notice in the newspaper and show up at the funeral," she shrugged. "But, maybe not. Who cares?"

"Mom. Listen." He held her arms gently. "This is nothing important in my life. In our lives. Jane didn't even come down. It's just a bit of troubleshooting to get things back on keel. I never even thought you'd be interested."

"OK, I'm not. My son is only written up in the newspaper as the savior of Seattle ..."

Paul threw his arms open in supplication to an unhearing deity. "Savior of Seattle! Shit, Mom, where do you get that stuff?"

"It's in the neighborhood. How proud everyone is! Paul will take care of it. Paul will fix things. That's all I heard this morning at the Delphi.

"But," she added. "Of course, I was not interested."

"OK, OK. You got me. I did wrong. I'm sorry. Let's lay a carload of guilt on me."

"I should hope. Now when is the swearing in?" she said, adjusting her hat.

The door to the office opened and a young man and a woman, neither of whom Paul knew, entered the reception room. They both went past, hurriedly, to their offices, evading this domestic *pas de deux.*

Holding his mother by the arm, Paul led her back to his office. "Yeah, Mom, come on back and take a quick tour of the office. Then we'll talk about that. "

She stopped and pulled away. "It's over, isn't it? It's done. They swore you in already while your mother was up on the Hill cooking breakfasts, and having to listen to what a hero her only son is."

"Cooking breakfasts. Since when do *you* cook anymore? You just sit at the cash register and gossip with the old men of the neighborhood."

"And women," she said proudly. "Any woman. Any time. By herself, can come into the Delphi and be welcome!"

"I know, I know, Mom," Paul said, remembering how his mother had scourged the male-dominated atmosphere of the Delphi after his father's death and made it a place where unescorted nurses and medical office workers on Capitol Hill were welcome. "Come on back. I'll explain . . ."

Paul had to half push and half pull his mother back to his office. Passing Mary Lynn Pierce's desk, he asked, "Mary Lynn, would you get Judge Hormsby on the phone please?"

Paul knew the nature of his mother's world. That she would not have witnessed her son's ascension to even the ephemeral position of caretaker prosecuting attorney was unthinkable. Paul had blown it, but, if Judge Hormsby were understanding of his plight, the situation was recoverable.

Superior Court, Department No. 12 was delayed until 10:00 A.M. that morning while Helen Andros, proud Greek mother, watched her only son be sworn in for the second time as the official, if only temporary, King County prosecuting attorney.

Gash n' go

FIVE

THAT SAME MORNING, twenty miles north of Seattle, in Everett, Cowboy Zack's Clothing Store opened at ten.

Terry Barnes, his hair now dyed dark brown, was the first customer of the day. He picked out a pair of light, rubber-soled work boots, a pair of jeans, and a red and black plaid flannel shirt. He went into one of the dressing rooms and changed into the new clothes and asked the clerk to wrap his black shirt and pants, white shoes, and gray sport jacket.

He then walked two blocks north to the Goodwill Store where he made a donation of the clothes in the Cowboy Zack wrapper and bought an oversized, ill-fitting, faded blue denim jacket and a blue polo shirt.

From there he went to the bus station and in a short time caught a bus to Seattle.

Walking east from the Seattle bus station, he kept pace with telephone workers on their lunch break from the telephone office building and walked across the freeway overpass up to Capitol Hill.

He was short of breath when he got to Broadway at the top of the long hill. He headed south past the coffee shops, restaurants, delis, and dry-cleaners until he got to Potter Street. A block just east of Broadway, he entered an older, four-story apartment building that had been remodeled several times. There were new doors and old doors to the apartments. It was apparent that the older, larger units had been rearranged to create additional smaller units. Terry was familiar with the layout. He took the stairs up to the third floor and knocked softly on the door of the street-front apartment.

There was no answer.

"Reeney," he called softly.

He tried the door handle but it was locked.

"Terry! Here," a voice down the hall whispered.

Terry turned and saw the still-swollen face of his number-one woman in the doorway of the right rear apartment. He strode quickly to her. Once inside he gathered the striking, dark woman in his arms. She was dressed in a loose, white, sleeveless undershirt and light pink nylon runner's shorts. She wore a set of tennis shoes to complete her version of the athletic look.

"Anyone here?" Terry asked.

She shook her head. "The girls who live here are at work. I told them I was afraid my old man was gonna beat me up again.

"Have you seen any cops around?"

"Just Jake. I'm scared, Terry-baby. I don't want to go back again."

Terry held her closer to him. He reached his hand under the open shoulder of her soft, loose shirt. He touched his palm over the point of her breast. The flesh of her pointed breast was firm, the nipple erect like a budding penis.

"Baby, baby," he said softly. "I'm scared too. But you'll be all right. Everything's gonna be all right."

She fit her hand into his neck and wriggled her body closer to him. Her left thigh began to move between his legs.

Terry grasped her shoulders and pushed her away from him.

"Reeney—Tangerine," he cooed softly to her. "Listen to me. Listen! They're gonna think we had something to do with that son-of-a-bitch persecutor's death. They're gonna be looking for us. We gotta move."

The woman said nothing. Her dark eyes studied Terry. The cut lip from three nights before was barely visible. She tilted her head and put her hands on his hips to draw him closer.

"Hah, nah, nah. Slow down," He held her at arm's length. "Slow down. There's trouble here, Reeney. Listen to me. We need money. I never used your money, Reeney. But now we need it."

She looked him in the eyes and said, "Honest, Terry-baby, I ain't got no bread."

Terry seized her by the wrist and moved around behind her. He pushed her arm into the small of her back in an arm lock.

She jumped forward. "Stop it, Terry."

"Go bitch on me and I'll break your fucking arm. I wouldn't ask if I didn't need it, Reeney. I need it. I'm busted."

"OK, OK. I got a little bit. But I'll just spend it as we go, Terry-baby."

"Sure, baby, sure. You know I won't run off with your bread. Where is it?"

"It's in a bank." She smiled, "How many black whores got their money in a bank?"

"Write me a check."

"I can't. It's in a savings account."

"Get dressed," he ordered.

"My clothes are still in the apartment. But if you watch the stairs I can go back in and get some."

Terry thought about Reeney's eye-catching wardrobe back in the apartment. "Nah, let's see what these other girls got."

"I looked. That's where I got this," she pulled at the thin, cotton undershirt. "The other one weighs like two hundred pounds, man. Her stuff goes around me twice.

"That'll do. We ain't in no damn style show. Come on."

Terry went into the bedroom and began rummaging through the closet. He found a mannish white shirt, and a pair of blue jeans hanging on a nail. Reeney followed him into the room. She stood by the bed pulling down her running shorts. She wore nothing underneath.

"Ohhh, Terry-baby, dress me. Dress me," she said, holding her arms out to him as she stepped out of the shorts.

Terry strode across the room to her. He grasped her right hand and put the clothes into it.

"Goddamn it, Irene. I don't need this shit. Take these clothes and put 'em on."

He left the room and went into the kitchen. He opened the refrigerator and helped himself to a Coke.

Reeney followed him into the kitchen, buttoning the shirt slowly and carrying the jeans. The shirt bottom stopped just short of her black pubic hair. Terry turned away and looked out the kitchen window.

"Terry," she said. "I can't wear these jeans. They're five times too big. I might as well wear a sack."

Terry turned back to look at her, his face grim. His voice almost sobbed with frustration. "Why is this happening to me? Shit! Why is this happening to me? Get those goddamn clothes on, Reeney. Can't you figure out that you can't go out on the street with those shorts folded into your cunt and your tits hanging out of that undershirt? Jesus Christ! We're up to our ears in shit and you play your little pussy power games with me! Have you lost your goddamn brains?"

"I'm smart enough to figure out you're gonna split on me, Terry," she said evenly. "Even I can figure out that you and me together, we'll be spotted in a minute."

Terry reached for her but she scurried away.

"Now, come on, Reeney, I wouldn't split on you. Three years? Huh? We been together three years."

She pulled on the jeans and buttoned the top. She pulled the waistband away from her stomach. The jean waist was almost twice as big as her waist.

"I said she was a cow," she said.

"Go find a belt. We gotta get going."

"I ain't giving you no money, Terry. And you know we can't split together. So go, jus go."

There was quiet.

Terry's mouth was a grim line. Reeney, expressionless, backed away and left the room.

Terry sipped on the Coke and followed as she went into the bedroom. There were several belts hanging beside the chest of drawers. He took down a cloth belt and turned to her.

Quickly, he wrapped the belt around her neck and pulled the ends tight.

Reeney did not utter a sound as she put her hands to her throat. The pants dropped to the floor. Her eyes stared at Terry without expression.

Slowly, Terry let go of the belt ends and walked out of the room.

Reeney rubbed her neck for some time. Then, she stooped to the floor, pulled up the pants, and slowly threaded the belt through the belt loops.

She went back into the living room as the front door of the apartment slammed shut. Her purse was open on the floor; her billfold on the couch. The so-called "hidden" flap—where she kept her cash—was torn, her money gone. She continued rubbing her neck and stared through the crack in the curtains at the blue Seattle sky.

Negotiating a
sharp Turner

SIX

EINAR TORGESON ARRIVED at the King County prosecutor's office at 3:15 P.M., Monday afternoon. He was a tall, thin man in his early forties. He wore a faded black polyester topcoat and carried a khaki rain hat. His suit was a patternless gray polyester and wool blend, with a white shirt and black clip-on tie.

The receptionist watched his prominent Adams apple bob up and down as he swallowed and asked, "Is Mr. Andros in?"

"Yes, he is. Are you Mr. Torgeson?"

Einar nodded slightly, as his fingers swept his straggly, graying hair across the top of his balding head.

"He said for you to go on back. Please take a right. His office is at the end of the hall."

Torgeson loped down the hall and nodded to Mary Lynn Pierce, whose desk appeared to guard the closed door of the head prosecutor.

Mrs. Pierce recognized the tall specter that occasionally visited the office during her tenure. "Hello, Mr. Torgeson. I'll tell Mr. Andros you're here."

Torgeson stood quietly, his stork neck extended, as she walked around him.

As soon as Mr. Torgeson's presence was announced, Andros came out of the office to greet him.

"Come in, Einar. Come on in," he said extending his hand.

Einar Torgeson shyly placed his long, thin hand into that of the newly appointed prosecutor. Torgeson's grip was surprisingly firm, but his face was expressionless as Andros led him into the office.

"Lyle Turner, I'd like you to meet Einar Torgeson," Andros said to a young man seated in front of Andros' desk.

Turner was a trim, brown-haired young man, wearing a tan suit, button-down white shirt, and a blue- and red-striped tie, all of which emanated an Ivy League manner and look. Turner rose and shook hands smoothly with Torgeson.

Turner remained standing and headed for the door. "Anything else, then?" he asked.

"Don't go yet, Lyle. Let's go over it again while Einar is here. I'd like him to hear this. Einar is going to be helping us out on Sherm Falkes death. Lyle here talked to Seattle PD about the motel bust before it went down."

Turner returned to his chair. Andros went around to the back of the desk. He motioned Torgeson to a leather sofa against the wall behind Turner. Turner arranged his chair so that his back would not be completely turned from Torgeson.

"Let's go back to late Friday afternoon, Lyle. Casey had gone home, you say, or he'd gone somewhere, anyway. Sergeant Gordon from Seattle PD came over and wanted to go over a prostitution bust he was planning. He had an idea about how to nail the pimp. Apparently, this pimp never went to the premises where the action took place. He would play the role of a satisfied customer and then tell the mark where he could get the goodies. Gordon wanted to know what would be wrong with throwing a scare into the madam, if you will, and see if she would draw the pimp back to the motel."

Turner nodded.

"You advised," Andros continued, "that you saw nothing wrong with this plan so long as they could get evidence to tie the pimp to what was going on at the motel."

Turner continued the story. "Sergeant Gordon had said he planned to send an undercover cop to the bar where the pimp was working. Get said pimp to solicit the cop, then send in a heavy to threaten the women. The women call the pimp. The cops wait until the pimp shows up, and once he's there they send in the guy who was solicited at the bar. If the pimp is at the bar and the motel we'd have a good start on a soliciting charge.

So long as the circumstances showed he was something more than a customer."

Einar Torgeson, motionless, sat listening.

"Did he tell you what this 'threatener' would say or do?"

"No."

"Did you ask?"

"No. I felt it was police business as to how to make the threat authentic."

"Authentic," Paul repeated. "Was Sherman Falkes here at the time you talked to Sergeant Gordon?"

"I don't know. Casey, the chief criminal deputy, is my boss. I scarcely saw Sherman Falkes," he said.

"OK. Was Casey here?"

"I don't know. I saw no reason to review this with other persons in the office."

"How long have you been with the office, Lyle?" Andros asked.

"Six months."

"Well, let me tell you what I'm thinking. What's bothering me is that I would think that Gordon would want to talk to someone who had been around a while, like Marty Schultz or Eric Smith. Casey's the chief criminal deputy, but there are other people who have been here for years who could advise him on his plan."

Andros consulted a list on his desk.

"In fact," Andros continued, "you are one of the newest deputies. On the other hand I know Sergeant Gordon. He's been around for years. He knows everybody here. How did he get to you? You said you just started doing felony work two months ago."

"What difference does it make, Paul?" Turner asked.

"I have no idea, Lyle. It just seems odd. Frankly, you seem defensive about it."

Turner looked over at Einar Torgeson who stared back blankly, his long hands motionless on the couch beside him.

"Well, I had kicked around the idea of a little bit more aggressive approach to prostitution with Chief Hellman, and Gordon works directly out of the Seattle police chief's office," Turner said.

"When was this?"

"At a couple of meetings."

"What meetings?"

Turner became exasperated. "What is this? Do I need a lawyer or something?"

"Do you?" Andros asked quietly.

"Of course not. I don't make a secret of the fact that I was not impressed with Sherman Falkes. I met Chief Hellman at a county police chiefs' meeting. I was the only prosecutor interested enough to attend. We got to talking and I guess Hellman was able to figure out that I was dissatisfied with Mr. Falkes' leadership. I guess that was why Gordon sought me out. In fact, Gordon and I had talked about the plan and worked on it a week or so before we had decided to recruit the out-of-town officers to make the contacts."

"When was that?"

"I had a brown-bag lunch with Gordon in Hellman's office a week ago Thursday. I was excited about helping put it together."

The room went silent as Andros wrote notes on a yellow pad. Andros thought about asking him why he went to work for the prosecutor's office if he was dissatisfied with Sherm's leadership. Andros hated disloyalty. But he looked over at Einar Torgeson's demeanor, calm and nonconfrontational, and decided to emulate his style. Maybe Lyle Turner knew what Sherm had been up to in the last days of his life.

"Why were you dissatisfied with Mr. Falkes' leadership?"

"Well, for one thing, he had a political stranglehold on the prosecutor's office. He should have been trying to move on for years, but he sat here like a lump, refusing to run for anything else or vacate the office. Other lawyers with political aspirations were forced to run for fire commissioner or auditor. Anything to get political exposure."

"What about Sherm's personal life? Were you concerned about that?"

"Frankly, I really didn't know anything about his personal life until today. The gossip that's going around the office from the police reports is that he was humping a sixteen-year-old prostitute."

Andros spoke sharply. "Have you seen the police reports? They weren't in when I asked."

"No, but I know they're in the office for charging. Casey's got them."

Andros got up from his desk, walked to the door, opened it. "Mary Lynn," he said. "Would you make sure I get two copies of the police reports on the Majestic Motel bust from Casey before you leave tonight?"

Andros smiled at Torgeson as he returned to his desk. "Got all the reports on Falkes' death, but I don't have those."

Torgeson stared back silently.

"Anyway," Andros continued. "You had no personal acquaintanceship with Falkes. How did you get hired?"

"I suppose it didn't hurt that I am a Yale Law School graduate."

"Yale. That's a law school? Somewhere back East?" Paul asked with a slight grin.

Turner closed his eyes briefly, refusing to acknowledge Paul's attempt to lighten the discussion. "Also, I worked on Carl Fraser's senatorial campaign right out of law school. We worked closely together during the campaign, and at its successful conclusion I asked him to contact Mr. Falkes as a favor for my efforts."

"You didn't meet Sherm during the Fraser campaign?"

"Not until after. Mr. Falkes arrived at the celebration party. Well after the results were indicating a Fraser win."

"When you and Sergeant Gordon planned the motel bust, did Gordon mention Falkes?" Andros asked.

"Are you kidding? Of course not. Falkes was the furthest thing from our minds."

"Did Perry Casey know you were working with Seattle PD on this?"

"No."

"Do you think you should have told him?"

"I don't know. I would have discussed it with him sooner or later. It is part of a prosecutor's job to advise the police."

Andros put down his pen and laid his hands on the desk in front of him. "Let me make it clear where it appears that Sherman Falkes and Perry Casey failed to do so. Your workload is assigned by this office. Your cases are assigned by Casey or the chief of whatever section you may be assigned to while working for Casey. Please, in the future, let him know if you are working on anything office-related that has not been assigned to you. Under me, only certain deputies will work with police departments on administrative or matters other than case filings. Clear?"

"Yes. Certainly," Turner said coolly.

"Advising police is tricky business. They tend to have a selective memory and a selective understanding.

"By the way," Andros added. "Because one of my law partners is a rather well-known and active Democrat, I have a delicate problem. I personally try to be nonpolitical. I often wish this office were nonpartisan, but, so long as it is partisan, I have to play the game. I've decided that, once a deputy has declared to run for this office, he or she will be required to resign."

"I hope that is not on my account, Mr. Andros."

Andros said nothing. He picked up his notes and went over them. Finally, he asked, "Do you have anything to add? Understand you're welcome to let me know if there's anything else you remember."

"I think we've been over it. Twice," Turner added as he rose.

"Thank you," Andros said.

Turner left the room, closing the door quietly.

Einar Torgeson waited for Paul Andros to speak.

"Do you mind helping me out for a few weeks, Einar?"

"No," he said.

"Are you ready to start?" Andros asked.

"I'll do what Burnside says," Torgeson said.

Paul was well acquainted with Ms. Marian Burnside, Chief Investigator of the Washington State Human Rights Commission, and knew that where Torgeson was laconic, Burnside was temperamental. No doubt she was angered by the call from the governor's office requesting Torgeson, and resented having to reassign Torgeson's heavy caseload. If she were unhappy, she could be absolutely savage in her retaliation against whoever she regarded as the cause of her displeasure. Obviously, Torgeson wanted no part of her wrath.

"What's her number?" Andros asked.

"234-2898 on SCAN," he answered.

Andros dialed the number, hoping he could direct her wrath upstairs, away from himself and Einar.

"Hello," a husky voice said.

"Ms. Burnside? This is Paul Andros."

"What do you want now, Andros? Secretaries? Cars? We just got two new cars this year after ten years. Would you like one of them? Both?"

Paul visualized her red-dyed hair in a tight bun. She wore a uniform of blue blazer, white blouse, and gray slacks.

"Look, I needed a good investigator who is outside of the King County law enforcement scene and who knows his way around. Einar did one of the finest jobs of investigation I've ever seen on that King County roads discrimination matter."

"Which you completely scuttled with your dealmaking, Mr. Andros."

"Wait a minute, Ms. Burnside. I admitted the police could do better, but I saw no reason why the commission needed blood. Your attorneys agreed to the disposition."

"Our attorneys are witless, green-behind-the-ears deputy AGs who don't listen to their clients and undermine our work."

"Well, sorry they're not up to your standards, but they're more than I wanted to take on, so we took an agreed order."

"Which they bumbled.... How long do you need Torgy?" she asked abruptly.

"I don't know," Paul answered.

"Well, I wouldn't have your job looking under rocks in that nest of snakes you've got up there. You look out for Torgy, now. And I want him part time on a few files, but we shifted most of his load. He can take care of what he's got left without interfering with this assignment.... Damn governor called me!"

"That was nice. Oh, and speaking of cars, I assume the governor authorized him to use his state car while he's up here?" Andros said.

"He can use it so long as he burns your gas. I'll let you figure out how to do that. And I want Torgy to know he doesn't have to be reassigned if he doesn't want to."

"Hold on, Ms. Burnside."

Paul did not cover the mouthpiece as he spoke to Einar Torgeson. "Einar, she wants you to know you don't have to be reassigned to me if you don't want to."

Torgeson ran his long fingers through his sparse, gray hair across his bald spot.

"I don't think he objects, Ms. Burnside, and I really need somebody from outside the local system," Paul interpreted.

"You tell him he does not have to stay and he may come back whenever he likes. Tell him!"

"She says for me to tell you that you don't have to stay and you may return to the commission whenever you want," Paul repeated.

"Regardless of whether you're finished using him."

"Regardless of whether I'm finished with the investigation or regardless of whether I want you to continue."

Torgeson nodded.

"He understands, Ms. Burnside."

"Good-bye," she said abruptly and hung up.

"Well, that's it, Einar. You're on."

"Better let me have a note pad, Mr. Andros. I probably shouldn't use state paper on a county job."

Paul and Einar set up a table in Paul's office for records and reports of the Majestic Motel bust and the preliminary investigation of Sherm's death. Paul hopped back and forth between office business and the files while Einar pondered each report. Paul knew that Torgeson was accustomed to working independently and could do his job without any supervision. Running the King County prosecuting attorney's office was another matter.

Estate of confusion

SEVEN

ANDROS AND TORGESON LEFT the King County Courthouse together at 6:15 P.M. As they walked to the county parking garage, Torgeson followed with his lanky, disjointed strides a half step behind Andros' compact movements.

Both of their cars were in visitor's slots on the first floor.

"See you there," Paul said as he got into his car, a new looking 1978 Volvo. Torgeson nodded and strolled across the aisle to his state-owned Dodge Dart of unknown vintage.

They were off to meet the mother of Sherman Falkes' children and to look over Sherm's apartment. When Carol Bennett, Falkes' ex-wife, had remarried and bought a home with her new husband, Sherman had purchased a condominium nearby. His children, a son and a daughter, visited Sherm whenever they liked and had free access to his apartment.

The Seattle police had called Carol and requested a time to look over the apartment. Carol had referred the police to Paul, as her attorney. Andros had arranged for the police to search the apartment the next day, but he was anxious to be the first to look around before the police got there. Paul had called Carol during the day and learned that, although Sherm had changed his will after their divorce, he had maintained Carol as the executrix. Carol wanted to talk to Paul and go through the apartment. She wanted Paul to serve as attorney for the estate, but, as prosecutor, even acting prosecutor, he could accept no private cases. They had agreed that Carol would retain Scott Turnbull in his place, and Paul would take over when his short stint as prosecutor was finished. She probably should have gone to another attorney, but she was insistent that he and Scott should handle the case. Paul decided to wait until an actual conflict arose before he made her go elsewhere.

As he drove toward Sherm's apartment in Magnolia, Paul reflected on his mistrust of the Seattle police in this affair. They certainly had caught Sherm red-handed in the Majestic Motel raid. Nothing wrong in that. Yet Paul had to admit to himself that he resented that the Seattle police had embarrassed the prosecutor's office. Also, Sergeant Gordon coordinated and planned the raid with the help of that supercilious little shit Turner right under Sherman's nose. But it was not just resentment that the prosecutor's office was embarrassed. Seattle PD was big and unwieldy, impossible to manage without meticulous rules and procedures. In some prosecutions the witness list often included ten or twelve different police officers working some part of a complicated case. Perhaps Seattle PD was not a quagmire of corruption like some other big-city police departments, but Andros saw it as nonresponsive to the community. He felt that, to be effective, policemen must avoid viewing themselves as a separate class. But after rousting drunks, sociopaths, and unmanageable juvenile delinquents, policemen begin to see the bad side in everyone with whom they have contact. Paul called it the "asshole syndrome"—everyone's an asshole. It is an attitude that can only be treated by constant education and responsible leadership that maintains and values police professionalism. Andros felt they were not getting either one.

Knowing police psychology, Andros knew they would be expecting a cover-up if anyone else except Seattle PD did the investigation, but, if left to their own devices, Paul knew they would concentrate on exposing the salacious details of the last evening of Sherm's life while stamping out any part of the trail that might uncover the details of his death. Paul wanted to stay in front of them.

Carol Bennett opened the door of Sherman Falkes' apartment. She was a dark-complexioned woman with elegant gray tips in her dark brunette hair. She was never without several silver bracelets and necklaces and she seemed to Paul to jingle and jangle like wind chimes in a breeze. Men were usually attracted to her exotic appearance, but Paul always found her thinking to be obtuse and elliptical. During and after her marriage to Sherm, she had a successful career as a commercial artist for Norbusch, a large department store chain. She had continued her active social life after her divorce from Sherman. Paul had heard that she was remarried to a well-to-do real estate broker.

"I couldn't skip work today. But my boss sent me home early. So I've been here since three o'clock," she said.

"I'm sorry I couldn't get here sooner, Carol. " Paul said.

"Who's this?" she said, spying Einar behind Paul. "God. I told you no police. Not yet."

"This is Einar Torgeson, Carol. He works for me at the prosecutor's office. I want him to help me go over Sherm's papers. I selected him because I felt him to be discreet."

Carol ignored Einar and directed her attention to Paul. "It's bullshit, Paul. The papers say that suicide is suspected by the Seattle police. Bu-ull-she-et. Sherm Falkes would not purposefully end his life, Paul."

She and Paul sat down on the modern sofa. Einar remained standing as Carol continued talking.

"I don't think it was any kind of accident either. I think somebody killed him. Sherm was killed by the hand of another. You should find out who killed Sherm. You really should do that." She touched Paul's arm as if catching Sherm's killer was as simple as passing her a tray of hors d'oeuvres.

"I'm trying to find out what happened, Carol."

"I know you are," she said. "Well, let's get going. I made some coffee about an hour ago, but I can make some fresh." She sat on the couch and put both her hands on Paul's arm. The silver bracelets bunched around her wrists. "Don't mind me. It's been like being locked in a morgue here all afternoon. This place is antiseptic as hell, but it still brings back memories..."

Paul broke in. "I want to get you out of here as soon as I can, Carol. What I wanted to do was inventory Sherm's papers, both for the purpose of helping you in administrating his estate and investigating his death."

Paul pointed to Einar who had seated himself on a straight chair across the room. "Einar and I will try not to pry unnecessarily into yours and Sherm's and the kids' private lives."

Carol set her mouth very firmly. "I'm not choked up over Sherm. I vowed long ago to shed my last tear over him. I will tell you that it was a shock to find the will and learn I was the executrix."

"Sherm never mentioned this to you?" Paul asked.

"If he did, it didn't register. I knew that he had made provisions for the children, and that I was trustee for their life insurance ... But ..."

"What other family did Sherm have?"

"I've written it down for you, in case you need it. His mother is still alive in Oakland. His father is long gone. Probably dead. An alcoholic. Mother linked up with the Pentecostal Something-or-Other Church when daddy abandoned her and Sherm. I never could stand her. That was one thing Sherm and I agreed on. He grew up in this little house on a thirty-foot lot in Oakland. As near as I could figure it out, she kept Sherm in tow until he was in high school. God knows how. Then he gradually broke away from her. His high school grades were good enough to get him into Berkeley with scholarships and student loans. He took student housing and moved out of Oakland over to Berkeley. He never saw much of her after that. Maybe he was afraid of her. I know I was. We took the kids through there when they were just infants. We stopped to see her. She wasn't really interested in them. Talked about Jesus and wouldn't even go out to dinner. Paul just packed us all in the car and said 'bye, Mama' and we left."

"Any brothers or sisters?"

Carol's eyes flashed and her jewelry jangled as she relaxed into a cocktail conversation posture. "Hey. When Mary Falkes discovered what she had done to bring about little Sherman's arrival in the world, she crossed her legs forever. I'd bet even her pee barely trickled out."

Paul tried hard not to laugh. He looked over at Einar who stared, glassy-eyed, as he held his ever-present notebook and pen in readiness for a significant note. If he saw any significance to Carol's reminiscences of her mother-in-law, he did not take any notes concerning whatever it was.

"Her address is on the list?" Paul asked.

"Yes. But the list isn't long. I guess that's why Sherm always adored Timmy and Lisa, because he had no family, no relatives, no brother or sister. Just him and his grim, old mama in Oakland—which is not exactly Cheerfulsville, California, you know."

"What did you find in the apartment here, Carol?"

Carol looked away from Paul and glanced at Einar as she moved forward on the couch and picked up the pile of papers on the coffee table.

"Let's see. I found a bar association insurance policy to the kids for fifty thousand. I know the county has a death benefit, but I couldn't find a policy. That's all the insurance. Here's the deed to the condominium here and the payment book. He owes sixty thousand, and it might be worth over a hundred, with the view of the Ship Canal and all. It's nicer than our house, but it's not too big. He had a money market account with Merrill Lynch with a balance of ten thousand five hundred dollars. He had a savings account at Sea-World of five grand, with a checking balance of nine hundred and fifty dollars. He was really doing pretty good, considering he paid child support to me of nine hundred and fifty dollars per month and had an eight hundred and ten dollar mortgage payment and a car payment of a hundred and ninety-five bucks. That's over two grand off the top before utilities. My God. I don't know what he used to live on."

"Anything else?"

"I found these papers on an apartment house in Capitol Hill."

"Oh?"

Einar paused from his note taking.

"Yes, to 'Sherman H. Falkes, a single man, and Jake Satello and Maria Satello, his wife.' I guess that means he's partners with a guy named Satello. There's a bunch of papers in a file in the desk and a bank book."

"Any rent receipts, anything with names other than Jake Satello?" Paul asked.

"Not that I saw," she said.

"What's the date of the deed?" Paul asked.

"November nine, nineteen-seventy-six. The papers said they paid three hundred thousand with ten thousand down. The payments are three grand a month, to some doctor. The bank account is in the name of Afterhours Group."

"Did he ever discuss this with you?"

"No. I just figured it out from the closing papers."

"But no rental records?"

"Just skimmed through. I couldn't find any receipt book. Just a record of deposits. The account has about fifteen thousand in it."

"I think we'll bundle up all that apartment house stuff and let Einar go through it before we meet with Jake Satello. We'll let the Seattle police know we have it," Paul said.

"Do you know him? This Satello guy?" she asked.

"A little bit," Paul answered. "He's a cop on the Seattle police force. A captain. I don't know his current assignment. I guess now your kids are Jake's new partner."

Carol stared at him blankly. She started to speak, and then looked down at the pile.

"I'm sure it will all sort out," she said. "Here's some car papers, car insurance. We should get enough from the insurance to pay off the loan."

"Did you find his cancelled checks?"

"Yes. They're in the desk."

"I'd like those bundled up for Einar as well. I think we better do it now. Anything else?"

"Just this. It was sitting over by the telephone when I came in." Carol handed Andros a one-page document—a Seattle police report. The victim was a twenty-two-year old woman—Martine Rodriguez. She had been mugged in the women's restroom at the Broadway Fred Meyers store. No suspects.

"Does this mean anything to you, Carol?"

"You know, the kids talked about going out to dinner and a movie with a girlfriend of Sherm's they called Marty. I saw the name and wondered if it was the same girl."

"Interesting. Anything else?"

"I think that's it."

"Could we take a quick look over the apartment, then?"

Paul rose and Carol jumped up beside him.

"Sure. Follow me."

It was a townhouse-type unit. The ceiling of the living room was two-story open beam and sloped upward from the front window toward the upstairs. There was an open staircase on one side of the living room and a fireplace on the other side. A balcony extended over the living room and marked the edge of the dining room and kitchen under the upstairs bedrooms. Beyond the kitchen was a bath and utility room.

Paul and Einar followed Carol on a quick downstairs tour. The apartment looked like a showroom for the Bon Furniture Annex. The kitchen was fully equipped, and the utensils and appliances were all a-shine. A full pot of coffee was still warming on the coffee maker on the counter.

"Oh, I forgot, that coffee. I'll make more fresh."

Paul and Einar stood aside without objections while she dumped out the coffee and the grounds and fixed a fresh pot. Paul opened cupboards and took out dishes, food, utensils. He examined and returned articles on each shelf.

Carol watched him intensely as the coffee dribbled through the coffee maker.

"Look, Carol. Einar and I want to search this place. Top to bottom. I would let you go home and leave us to it, but

I really need you here as another witness and to answer further questions."

"No problem. The kids are with Jack, my husband. So take as long as you like."

They drank coffee and proceeded to work through the apartment. It appeared not to be lived in. The master bedroom upstairs had Sherm's clothes and the two smaller bedrooms each had a few clothes and personal belongings of Timmy and Lisa. There was a TV and stereo in the living room with a library of classical music and soft rock tapes. There was no sign of anyone else in the apartment except Sherm and the kids. Sherm had established a work area in the living room where he kept his financial records. His apartment partnership records appeared to be in good order, except there did not appear to be any rent receipt records. Paul and Einar packed up the apartment records and Sherm's personal bankbook and cancelled checks in grocery sacks to take along.

"I think that's good enough for us amateurs," Paul said at 8:45. "Let's lock it up."

"Funny" Paul said. "No cash or valuables around the house. None whatsoever."

Paul looked casually at Carol. "Did you find any cash when you came over on Sunday? Put it away or something?"

"Me?" she said. Her wrists tinkled as she put her graceful fingers to her bosom protectively. "No. I didn't find any money... I looked around, but I assumed any cash he had was on him when he died."

Andros felt sure she was lying. "Did you come by yourself?"

"Yes. Jack stayed with the kids."

It didn't make any difference to him that she found some cash and appropriated it. But it would be interesting to know how much cash Sherm had laying around the house in addition to the fifteen thousand in his bank accounts.

They looked briefly through the garage, but even it was model-like, as neat and apparently as little used as the apartment. Not even a grease spot on the floor.

Paul sent Einar on for his long drive to Olympia and told him not to show up until after noon the next day. He stayed with Carol while she turned off the coffee and the lights and locked up.

He was walking her to the car when she said, "Just a minute, Paul. I just thought of something. Could we go back in for a minute?"

"Sure," he said reluctantly. It had been a long day.

He followed her as she unlocked the front door and went through the hallway to the kitchen and from there to the garage. She headed to a medium-sized workbench with tools hanging neatly on a rack above an ample worktable. There was a bank of drawers on the right. Einar had opened and closed the drawers when they were previously in the garage. Carol put on a pair of rubber gloves that were sitting atop the bench and opened the second drawer from the top. She removed sticky cans of glue and paint from the drawer, and a brush with some sort of thick sticky substance on the bristles and the handle. She put them on the table surface. Then she pulled the drawer out as far as it could go, which Paul could see was not the full width of the table surface.

"Oh, I see. It's short-drawered."

"He did that for me with a kitchen drawer when we were married. For my jewelry. But I never bothered with it. He stored a few papers and stuff. I noticed it before you guys came."

"Did you look inside?"

"I was going to come back. But it's late. I'm tired. And I'm terrible at lying if there was something in there I wanted to hide."

She took down a screwdriver from the tool rack. "There's a cleat that is screwed onto the back of the drawer. That's what holds it so it won't open. See the screw there? I'll loosen it and the cleat will fall off or move to the side and, voila, a place to store valuables."

She removed the drawer. The vacant space was enclosed with thin plywood on the back, bottom, and sides. Paul could see a pile of papers, cash, and checks.

"Would you remove everything for me, Carol? Don't remove the gloves."

"OK," she said quietly. She piled up the papers, police reports, the checks, and the cash on the bench top.

Paul had taken a notebook out from the sack of other papers he was carrying. "Count the checks, please."

There were ten checks for two hundred ninety-five dollars and six for three hundred ninety-five dollars made out to After Hours, Inc. "That's five thousand three hundred and twenty. Would you count the cash, please?"

There were thirty-five 100s, sixty-two 50s, and two hundred and fifty 20s. "That's eleven thousand, six hundred and forty. Lots of renters paying in cash. I wonder how big that apartment house is. Carol, have you taken any cash? It's important."

"I opened it up and saw it in there and I certainly thought about it. But I didn't touch it. It all belongs to the kids anyway."

"So you didn't take anything."

"Well, no . . ."

"Carol, you can't be vague or cute on this or the Seattle police will eat your lunch."

"No . . . no. It's just I thought about it."

"You told me that. So you didn't take anything."

"No. No!"

"Where were you Friday night?"

"Thank heavens, I'm so relieved you asked. Jack and I and the kids went to Long Beach Thursday evening. We were going to stay 'til Sunday, but Jack thought we'd better get back when we heard the news."

"Look at those police reports. Do you recognize any of the names?"

There were eight police reports. Paul looked over her shoulder as she went through them. Three dated back to 1973 and 1974, just after Sherm had been elected.

"Eww," she exclaimed. "Look at this. James R. Ferranti. That rings a bell. DWI? I never heard about that."

"That might be the reason the report's in the drawer, Carol."

"Oh ... oh!"

She didn't recognize the other names: some fifty-five-year-old man suspected of making a homosexual solicitation to a kid at Volunteer Park. A sixteen-year-old girl with a Laurelhurst address busted for marijuana. Three were King County police. The other five were Seattle police. The first was dated 1976, the same year, Paul thought, that Sherm got involved with the apartment house.

"I know this one," Paul exclaimed. "Old Jennings Fairhurst. Thirty-two years on the force. Came in a patrolman. Went out a patrolman. Everybody liked him, but he was thick as a post. DWI. Looks like Mr. Falkes mixed compassion and politics in losing police reports."

"Huh?"

"If I had to guess, Carol, I think these are reports that just somehow didn't get properly charged by the prosecutor's office."

"Is that as bad as buying sex from sixteen-year-old girls?"

Andros realized this was the first remark from Carol that indicated any emotion over the circumstances of Sherm's death. "I can't answer that," he said carefully.

"Well, I can. And thank heavens Jack is willing to adopt the kids so they can change their name."

Keeping cool, staying hot

EIGHT

THE LAST THING TERRY WANTED TO DO that night was return to the Majestic Motel. He was afraid that it might be staked out with squads of cops. His reason told him that his fears were unwarranted, but he had no desire for any further contact with the police. No way.

Reeney had gone bitch on him. Only eight 20s in her purse. There was a stash laid away in the motel, and he needed it.

He walked to a luncheonette on First Avenue and ate fish and chips and drank coffee slowly until late afternoon. The weather was clear when he left the restaurant, and he decided to hike across town to use up time until dark.

It was sundown by the time he made it to the east end of the block where the Majestic was located. He strolled by the Third Avenue side of the building. He kept looking for cops or cop cars. He walked a block south past the parking lot and continued around the block to the south so that he could approach the motel from the west on Doris Street.

He didn't see anything suspicious, but the absence of police cars meant nothing. The narcs used unmarked vehicles and dressed in unlikely clothes, like the narc that beat up Tangerine. He had to be a narc, or some dude the narcs were using.

He walked slowly until he spotted a middle-aged couple getting out of their car in the parking lot. He timed his pace so that he held the lobby door open for the woman.

Terry smiled at the husband. "Looks like no rain tonight."

"Yes. It is pleasant," the man replied.

They entered the lobby together and the couple walked toward the east wing. Terry followed until they got to the beverage machine where he stopped and made a show of fumbling for his change. The couple disappeared down the hall.

Terry continued to move coins around his palm while he looked over the small lobby and the hall leading to the west wing. No one. Nothing suspicious. He opened the fire door to the east wing stairway leading to the second floor. The corridor was empty. Things appeared to be slow. It was early Monday night.

He moved quickly down the hall to the ice machine alcove on the west wing. He had his pocketknife with the screwdriver blade ready and quickly disassembled the casing over the top of the ice storage bin. The clear plastic bag of white powder was still there, saddled and taped over the copper piping. The bag felt cool as he lifted his sweater and put it inside his shirt next to his skin.

"Keep me cool while I stay hot," he murmured to himself.

He refastened one of the screws to hold the casing and hurried back to the east wing. He avoided the lobby and headed toward the emergency exit at the end of the hallway. Before opening the door, he removed the globe over the hall light and unscrewed the hot bulb. He took off his denim jacket, rolled it up, and put it under his arm.

He pushed the door bar quietly and moved swiftly into the night. The parking lot was to his left and there was an alley to his right. He walked down the alley until he found an opening through the parking lot of a deserted building that went through to the next street north.

He continued working his way through openings in the middle of the block until he came to the Kingdome parking lot. Before crossing the street, he put on his denim jacket.

He headed west for the understructure of the Alaska Viaduct. A patrol car slowly cruised on Elliot Way. Looking for him? He assumed the worst but walked on at a steady pace. He skirted around Pioneer Square and headed up Third Avenue to University. He walked east to the Park Northwest Hotel.

A stack of cabs six deep idled in front of the hotel. Three drivers, two white, one black, were standing by the fourth cab back waiting to move up. They looked up expectantly as Terry walked toward them.

"Cab, mister?" asked the black cabby.

"Yeah," Terry said tentatively. The driver led him to the rear cab.

Terry pulled out a five-dollar bill and held it out. "Hey, man," Terry said, "what I really need is a snort. I'm just off the boat. I gotta find me some whee."

The black man's face hardened. "I don't know what you talkin' 'bout. You wanna go some place or not?"

"Jesus, man. I'm no narc. Do I look like a narc? Jeez."

Terry started to walk away. Then he turned around and came back.

"Look. Just tell me someone I can talk to," he said, the fiver still in his hand.

The black man reached for the note belligerently. "Man, I don't know what you talking about. Go in the big hotel, there. Somebody there can help you, I'll bet."

"Who, dammit?" Terry still held onto the note.

"If a man go in that hotel, he need some luggage. Yeah luggage's what he need," he mumbled.

He looked into Terry's eyes and grinned as he pulled on the note. Terry released his grip.

"Which one?" he asked.

The black man still smiled.

"What you want, man? You want me killed? You a smart-looking cat. Go in there and look around. You'll connect."

"Thanks for nothin'."

"Go on. Go on. You'll connect."

Terry decided he had been dumb in this blind approach. He had wasted five bucks. Smarten up, he thought, entering the hotel.

But the cabby had been right. Spotting his man was no problem.

There were two bellhops. One, with wily eyes, looked over fifty; the other, trim and young, with styled black hair, wore black suede, cushion-soled shoes.

Terry waited at the lobby newsstand until the older guy went off and the younger bellhop was at his little desk outside the corner of the registration desk. The young man watched Terry as he crossed the lobby.

"Yes, sir?" he asked. His helpfulness was restrained, as if he would have to carefully evaluate whether he would perform any service Terry requested.

Terry spoke low. "Look, you little shit. You have just stumbled into the buy of a lifetime. I can be here in fifteen minutes with twelve ounces of coke. Good stuff. I need money and I need it fast. My contact's busted, and some creep at the bus station wants me to fire sale it for fifteen hundred bucks. If you want to do better, it's yours."

The young man laughed and walked around from the short counter. "I don't think I understand you. Do you know anyone I know?"

Terry said, "I know Joe, the bartender at 21 Palms in Pioneer Square. I know Maurice at the Frontwater."

The young man's eyebrows lifted. "Hold on a minute. What's your name?"

"Terry. But tell him I dyed my hair."

Terry returned to the newsstand. The young man disappeared, soon returned, and reached into his pocket. Ten twenties were clipped together.

"I've got two hundred bucks here, and you're hot. Maurice says the man is all over town looking for you."

"Ok. Try two ounces. If you like it, I'll come back later tonight."

"I don't want you near this place. I can get together five hundred. I'll owe you twelve hundred."

"Owe me? What are we here, lovebirds?"

"Look. You can carry it around and have it on you when you get busted or leave it with me. Maurice says you are very, very warm."

Terry reached deep for a past coolness he had lost since Friday night.

"Look, motherfucker," he said. It's fifteen hundred now or I walk."

The punk studied him carefully. "Come on."

Terry followed him across the lobby and watched as he unlocked a door to the baggage storage room at the far end of the registration desk.

"Stand in the doorway." He reached inside his coat pocket and turned his back to Terry. When he turned around again it was to show Terry a fan of fifteen one-hundred-dollar bills.

Terry silently reached inside his shirt for the plastic bag.

"Stand there" the young man said as he took the bag. Quickly, he untaped the bag and reached a wetted finger inside. He licked the white powder. He handed Terry the bills.

"Pleasure doing business with you, Terry," he said, smiling.

But Terry was gone.

Falkes
and figures

NINE

H. Scott Turnbull possessed a legendary appetite. He broke fast in different restaurants all over Seattle while he met with clients and associates or while he languished over whatever legal file had seemed particularly unmanageable the day before. On Thursday morning at 7:30 A.M., he sipped his coffee at the Delphi Café on Capital Hill as he picked out salient points from a doctor's report for a settlement offer in a personal injury case.

"Some day I'm going to get up early enough to beat you here," came Andros' voice as he took a seat at the corner booth.

"That would be a vain attempt. I sleep no longer than nature's first call to the pissoir, and that, my boy, comes very early."

Scott cleared his papers away from the place setting across the table. The craggy bags underneath Scott's heavy-lidded gray eyes pointed down to his cheeks. His dark blue double-breasted suit was bulky in front to contour around his glasses case, pocket calendar, and various legal papers stuffed into both inner pockets. He never worried about his diet, and was surprisingly fit, but his loose skin gave him the appearance of a heavy man who had just lost weight.

"Make yourself comfortable, Paul, and tell me: how you would summarize your first few days as His Prosecutorial Highness? Have you cleaned the streets of scum and vermin? Have you restored our community to its righteous and law-abiding citizens?"

The words rolled around his jowls like as if he were intoning some religious liturgy.

"Sure I did. I should be ready to get back to the office by the end of the month."

"Before you leave office I have a list of little corruptions you can put a stop to, like radar speed traps and police-sponsored charities. Like who the hell wants to pay fifty bucks to watch donkey basketball? And while you're at it, why don't you put a stop to pandering to the rights of thieves, whores, muggers and murderers? What an absurd idea that anti-socials have rights! The only reason we put ourselves to any trouble for them is because our judicial so-called intellectuals fear a police state more than social anomie. And in this worst of all possible worlds we end up with both."

"Better that ten guilty go free than one innocent person be prosecuted."

"Damn foolishness. Ten maniacs should be let loose to maim and kill and endanger our personal safety to protect one guy's ass who was in the wrong place at the wrong time or looks like someone else?"

"Easily said unless you're the innocent guy."

"Bosh. As I've always said, the real reason behind all this pandering is that our judicial policymakers fear to embrace the French and South American banana republic system, where the police haul in the guilty and the courts rubber-stamp the arrest and determine the sentence. That's the way to keep law and order."

"No Magna Carta? No English legal traditions? No civil rights?"

A soft voice broke from behind Paul. "No civil rights? You going to eliminate the people's civil rights in your new job?"

Andros turned to greet the smiling, white-haired black man clearing the table behind them. "Jimmie. How the hell are you? Helen still cracking the whip?"

"Your mother never got the word about emancipation," he said.

Paul moved over and motioned for him to sit. Jimmie was very thin. He moved slowly as he sat down beside Paul.

"Scott, you've met Jimmie Smith."

"Paul, you have introduced me to Mr. Smith at least a dozen times. How are you, Jimmie?"

"I'm fine. But I worry about all this mess Paul's taken on. His mother's swollen up about his being new prosecutor. But what's going to happen to his work with you, Mr. Turnbull?"

"Nothing. It's temporary, two jobs for a while. That's why we're meeting here this morning."

Jimmie Smith turned to Paul. "What's it like to go back to work at the prosecutor's office after all those years?"

Paul knew that Jimmie's question was not just polite conversation. Smith was an articulate man, soft-spoken but deeply observant of the character and dimensions of the people around him. His co-workers at the Delphi suspected there was a mystery about Jimmie Smith, but it was an unwritten rule to avoid probing questions about his background. Paul always felt an inexplicable respect and closeness to him.

"It's hard to say. Everything's moving so fast that I haven't had time to collect myself. It's more like starting to work on a new case than settling in on a new life."

"Paper said you were only going to be temporary. I wasn't sure it was true."

"It's true, Jimmie. If I left Turnbull, Padgett, and Andros, Mr. Turnbull here would have to be marched off to the old-folks home. Provided they'd have him."

Scott snorted.

Jimmie Smith smiled at Scott. "Don't sound like he's too respectful of his elders, does it?"

"I don't care whether he's respectful of his elders, so long as he's respectful of his betters. In present company, Mr. Smith, he has every reason to be respectful."

Jimmie Smith avoided the banter. "What was Jane's feeling about you taking all this on, Paul? She and little Bea probably see scant enough of you as it is. Should you be taking all this on? Your daughter will be gone before long. You should be thinking about that."

He stated it as fact, not rebuke. He smiled. "Well, I'm not criticizing. Not my place. But I'm an old man. I know how fast life slips by. I want you to know that."

Andros didn't answer. They ceased chatting while the waitress brought Andros a cup of coffee and refilled Turnbull's cup. Jimmie slipped out of the booth.

"Take care, Paul. Your mother will be sorry she missed you. Everybody around here sure wishes you well."

Paul and Scott sat in silence for a moment, thinking about the old man's words as he watched him carry a tray of dishes back to the kitchen.

"Did you get an autopsy report?" Scott asked, bringing him to the point of the meeting.

"Yeah, finally. It is confirmed that Sherm Falkes did not commit suicide. He was murdered."

"'Murder'. Now there's a potent word. The papers will love to make a great deal of it. 'Homicide' is always less inflammatory. What have you got to prove murder? And who is a likely candidate to accuse?"

"At this point, proving murder is the easy part. The autopsy shows no smoke or burns in his lungs, so he wasn't breathing when the car burned up. I wasn't surprised. My gut feel is that no matter how badly Sherm was personally or politically embarrassed by being caught in a whorehouse, he would not commit suicide. His ex-wife shares my opinion. She knew him better than I did.

"Regarding a likely candidate, the police are frantic to get their hands on the pimp, Terry Barnes, who got caught in the motel bust. I guess they think Sherm knew him and got into an argument over protection, or the lack thereof. Carol Bennett, Sherm's ex-wife, showed me a hiding place in Sherm's condo where he had stashed some police reports on various people that I suspect did not get followed up on in the prosecutor's office."

"Deliberately lost?"

"I'm almost positive. It will be easy to check out. Maybe Barnes expected the same kind of treatment and Sherm told him it wasn't going to work. The argument gets out of hand, and Sherm ends up dead. But there was no sign of any struggle at Sherm's condo. Except for the stashed reports and some cash the apartment was clean as a whistle. The cash was interesting. There was a lot of cash and some checks that I think were rent receipts from an apartment house he owned with Jake Satello, a Seattle police captain. Einar checked the assessor's records and found that after some recent remodeling the apartment house has 24 units. There were checks for five thousand three hundred twenty dollars covering sixteen units. That's less than four hundred bucks a unit. Suppose the rent for the other eight units was paid in cash at four hundred per unit, that's thirty-two hundred. We found eleven thousand, six hundred and forty in cash. That's more than eight grand over the monthly rent receipts. What the hell is that about, Scott? Could Sherm have been holding out on his partner? I'm having Einar find out everything he can about that apartment deal. But Sherm's dealings with Satello is every bit as interesting as whatever dealings he had with the pimp."

Scott Turnbull's eyebrows lifted. "Who is this goddamn Einar Torgeson that you set such store by? Why not just let the police investigate the damn thing? It's getting complicated. You've got enough on your plate."

"Einar is one of those famous Norwegian bachelors Garrison Keillor talks about. He's also a damn good investigator. He beat us up real bad when I was with the county. A black employee complained that the county's supervisor selection process for road crews was discriminatory."

Scott Turnbull grunted. "WASP selection committees selecting WASPs. The proposition is self-evident."

"Well, Einar Torgeson has the ability to prove it. He's an astute interviewer. He has a kind of bland, self-effacing manner that conceals his ability to get beneath the surface of things. Unlike you, he listens to people instead of arguing."

Scott lifted his eyebrows in mute opposition to the criticism. "What else are you looking at?" he asked.

"For one thing, Scott, I think that Sherm was into things more serious than dipping his wick in young girls."

"That seems likely enough."

"No. There's something fishy about his apartment, his finances, his lack of involvement in the office. I think that Sherm had fallen apart below the surface."

"What about his finances?"

"I went over his check register and paychecks last night. I just skimmed it, but his pay stubs show he cleared about forty-five hundred after taxes, social security, retirement and medical. I figure he had well over three grand in fixed expenses. Like he paid over a thousand per month on his condo with utilities and association fees, nine hundred fifty in child support, two hundred on his car payment without gas and oil and insurance, so say four hundred in auto expenses. He had over three hundred per month payments in furniture and bank cards. He put a few hundred dollars a month in bank accounts that he never touched. There's a bunch of money in an apartment house account. Then there's all that cash. I can't see where he could afford to eat, and there he is with all that money running around buying ass."

Scott Turnbull removed the last biscuit from the napkin-lined basket. He split it and proceeded to spread butter and jam upon it as he asked, "What makes you think he was *buying* ass?"

"Exactly, Scott, exactly. I'm thinking he was involved in that girlie operation or was being paid off in *merchandise*. He used his salary income to purchase a respectable condominium where his kids could freely come and go and stay whenever they liked. He banked his paycheck, paid the fixed bills, and had a savings account. But all of his out-of-pocket expenditures, like food and clothes and vacations, were paid from his extracurricular activities."

Scott sipped some coffee to top off his biscuit. "What would Sherm have had to sell?" he asked speculatively.

"Item one. Sherm could use his position to deep six certain police reports that came to the office for charging. We did a quiet check at the office. Of the eight reports we found at his house, there were either no charges or minor misdemeanors. There could be other crimes charged at less than the facts warranted, or cases could be plea-bargained down to minor infractions. That gets hard to check. But Casey says Sherm always went over the police reports before giving them to him, so he can't say for sure what came in unless whatever agency that submitted a report checks on its status."

"Casey?"

"Chief criminal deputy. And Sherm could easily tip off interested persons as to search warrants and police raids. It's the prosecutor that presents search warrants and gets them signed by the judge."

Scott Turnbull placed both stubby hands on the table and squared his body evenly in the booth.

"None of those feels completely right to me, but you are going to have to check them out.

"It seems to me," Scott continued, "that a prosecutor works too much in the light of police, judges, other prosecutors, and even defense attorneys, to manage an extensive justice perversion operation. He could do something odd every once in a while, but I'm sure if you accosted him on the eight police reports, he would have had a ready explanation. It does seem to me that Sherm could sell his knowledge of the law-and-order game and the players, rather than perform specific acts of defalcation. Certainly, preknowledge on execution of search warrants would be a marketable commodity, but he'd have to be careful."

"Kind of a broker? Work through one trusted police officer?" Paul asked.

"Uh huh. Like this apartment house partner. Who's this guy Jake?"

"Jake Satello? He's been around a long time. Seattle PD. He's a captain, I think. I just remember he used to come by the office quite a bit. He and Sherm were pals. I always thought it was political stuff."

"So what, counsel? What's the difference if Sherm had some pals on the police force?"

"Nothing at all, counsel. Except it confirms what I observed when I worked with Sherm. Young prosecutors often get all caught up in the cops-and-robbers game and begin to acquire the police mentality. Rather than seeing themselves as lawyers and officers of the court, they become instruments of the accuse-arrest-and-detain process. Sherm was always a Hessian. Terrill Bascom was always lecturing him about making more judicious charging decisions. Sherm's idea of reasonable cause was just getting your name under the suspect heading on a police report. Never grew out of it. His political base certainly wasn't the Urban League or the Washington Business Association. He pandered to every police association in the county that would give out an endorsement. If you look at his public disclosure files, you'll probably see a pattern of workers and police buddies in Kirkland, Bellevue, Seattle, Renton, King County. A man could cash in on a friend or two developed through that network a whole lot more productively and safely than losing a few files or playing round-heels to defense attorneys. Call it brokering, or maybe an early-warning system. I don't know."

The waitress offered to top off their cups. They assented and pushed them toward her.

"Well, it sounds like you're gonna get busy on investigating Satello and the police will chase down the pimp."

"Yeah, the police are enthralled with him as a suspect. He got out on bail from the Majestic bust before Sherm's body was discovered. It's possible he could have gone after Sherm. But it seems to me that Sherm would have been as put out about the police raid as Mr. Barnes. Anyway, the police are all over that lead, but so far he's on the loose."

"He'll turn up. Maybe the police will rubber hose a nice confession out of him, as well they should, and you can be on your way. Now before you go, Paul, I would like to ask a favor. Would you mind calling Mrs. Arabella Ramey Fucking Carter about her father's estate? We've got the audit coming up and she's got herself in a nervous snit. She's your client; I simply cannot talk to that woman. So what if she has to pay the IRS a few bucks more estate tax?"

Paul realized that last week's private practice problems had drifted miles away. He forced himself to concentrate on the problems that Scott began to recite, but he promised himself to return to Einar's investigation of the murky relationship between Sherman Falkes, Terry Barnes, and Jake Satello.

Cross currents

TEN

EINAR TORGESON IDENTIFIED HIMSELF into the intercom at the grim side entrance of Anderson Juvenile Center. A buzzer sounded and he pushed his way into the gray, foreboding building in which juveniles were, in caseworker parlance, "detained." The hallway was small and devoid of chairs or seating of any kind. To the right, a glassed-in room that looked like a theater box office. Einar stooped down to peer into the window. A young woman smiled back at him.

"Mr. Strand will be here in a moment," she said.

Einar nodded patiently. It had been over ten years since he had brought youngsters to this place. As he looked around at the scuffed and dirty walls of the "detention" facility, he recalled why he had answered the announcement looking for experienced police officers to join the State Human Rights Commission. Einar knew immediately that he wanted out of the life of a city police officer: he hated the use of force. It was not that he could not handle himself or protect himself. He just did not like to force other persons to do something against their will and he was not all that good at the con or the jolly. He always said what he meant and tried to cut through the crap in what other people said.

A buzzer sounded and a steel door to the right of the glass box office opened. A fit-looking young man stepped out into the waiting room. He was dressed in a beige corduroy jacket, button down blue shirt, blue and red striped tie, and blue jeans.

"You called about seeing Margie Cross?" he said brusquely.

"Yes. I'm Einar Torgeson," he said, extending his hand.

The young man shook Einar's hand briefly but did not offer his name.

"Come into the interview room. Could I see your credentials, please? It's procedure."

"Certainly," said Einar, quickly removing from his wallet a laminated photo accompanied by the signature of the Secretary of the Washington State Human Rights Commission.

"You're from the prosecutor's office?" he asked.

"I'm on loan to assist in the Sherman Falkes death investigation."

"I guess that's OK. Anyway, I don't know what you'll get out of the little dolly here. A man and woman team from Seattle PD gave up yesterday. There were two or three detectives before that. She just tells them she wants her lawyer."

Einar did not respond. He entered a room marked "Interviews," put his notebook on the table, and sat down.

"I'll bring her down," the man said.

One wall of the room had a glass window through which Einar could see the young woman behind the box office across the hall. It was a sort of control booth through which she watched the room he was in, as well as two others. Einar could see through the other side of the control booth into a large room, where youngsters who looked to range in age from ten or eleven to sixteen or seventeen lounged. It was difficult to observe what they were doing, except perhaps watching TV or glancing at magazines.

The door opened. The last person known by police authorities to have seen Sherman Falkes alive walked into the room. She was washed and innocent looking. Her clothes were a loose crew-neck cotton sweater and a pair of khaki pants. Still, Margie Cross was an attractive girl. She had light brown eyes and long auburn hair swept back and tied with a red ribbon. Soft wisps of hair escaped artfully from the hair tie. She glanced at Einar shyly and seated herself sideways in the chair, her hands in her lap.

"I'd like to have a lawyer," she said.

Einar's long fingers pushed his gray hair across his bald spot. His index finger stopped at a bushy place above his ear and he scratched. His voice was barely audible as he spoke.

"A lawyer is not necessary for you to talk to me. I'm only here to talk about the man you were with the night they brought you here."

"I didn't know him," she said.

"Well, he died not long after he left you. Did you ever know anyone who died before?"

She thought about Einar's question. "My grandma."

Einar did not smoke, but he had brought a pack of cigarettes and opened them before the meeting. He took them out, lit one, and put the pack and matches on the table. He pushed them across to the girl. She took one, lit up, and inhaled expertly. Einar wondered if the woman in the control booth would come in and take the cigarette from Margie. He doubted it.

"Where did your grandma live, Margie?"

"Tacoma. I used to go there and stay with her, but she got so sick."

"Did you go to school there? In Tacoma?" he asked.

"Sometimes."

"What did you like in school?"

"Oh, stories. When I was small, they used to read stories."

"They don't do that too much when you're older," Einar said. "Maybe that's too bad. Where else did you go to school besides Tacoma?"

"If I talk to you will I get in trouble?"

"No. My name is Torgeson. Einar Torgeson. Let me give you my card, and that way you can call me anytime you remember anything about the man you were with on Friday night. That's the only reason why I'm here. I want to find out what happened to that man. Had you ever seen him before?"

"The man? Oh, yeah. He was with Terry and Reeney lots of times."

"Did you like him?"

"Oh yeah. He was funny."

She looked down at her hands.

"I'll bet he really liked you too, Margie," Einar said. "Did he give you any money?"

"Not Friday."

"Well, I know the police were there. But what I mean is was he a boyfriend, like Terry?"

She looked up, her hand went out to the edge of the table. "Terry's not my boyfriend. Besides, I don't know any Terry."

"What about Reeney, then?"

She laughed. "What do you think? I'm lesbo?"

Einar smiled. "No, like friends. Like people you meet who you like and you can talk to. Did you talk with the man, Sherman Falkes?"

She put her hands back in her lap. "Sure," she said.

"What did you talk about?"

"Just stuff you talk about on a date. You know. Why have I gotta talk about this stuff?"

"You don't have to talk about it, but you'll help his family if you do. They all want to know what happened to him."

She looked up blandly. "He's dead. That's what happened to him."

"True. But think about it, Margie, maybe somebody killed him. And if they think you know something, maybe they'll kill you. Even if you don't really know anything."

"What people want to kill me?"

"That's what I'm trying to find out."

She looked at Einar anxiously. "I didn't see Terry or Reeney after they busted me. They just put me in a car and brought me here."

"Maybe if we just talk about things before Friday night that will help. I know you don't know what happened after the man left your room. By the way, was that *your* room he was in?"

"My room? I don't know, I guess so."

"Say, I'm just going to ask you some questions, and you can answer them or not, as you please. Whatever you want to do. We'll see if maybe I can ask enough questions about you that we work our way back to your grandma in Tacoma."

She smiled and sat forward in her chair, interested in the prospect of a game.

"When did you first move into that room in the motel?"

"We checked in on Tuesday."

"Where had you been before that?"

"In Seattle. Only we were out by the Center at the Windsor Hotel."

"How long had you been there at the Windsor?"

"I don't know how long the others had been there. I had only been there about two weeks."

"Where had you been before that?"

"I was staying with a friend of my mother's in Queen Anne."

"You met Terry, then, about two weeks ago?"

"Tangerine. I met Tangerine."

"OK, Tangerine. Look, I don't care whether Terry or Tangerine get busted. I want to know about the man in your room. When did you first meet him?"

"At the Windsor Hotel. We had a date."

"What night?"

"Sunday night, I think. I had my own room. He came after we got back from the Center."

"Did you and he go out?"

"No."

"Had you ever seen him before Sunday?"

"No."

"He came into your room?"

"Yeah. Reeney brought him."

"Reeney is Tangerine?"

"Yeah."

"Did you see Terry with the man? By the way, what did you call the man?"

"John. He wanted me to call him John. He was kind of sad. Reeney said he needed cheering up."

"When did you see him with Terry?"

"What makes you think I did?" she said suspiciously.

"Did you?"

"Those other cops kept asking me that. Why should I narc on my friends?"

"I don't know. That's for you to decide."

"They said that Terry and Reeney weren't my friends—that they just wanted to sell my body. But I don't care. That's all everybody else on the street wanted and they weren't even nice. Terry was nice. Reeney was nice most of the time. They bought me clothes. They let me pick out something, then they'd pick out something. I never had so many new things in my life. I didn't want to take the price tags off."

"Didn't your mom and dad ever buy you new clothes?"

"Grandma died. Mom's an alcoholic," she said flatly. "She doesn't care about clothes for herself or anybody."

She looked defiantly at Einar as she spoke. "I don't drink."

Einar eased back in his chair.

"Good. That's good, Margie," he said.

The room became silent. Einar wondered if his long experience as a discrimination investigator might be hampering the interview. His style, and the approach he was trained in, to allow the feelings of the interviewee to come forth unfettered and undiscouraged by the interviewer, was to efface himself from the interview. Never incite. He could not change now, and, even if he could, he would not bully the girl. That had apparently been tried by the police and had failed.

"Did Terry or Reeney want you to drink?"

"No," she said abruptly.

"Did any of your dates want you to drink?"

She smiled. "Oh, I could handle them."

What then, he thought?

"Did Terry or Reeney want you to turn on?" he ventured.

The girl became visibly excited. "I never saw so much stuff. Coke. Grass. Pills. Reeney's room was like a drugstore. And the other girls were in and out getting stuff all the time. I was scared."

Apparently, the cops had only asked about Terry and Reeney's pimping.

"Why were you scared?"

"Reeney wanted me to deliver some pills to a guy in the Queen Anne business district up by the Center. I said I wouldn't and she slapped me, but then she hugged me and said she was sorry, she just lost it. I told her it was OK but I was scared to carry drugs or be around them with my mom an alkie and all."

"The man who was with you. John. Did he have any drugs?"

"No. I could smell booze, but he didn't seem like he was using."

She folded her arms and sat back. "Are they gonna let me out of here?" Tears came in her eyes. "I don't want to go to my mom. But I don't want to stay here."

"Where's your dad?"

"I don't know. Nobody knows. I don't think I had a dad."

"I suppose that's possible, but they have to release you to someone responsible, Margie. Do you have any aunts or uncles?"

"I have an aunt in Wichita. Wichita, Kansas. And two cousins. Grandma and I visited them once."

"What's her name?"

"Virginia Hawkins."

"Do you know their address or telephone number?"

"No."

"What's your uncle's name?"

"William Hawkins."

Einar made a note.

"If you went to Wichita, you'd have to stay off the street. Go to school. What grade are you in?"

"I could go to Continuation," she said.

"Well, those things could be worked out. Tell me where you lived before you lived with the lady in Queen Anne—what's her name?"

"I was at a foster home. The Tuckers. In Kent. She just wanted a babysitter. It was way out in the country."

"Where were you before that?"

"I was at another foster home in Tacoma. She was nice but ... I left."

Einar studied her large brown eyes. Apparently innocent, but looking out at a world with catches and snags at every turn. A friend in Queen Anne with no name, a foster home with a nameless but "nice" foster mother, but what else? A foster father who groped for her in stolen moments in the car or when his wife was gone? None of this told Einar much about Sherman Falkes, except to help Einar understand how an underage girl came to be in a hotel room with a forty-five-year-old man.

"I'll bet we're getting close to your grandma. When did she pass away?"

"I don't know. It was about two years ago, maybe longer?"

"What was her name?"

"Anna Burgess."

Einar made some notes on his pad, summarizing the times, events, and names she had given him. He tapped his pen on the pad.

"You first saw Sherman Falkes last Sunday night?"

She nodded.

"The second time you saw him was Friday, the night the police came?"

The brown eyes flickered.

"When did you see him again after Sunday night?"

"I saw him again on Friday. Yes."

Einar pushed. "Friday night?"

"Yes."

"When Friday night?"

"When the police came."

Her arms folded. Her eyelids lowered. There was something else, but how to reach it?

"You've had a lot of tough luck, Margie. Losing your Grandma. A mom that doesn't care, falling in with bad company who want to take advantage of you."

He turned his pencil between thumb and index finger. He did not look at her but gazed toward a corner of the room.

"I have to tell you for your own sake that you are in the hub of dangerous men and women who are scared, too. And these people become more dangerous when scared," he mused. "I'm not bargaining with you—a piece of candy or a cigarette in exchange for telling all you know. I am telling you that, if someone found it necessary to kill Sherman Falkes, it is going to occur to that person that Reeney and all the girls who worked for them might also have to be killed. I just want you to be safe. I think you're old enough and smart enough to think about your own safety."

She shifted in her chair, gazed down at her worn tennis shoes. "I didn't hurt nobody," she said.

"But you were there, Margie. You saw things. Other men who visited you? Other men who visited Terry and Reeney?"

"Terry wasn't there at night, except late when we were done. Most of the guys were really nice. Reeney said that Terry was real careful. No weirdoes."

"What about the grass and the drugs? Where did that come from?"

"It was just there. I don't know. Once, in the morning, Terry and Reeney went out. It was early, but I heard them. I could see Terry's van from my room and watched them drive out of the lot and I saw a black car follow them. I thought it was a cop car and they were gonna get busted. I was scared. I got my stuff together to leave, but I waited and pretty soon I saw them come back and park the van. The black car was gone though."

"When was that?"

"Day before we got busted."

"Could you see who was in the black car?"

"No, but I think it was a man I seen John with. I was in the market Friday noon and saw John there with another man."

"What did the other man look like?"

"He was fat, dark hair, a black raincoat. I don't know. He looked sort of ... stuck up."

"Where in the Market did you see him?"

"They were eating."

"Did John recognize you?"

"I sort of looked past him and pretended I didn't see him. I don't know whether he saw me."

"What makes you think the other man was the man in the car that followed Terry?"

"The black coat. I could see the coat sleeve, and the car moved slow, like the man did. When I saw them together John was talking, but the other man didn't move. It just *felt* like the same man."

"Anything else you could see about the man?"

"No. I just had a feeling."

"Did you see his face?"

"Not really well. Terry was stooped over to talk to the man inside the car. I was too far up."

Einar made some more notes.

"Now, Margie. Did you see John or the other man any other time before Friday night when the police came?"

"No."

"Margie, may I come and see you again? I want to talk to the people here about maybe getting you down to your aunt's in Wichita. Would you stay there if we could?"

She pushed back a soft wisp of hair from her eyebrow. "Sure. I'll do my best," she said.

"I will too, then," he said.

The girl reached across the table and lightly touched the back of Einar Torgeson's hand. "Where did you get those?"

There were barely noticeable scratches on the back of his hand that were almost healed. "Oh, I had to clear a path through some blackberry vines to get to the tool shed at the cabin."

"Cabin? Where?"

"My mother's place. She's old now. In a retirement home. It was our family's vacation place when I was growing up."

"Where is it?"

"On Hood Canal. North of Shelton.

"I've never been to Hood's Canal. What's it like?"

"Oh, it's like the Sound. Only calmer. Like a big lake."

"Do you have a boat?"

"Sure. A small one. And a canoe, I like to canoe."

"I like boats," she said. "Why is your mother in a home?"

"Because I can't take care of her any more." He looked down at the scratches on his hands, thinking back to that Saturday when he had jumped from the car and worked with manic energy around the cabin to clear his mind and feelings.

"How's she doing?" asked the girl, watching him.

Einar thought about it. "Better than I expected. She seems to enjoy the company. I was out of town a lot anyway when we lived together."

"Are you a mama's boy?" the girl asked, smiling.

Einar's jaw dropped. He shook his head in denial, but he said, "I suppose I am. I suppose I am."

"I'll bet you never got married."

"No, wrong there. I was married once. Years ago."

She looked at him inquiringly.

"Nice person. We just drifted apart. It happens to young cops all involved and gung-ho about learning their trade."

"So you lived with your mama. Now you live by yourself," she said simply.

Einar did not acknowledge or deny. "I'll get back to you," he said. "If you think of anything more about John, or the man in the car, call the number there on my card. Those numbers are for my Olympia office."

"Olympia ... Where's Hood's Canal?" she asked.

"It's Hood Canal. Oh, it's not too far from Olympia. A little west."

"Oh, *Hood* Canal," she murmured.

Einar waited patiently as the girl in the control booth procured the young man in the corduroy jacket to escort Margie back to her room, or cell, or pod—or whatever they called it.

Without asking, Margie put the cigarettes in her pants pocket. They sat quietly, waiting.

As a young patrolman for Seattle PD, Einar had met many hookers. He had liked talking to them. They knew how to talk to a man. That was their job. Einar had that same feeling when talking to Margie. Maybe she was just a kid, but had he just interviewed her, or she him?

At the gates
of Hellman

ELEVEN

Arnold Hellman, Chief of the Seattle Police Department, fumed. Captain Jake Satello and Sergeant Hal Gordon sat calmly but attentively across his tidy desk. Hellman himself was turned out as trimly and neatly as his desk. He preferred his uniform to a business suit, and he was wearing it that morning. He had dark brown eyes and thick graying hair that he kept just long enough to part and paste down.

"What's this all about, Jake?" asked Chief Hellman. "This guy Andros wants to ask me some questions about you. He wants to see your jacket. Why is that? I don't like surprises. I definitely don't like surprises. And I don't like whorehouse prosecutors coming over here and looking at my guys' files."

"So show him the file, Arnie," Satello said placidly. "I don't care if he looks at the file."

"I don't fucking care whether you care. *I* care. *I* don't like it. First, he brings in that Torgeson character. Some guy that's not even police. He's not a dick, and he brings him in to investigate our bust!"

"Wait a minute, Arnie," said Gordon. "He's investigating Sherm Falkes's death, not our bust. But I don't like it any more than you do."

Sergeant Gordon was a medium-sized man with a balding head of reddish gray hair. Although he worked mostly in the chief's office, he wore blue coveralls—by which he indicated to other department workers the utilitarian nature of his assignments, such as administering lie detector tests and investigating accidents involving police vehicles. He was Chief Hellman's right-hand man, and one of his privileges was to dress as he pleased.

"Well, what do I do? Do I slam the door? We're not under any suspicion here. Whyn't he clean up his own goddamn house before he comes nosing around over here?" asked Hellman.

"Maybe he wants to know about the apartment house, Arnie," said Satello.

Hellman stared at him in mute inquiry.

"Me and Sherm bought an apartment in Capitol Hill," Satello continued. "We fixed it up in our off hours. Rented it. You know, an investment."

"You and Sherman Falkes. When was that?"

"Couple of years ago. Maybe three or four."

They sat quietly. "Anything else?"

"Anything else what?" asked Satello.

"Well, any other business ventures with Falkes?"

"Naw. I helped him with his campaigns. I raised money. We just got to talking about investments and decided an apartment house would be really good. Depreciation. Keeps up with inflation. So we did it."

Chief Hellman gazed out the window at the dark blue water. The Chief's office was located in another building next to the courthouse and had a view similar to the Prosecutor's office. OK, he thought, maybe it's better to relax and see where this all is going.

"OK, Jake, OK. If you're not gonna object, I'll show the prosecutor your file. So give it to me, Gordo. You two can go on, but, Jake, you stay around the building in case something comes up."

Hellman was a compromise Chief of Police, selected seven years ago after a brief Reign of Terror engineered by a grim-faced import from San Francisco. He'd instituted brutal internal investigations and detailed responsiveness to citizen complaints. His by-the-book approach made him unpopular with cops, who felt that their effectiveness and personal safety were based on unquestioned authority on the streets. Ironically, his thoroughness also made him unpopular with the complaining citizen groups, since by the time a response to a citizen complaint was

vetted by the city's lawyers for liability and labor relations impli-
cations, no law enforcement wrongdoing was ever admitted
or remedied. Mayoral support by the Police Guild in the next
election had been conditioned on his ouster and replacement
with a new chief more understanding of the policeman's
unhappy lot. Hellman—honest, reliable, compassionate for others in the force who erred either in laxity or excess zeal—had
been just the man. Rather than punish incompetence, he preferred to reward competence. When his "problem children" got
into trouble, he would make loud disciplinary noises, which
translated into re-assignments or, in extreme cases, days off.
He was popular, but his critics called him "the pistol that shoots
only blanks."

The chief welcomed Andros in a friendly manner. They had
met a few times when Hellman was a captain and Paul was a
prosecutor. "Paul," he said, offering his hand. "It's good to see
you again. I sure admire you for jumping into the thick of things
when you were needed."

"It's hard to say whether I was needed or not, but it's a hell
of a time for everyone in law enforcement. There's a half a
dozen guys in the prosecutor's office who could have taken over,
but the county council thought it would be better to have someone from outside for a little while."

"Good idea. Say, Paul, I know it's probably a big financial
sacrifice for you, but we in law enforcement really appreciate it."

Paul picked up on Hellman's subtle hostility: his compliments were barbed, overdone. So he got down to business.

"One of those things that has to be done by somebody,
right? Did you get that file for me, Arnie?"

Hellman smiled on. "Sure. No problem. Got it right here."
Hellman patted the file on his desk but then kept his hand upon
it. "But, Paul, what have you got? Jake's okay, isn't he? Should I
get on his ass about something?"

"Not as far as I know," said Andros. "I'm trying to put
together Sherm's life over the past few years. He and Jake

Satello were in on a business deal together. I thought I'd like to review Captain Satello's career record before I talk to him."

"What kind of business deal?" Hellman asked off-handedly.

"Apparently they were co-owners of an apartment in Capitol Hill."

"Yeah? So what the hell's wrong with that?"

"I don't know that there's anything wrong with that."

"Well, what do you want? Exactly? You want to see the jackets on everybody who knew Sherm Falkes?"

Hellman was beginning to stoke himself up. Andros paused to gauge the chief's escalating emotional level. "No sir," he replied evenly. "But if there are any other police officers who were involved in moonlighting ventures with Sherm Falkes or anyone else who socialized with him, I'd like to see their files and I'd like to talk to them."

"I'm going to tell you something, Mr. Andros. Demanding to look at guys' files is no way to initiate a friendly conversation about a pederast. The only reason I'm going to let you see this file and talk to Jake Satello is because Jake has no objection. If it was up to me, I'd tell you to stick it up your ass."

Paul stifled an impulse to respond in kind. He swallowed, spoke softly.

"Frankly, Chief Hellman, I think that's a commendable attitude. You *should* be protective of your men. And *I* should be attempting to investigate the death of Sherman Falkes. Now, may I see the file?"

Briefly, their eyes locked. Hellman tossed the file over to Paul, then sat back, arms folded, and stared at him. Obviously, he intended to personally supervise Paul's review of the file. Paul calmly disregarded the intimidation and opened the folder. On the left side was Satello's employment application, along with personnel action memos.

Jacomo Richard Satello. Born March 10, 1936. Graduated Seattle High School, 1955. U.S. Army, two years. Honorable Discharge. Commercial fisherman three years. The first personnel action form in the file showed that he started service with Seattle PD March 31, 1960. He made lieutenant in 1972 and interim captain in 1974; confirmed 1977.

"He's done all right for a guy without a Police Administration or Public Administration degree," Paul commented out loud. "Only a few quarters at Seattle Community College. Did real well on all his various civil service exams."

"I've always known Jake to be a hard worker," Chief Hellman conceded. "Knows a lot of people, really gets around," the chief mused.

"Active in the Guild?"

"He was on the bargaining team every year as long as I can remember. Until he made captain."

"What were his various job assignments?"

"Everyone rotates, of course, but Jake less so. For the last few years he's been in charge of support services—records, logistics. He's had court liaison since he was a sergeant. And prosecutor liaison. I suspect that's how he got to know Falkes so well. You remember him from the prosecutor's office?"

"Vaguely. I was more involved in the civil department."

"Yeah," said Chief Hellman definitively.

Paul continued to read the file. His life insurance beneficiaries were his wife, Maria Satello, or, in the event of her demise, his children, David, Samuel, Tammy, and Virginia Satello. He lived in the north Queen Anne area. Paul memorized the address.

He had one commendation related to a shooting in a shopping center. In an armed robbery of a jewelry store, a man had fired shots. "Mindful of the safety of others," Satello had waited until the suspect was in front of a brick background and citizens were out of the way before returning fire, wounding the assailant, making the arrest, and recovering the jewelry. Sound police procedure commended, Andros suspected, in order to encourage similar responses from the other, less prudent, members of the troops who have to be constantly reminded not to fire indiscriminately and to know what they are firing at.

"I see a commendation in here but no reprimands, no time off, no suspensions. No trouble?"

Hellman briefly appeared to want to discuss Satello. "Not that I recall," was all he said.

"What about Internal Investigations?" Paul asked.

"I personally shit-canned I-I, Mr. Andros. Why should we waste good men's time chasing bullshit complaints from malcontents when those same guys could be out investigating real crime? People who got complaints can talk to me. If something needs to be investigated, I assign it," Hellman said, arms still folded.

Andros did not debate the point. "What about the department's own files—notes on disciplinary actions? Not everything gets in the personnel file."

"Andros, if there is such a file, I would consider it the personal property of the chief, and I damn sure wouldn't discuss it with you."

"Relax, Chief. Satello isn't charged with anything. Listen again: all I want to do is talk to people who knew Sherm."

"You're talking to one."

"OK. The accident reconstruction people are reviewing the car crash that killed Sherm. You probably know that the indications are that Sherm's death was not an accident. If he *was* killed, would you have any speculation, note I say speculation, as to why? Any unsavory associates?"

"'Why' leads to 'who,' huh, Counsel?"

"Well, I think we need to understand Sherman Falkes a little better if we're going to accomplish anything in the investigation. I kind of lost contact with him after I left the office. Frankly, his conduct at the Majestic was as shocking to me as his death."

Chief Hellman snorted, "Could happen to anybody. In the old days, before we all got so chicken-shit sanctimonious, we'd tell him to get the hell out and go about our business."

Andros considered whether Sherm believed that being let go was a possibility. The police reports of the bust had said that he was in a room with Margie Cross, but the reports didn't show up until Monday, after his death. Was he sure at the time that the reports would name him? He would have to ask Einar to talk to Gordon and the other arresting officers about whether there was any indication of whether he was or was not going to be named.

"Gordon was in charge of the raid. He's your right-hand man. He apparently didn't feel that way. The reports said he was there."

"I know, I know. That's the reason he's my right-hand man. Gordon is a prick. If there's gonna be a good guy in this department, it's gonna be me."

"Well, be a good guy. What was the gossip about Sherm?"

Hellman mused a moment. "I can't say that anything got to me."

"Tell me about Sherm's deputy, Lyle Turner. He says he worked on the raid with Gordon. Turner said you sat in on the arrangements."

Hellman paused enough for Paul to sense that the Majestic Motel preliminary arrangements were something he wouldn't have brought up if Paul hadn't. "You did sit in on that didn't you, Chief?"

"Yeah I did. The kid, Turner, likes to make a big deal about things. So he comes over and talks to me after Gordon did all the preliminary work to set up the raid. We only contacted the Turner kid to find out our legal ground if we pushed around the female a little bit in order to get the male to come back to the motel. All of a sudden Turner's over here acting like he's running the whole show."

"What was his legal advice?"

"He said we might lose her, but we didn't care. It's usually hard to nail the pimp, and we wanted him."

"Any background on the man, this Terry Barnes?"

"Not much. We sent it over with the reports. What? Disorderly. Assault. Small-time forfeiture stuff. I know there was no prior pimping. I looked. No girlie stuff. "

"Dope?"

"Just a misdemeanor possession. Marijuana. A fairly careful operator. Never done time."

"Do you have any evidence that he and Sherm knew each other?"

"I asked that same question after the bust. Nothing so far as anyone knew. Sherm being there was one great big surprise."

"How did you get a line on this Terry Barnes' operation?"

Hellman paused. "That was me. An accident. My wife and I were having dinner with Chief Brewster and his wife from Kirkland. While we were waiting for our table in the bar, Brewster and I watched the son of a bitch operate. He was talking to different marks and they'd leave. It was fucking embarrassing. Brewster and I have both worked vice and we knew exactly what was going on. Brewster said something about where's a vice dick when you need one. Pissed me off. I had Gordon look into it. Gordon got the line of jazz from one of the marks. He would say to the mark that he had just got a helping of some real swell stuff at the Majestic Motel, or wherever, and he'd tell the mark to ask for this Tangerine woman and she'd fix him up. Terry would make out that he was nothing more than a happy consumer, giving out testimonials. So we figured if *his* piece got threatened by some other pimp that would bring him home, and it did."

"Did you guys find any drugs?"

"Drugs? Nothing in the report. I'm sure they looked."

"Anything else about Sherm? What was your observation of him the past year or so?"

"Frankly, my impression was that he wasn't going anywhere. Sherm was always rah-rah law enforcement, OK, but he didn't seem to be looking for any other political office, a judgeship, Congress. He'd been there what? Fourteen, fifteen years? Elected for a second term. Looked like he was gonna be there forever."

"The cops all seemed to like him."

"Maybe they did in your day, but the chiefs were getting disenchanted. He told the police rank and file what they wanted to hear, but it was all that shit about how the judges are screwed up. Sure the judges are screwed up, but where do you get by groaning about it? They make the rules and we're cops. Cops are supposed to follow the rules. That's why I encouraged Turner. He's kind of a stuffed shirt, but he was ambitious to make a name for himself as a law- enforcement man. I'm not opposed to that."

For the first time since sitting down, Andros sat back. "I admit, I have mixed feelings about Turner. I don't warm to him personally and I don't forgive him going outside office channels without coordinating with the chief deputy. But he did show initiative." Andros smiled. "Maybe I should fire his ass, but I can just imagine the fracas he'd make about it if I did."

"If he was one of my guys I'd say you don't have jack shit to can him, but then you don't have Snivel Service to deal with. I envy you guys that operate with the spoils system."

"Don't forget the discrimination board and the union."

Hellman snorted. "White, black, yellow, or green. You can pick your people, Andros. That means accountability. I am personally accountable to the mayor for everything I do. Are my people accountable to me? Shit, no. Not unless it's all laid out in some bullshit rule that some shithouse lawyer for the union tears apart five minutes after it's posted."

"I've got another question, chief. Go back to the raid for a minute. You say you spotted Terry Barnes in a bar? Was a contact report filed?"

"Naw. I was pissed off about it. Here's a pimp parading around like some kinda movie star. Dyed white hair. Black suit. What the hell was vice doing, for Chrissakes? I told Gordo to confirm it but keep vice the hell out of it. Then I was gonna have a word with those fuckers. Brewster even loaned me one of his young officers to be the mark."

"That's how Gordon got involved, then," Andros stated. "You organized the operation directly out of this office."

Hellman rocked slowly and nodded.

"Gordon, your administrative assistant, chose the men himself. No vice people?"

"Definitely no vice people," Hellman confirmed dryly.

"Only street patrol as backup? And that was ordered at the last minute?"

"Yes."

"The whole operation utilized none of your usual departmental apparatus and procedures?"

"Whatta you mean, 'apparatus and procedures'? I'm still a cop. Gordo's a cop."

"I mean no records. No memos. No channels to the prosecutor's office, except the little shit Turner who made it his personal project and didn't tell anyone in his office."

Hellman nodded.

"Chief, why'd you do that?"

Hellman cleared his throat. "Shit if I know. It just seemed to develop that way."

Andros stared silently at Hellman until he volunteered, almost apologetically, "Maybe it was the way it got started, dinner and all. Chief to chief."

Each man sat for silent moments with his own thoughts. Then Andros closed the file and placed it gently on Chief Hellman's desk.

"I'll talk with Jake later," he said quietly. He stood, moved toward the door, turned. "Chief?"

Hellman's eyes were glazy.

"Chief, how long have you been a police officer?"

"Twenty-eight years," he answered.

"Ever hear of police intuition? What makes a police officer drive by a half-dozen citizens out for a morning jog and stop to question the one guy who turns out to have robbed the local 7-11? What did you think would have happened on the

Majestic Motel bust if you had turned the investigation over to vice?"

Hellman offered no reply. The meeting had been a revelation for them both.

Andros closed the door and went back to his office. He and Einar would do some more research. Then talk to Satello.

An aunt

in his pants

TWELVE

URBAN AIRPORTS BRING WITH THEM diverse environs of deterioration and renewal. Sea-Tac is no different. The residential areas are largely apartments, appealing to transients and singles seeking a low-cost home base to store stereos and sweaters. Most family people engaged in airline- or airport-related business live and commute from elsewhere. The commercial areas offer hotels in various conditions, from the new and modish to feed, entertain, and rest the jet and Gold Card set, to the rechristened and redecorated, in their waning years, servicing group tours and bargain hunters. Terry Barnes' bus sped past the parking lots, car rental shops, and hotels to its early morning Park-and-Ride rendezvous with the commuters south of Sea-Tac, readying to return to downtown Seattle. Terry's destination was the no-name corridor between Seattle and Tacoma, south of the airport. He had holed up for over a week in a cheap motel in South Everett. He had seen every flick at the mall and watched hours of TV. He had finally decided that it was time to move. He had caught the first morning bus to downtown Seattle and transferred to another bus routed on Old 99 south past the airport toward Tacoma.

At 6:00 A.M. the bus pulled over to let him out at the South Breeze Mall. Hands shoved in his jacket pockets, he loped west on Mapleview Avenue. He walked fast to ward off the chill

It was 6:30 A.M., just beginning to get light, by the time he could see the corner house with the brick lattice fence, a landmark from previous trips to Aunt Steffie's when he was growing up. He continued on along Mapleview, past her street, glancing down the block. Unlikely that the police would stake out her house. But everything else had gone wrong in the past weeks. He turned north at the next street corner, walked to the next corner, double-backed on a street parallel with Mapleview. He turned down Aunt Steffie's street and walked purposefully past her house, without stopping.

There were no parked cars in the area, nobody in sight sitting around watching her house. Her old Buick was in the driveway, blocked by a new black Toyota with lopsided dealer plates. Steffie was entertaining overnight company. He hoped it was not a live-in.

He continued back to Mapleview Avenue, easing his pace. Traffic was building.

He walked a block east and doubled back again. This time he checked for houses without any morning activity or signs of life. A self-absorbed jogger went past him, the tinny blast from a headset audible in passing. Dogs barked in fenced yards.

The area around Aunt Steffie's house had become a labyrinth of streets as newer subdivisions were developed and connected to the north. Aunt Steffie's house was in the first subdivision in the area. It was probably over twenty years when Terry first stayed with her. She was married then, but Terry didn't remember her husband. Yeah, then there were many, many "uncles" he didn't remember, either...

Curiously, her block appeared to be the most placid. He noticed an old Ford LTD parked outside an empty carport across the street from her house and three houses north. The lawn was ill-kept and the house looked deserted. Would it start if he hotwired it so that he could get out of there and avoid Aunt Steffie? What if he got stopped with a hot car? He decided to keep walking.

The black Toyota was still there, but the lights in the house were on. Terry walked back to Mapleview and started around the block to the east again. He had just turned onto the next street east when he looked back to see the black Toyota heading east on Mapleview. Terry continued at a leisurely pace around the block from the other direction.

Aunt Steffie's house was dark by the time he walked around the block. He went around to the back door, knocked softly.

She had not gone back to bed. She was at the door almost immediately. She glanced through the window, opened the door, and pulled him inside. She shut the door and immediately put her hand around his neck and kissed him as she pressed her body against him. Her tongue searched his mouth. Terry relaxed and let her explore.

She put her arms around his back and pulled her hips to his in a few masturbatory thrusts. "Oh, God!" she gasped. "I'm glad to see you, Terry-Boy."

She was wrapped in a dark green robe with white lace lapels. She was a taller than average, medium built woman, almost head-to-head with Terry. She adopted her hair to dark blonde, which complemented a smooth face, not tanned, but of a dark complexion. Terry knew that beneath the robe were her long, slim legs, which were, she knew, her best feature. She had probably been one of the first to wear a miniskirt, and as fashions changed she had never accepted longer hems.

Terry sniffed down the front of her robe. "Auntie needs a bath, doesn't she?"

"Oh, Terry-boy," she said. She grasped him around the waist and pulled him close as if she were going to front-lift him. "I'll bet Terry-Boy needs a bath too. Does Terry-Boy want Auntie Steff to give him a nice warm bath?"

Terry stroked the back of her neck, trying to relax his own inner turmoil. He had never been able to release himself to her. When he was ten years old, she had taken him into her bed. Before he could ejaculate, she would play with him, tease him, put him inside her, suck him. It would have been a teenage boy's dream, except to a ten-year-old it was only tiresome—something he wanted to get over and away from. Yet he had clung to her and the opportunity to stay with her here as the only safe harbor from his mother's studio apartment in the Broadway District, where he slept on a couch and had one drawer in her chest of drawers for all his clothes and belongings. Here, when Aunt Steffie was off to work, he could do as he pleased, with the whole house to himself and this suburban neighborhood to roam.

She moved her head into his hand and brought her hands up to pull his face to hers. She kissed him fully and pulled his head back.

"What have you been up to? Your hair's all black and icky."

"Police are looking for me, Aunt Steff."

"Well, you know you can do no wrong by me. But I don't want no trouble, Terry!"

"It's cool," he said softly. "I walked here. Nobody saw me come in. I waited until your friend left."

She let go of him and went to the stove. "Let's have some coffee, and you tell me what the police want with my Terry-Boy."

"Sure. I could eat something too."

They set about making breakfast. When they had finished eating, Terry told her a garbled version of falling in love with a woman who turned out to run a prostitution ring. And how the woman was somehow involved with that prosecutor who was killed in the car wreck on Queen Anne.

"So the police think I'm involved with her prostitution stuff, and I know they're gonna try to get me involved with that prosecutor guy. So I gotta get outta here, Aunt Steff. I gotta move. But I gotta have a car. They took my car for bail. Can you get me a car? I'll pay you back as soon as I get settled."

"What will the police say if you're driving my old car?"

"Nothing. I'll just say I took it."

"Come here," she said, loosening the belt on her robe. "Terry and Auntie Steff need a bath."

The point

of the bop

THIRTEEN

ANDROS' TENURE AT THE PROSECUTOR'S OFFICE had settled into a routine. After the first few weeks of dealing with office fires and interviewing the staff, he had finally taken time to discuss the Falkes case with Einar. Scott Turnbull was also present, ostensibly for the purpose of considering whether to appeal an IRS revaluation of a wheat farm in Eastern Washington that was part of a large estate Paul had been probating. He had quickly set that aside to participate in the more interesting details of the Falkes case. Einar had been gone for two days on state business, and while Andros and Scott argued their theories and suppositions, he was studying police reports. They were waiting for Alton Williams, a Seattle Police Department forensic expert, who had agreed to meet with Paul to discuss his investigation.

Williams was fifteen minutes late when Mary Lynn Pierce escorted him through the door of the prosecutor's office. Pale, youthful-looking, with long black hair, he wore round steel-rimmed glasses that looked odd on his angular face. His clothes were casual. Paul wondered, was the Cal Tech emblem on his sweatshirt part of his background, or had he selected it off a sports shop rack?

Williams observed this appraisal of his outfit. He pulled at the front of the sweatshirt and said, "Only a three-day conference on automobile design. I'm just a Cougar, fresh off the Palouse."

"Paul Andros," Paul said, extending his hand. "This is Einar Torgeson. He's a special investigator helping on the case. This is Scott Turnbull, Courthouse Kibitzer."

Williams, disregarding the formalities, dumped a disheveled file on the conference table and collapsed himself into a chair.

"Well, gents, this bop denies the laws of physics and chemistry and everything else. You got any money to bring someone else in? I'm having a hell of a time figuring out what happened here."

"Why don't you tell just us what you got, Alton?" Paul asked carefully.

"Sure, sure. See, I was out there the night of the wreck. Got there when they were removing the overdone remains of one S. Falkes. Talking Mr. Yuk.

"Going up and down the hill, the beat guys had mucked up the path of his car but I kinda could pick it out."

He pulled some photographs from the folder.

"Okay. Here you are looking north on Simmons. The grade is down. Simmons dead ends to that alley and the arterial turns east up the hill on Twenty-Second. Kind of a swale where Twenty-Second and Simmons meet. Well, you've probably been out there.

"Anyway. The Falkes' vehicle, a seventy-eight LTD, heading north, cuts across Simmons street onto the lawn of the first house south of the guardrail. The guardrail is designed for traffic coming down the hill on Twenty-Second. Not for some schmo to cross over the centerline of Simmons and get behind it from the south."

"Speed?" asked Einar.

"Not fast. Could be twenty-five or so, less if you discount acceleration from the fall. But the drop is like fifty feet of almost free fall. There's a big drain pipe that takes the water for four blocks south of Simmons and, of course, Twenty-Second. Fire and other emergency crews accessed it from below. Like I say, it's a swale, and the drainage has eaten away the side of the hill. I'd say the grade is one to one at least, maybe one half to one. One of the beats tied a rope to the guard rail to help us get up and down. But it wasn't a free fall for the car. It rolled counter clockwise. Kind of corkscrewed its way to the bottom. Here's a picture of the point of bop. On its side. Driver down. Gas is draining from the gas tank. Something ignites it and poof. Falkes flambé."

As if relishing the grisly effect, Williams removed a picture of a blackened shape that resembled a human form.

"And I'll tell you what, pal. It did not smell good. I hadda keep telling myself: I do not get sick; I do not get sick ... But whew, did I get sick!"

Williams paused.

"Crime scenes are rough," Paul mused. "You're out there. Out of your element. The cops love it. They live to see a lawyer or any kind of young college boy lose it. Reporters especially ... So anyway, the car rolled over on the way downhill. Any idea how many times?"

"I'd say a definite two times. There were two sets of indents on the driver's side door. I tried to figure out why it rolled. That was before the autopsy told us there was no evidence of smoke in his lungs. He was already dead. Like why didn't it just nose-dive? It might have if the wheels were turned toward the drop. But the wheels were directed *away* from the drop. The car moves transverse across the grade, like a spider on a wall. Then it gets to where the grade is too steep, about by the outfall of the drain and the car starts rolling. That's what it did—went over. Interesting. What would have happened if it had been steered more downward ... would the car still roll? I don't know. If you've got three or four cars laying around, we can do some experiments."

Scott wheezed appreciatively at the idea of destroying three or four cars to determine the path of the car's descent.

"What was the condition of the vehicle?" Paul asked, refocusing the discussion.

"Left front fender was the point of the bop."

"What do you mean, 'point of bop'?" asked Scott.

"Impact. I'd say it hit the ground at an angle and settled on the driver's side. The car body was gouged and dented, but no extreme distortions like you'd get with a high-speed impact. Primarily a caved-in left front fender."

"How did the fire start?"

"Now that's what gets interesting, gents. There was no damage to the fuel tank, but the gas cap was off. It was found about 15 feet from the car. But even so, there's a little backwash gate that should keep the gas from gushing out. So there shouldn't have been a great deal of gas just because the cap was off. And where's the ignition source? Car slides down a steep hill, turns over, lands on its side, gas tank cap coincidentally missing, little bit leaks out, and poof, the whole car's in flames. Gotta have an ignition source. *I'm* sure the car was torched."

"How do we prove it?" asked Paul.

"I'm not a fire investigator. But I got our torch guy to look it over. Seems that to prove a torch job you work backwards, like I did. Eliminate accidental and natural causes. Short circuit in the electrical system? I checked the battery, it still had a charge which means there probably was no drain from a short. Fuel system? Fuel lines all connected. Like I said, the fuel tank was fine. There was no evidence of any problem in the engine compartment. The fire burned inside the passenger compartment and all around the trunk. No engine fire. This is the tip off to me. The backwash gate on the gas tank access made it unlikely that a large amount of fuel would escape in any great hurry. Yet there was a lot of burning around the trunk. And there was also burning inside the passenger compartment. It appears that the fire started in two places—inside the passenger compartment and outside the trunk."

"How can you tell?" Einar asked softly.

"Because the interior of the car was doused with gas," answered Williams. "Before starting the car down the hill, our invisible man opens the front windows for a little ventilation and slops around a little gas. Sherm Falkes is immobile. The car is upright when Mr. Invisible is dousing around the fuel. So a good place to look for residue is the floor carpeting. Also, of course, the seats. Sherm's clothes, too, but I can't get any samples from the coroner until you okay it. So I collect floor carpet samples into the good ol' ever-ready sealed plastic bag and hurry back to the lab to the good ol' gas chromatograph.

"By the time I got to the lab and unsealed the bag even just a bit, brother, I smelled gas. It was rich. No need for exotic distillation or washes to extract the flammables. I just took a sample of the atmosphere in the bag with a syringe and injected. Sure enough the test of the floor carpeting of the Falkes vehicle shows a combustible liquid residue. Now, gents, how does flammable liquid get on the floor of a car sitting on its side? Some defense attorney gonna tell us that better-built-by-Ford means gasoline in the floor carpeting all ready to burn up the occupants?"

"Why didn't the gas burn up in the fire?" asked Paul.

"Remember, gents, to get fire you gotta have heat, oxygen and combustible materials. Combustibility is relative. Burnables burn more so or less so. Nothing burns to a state of total disintegration. I'd guess..."

"Don't guess," interrupted Scott.

"Just a manner of speaking."

"Alton," Scott said, "if you're going to become a good expert witness, and I have no doubt you will one day, remember that opinions are either guesses, which are not evidence, or opinions which are an interpretations of evidence by a qualified expert. If the expert can say that his or her opinion is more probably true than not true, then it is evidence."

"I knew that."

"Good. Act like you do."

Alton looked back at Paul with a who-is-this-old-guy expression and continued. "Okay, okay. It is my opinion, more probably than not, that the surface of the carpet was only slightly singed and the gas which doused the fibers was not oxygenated sufficiently to burn well. Another factor was that the firemen put it out relatively soon.

"All I'm saying is that if a combustible liquid was poured in an unlikely place, we have techniques to detect that by carefully washing or distilling extracted samples from debris. Here, I got a patch of floor carpet debris, put it in a sealed bag, and the atmosphere in the bag tested positive for combustible liquid, more probably than not a motor fuel because the chromatograph is closer to unleaded gas than charcoal lighter or kerosene or something like that.

"I'd guess, yes I mean guess, that samples of Sherm Falkes' clothing debris, when carefully prepared, will test for the same combustible. This will make it unlikely that Ford Motor Co. employs a manufacturing technique of saturating car carpets with combustible fuel. There goes Sherm's product liability case."

"What was the position of the body?" Einar asked.

"He was still in the driver's seat when they removed him."

"Was there anything left of the seat belt?"

"Not much, but the seat buckle was clasped. I'd speculate that if Mr. Invisible wanted to torch him and send him over the cliff, he'd buckle Sherm in to keep him in the driver's seat."

"Imagine you were sending the car and Sherm over the hill. How would you do it?"

"Okay. First I gotta have Sherm immobile. I'd do Sherm first. Then I'd drive up on the northeast corner of the yard to the south of the drop. The car is headed behind the guardrail. In park, motor running. By the way, I verified this part. The tire tracks show that the car stopped before it went over. It's grassy, but fortunately, the ground is soft enough to show scarring from the wheels of the car. The imprint definitely shows stop and go, a deep impression where the car took off. Anyway, I'd move Sherm into the driver seat and buckle him in. Put his foot on the gas pedal. I'd open the gas tank and take the cap off, but I'd need some gas from a gas can. I'd scatter gas from a gas can here and there. Open the windows. Walk around to the driver's side, shift the automatic transmission to drive and watch it shoot off down the hill.

"Question is how do I start the fire and reach in to set the transmission to drive without burning myself. Gas isn't like kerosene or charcoal lighter. Gas is explosive. It's hard to light without getting a face full of flame.

"So what I'd do is tie a strong twine to the cigarette lighter, time how long it takes to heat up, run the twine over the back seat through the open back window, push it in and set the car in drive. Then, hold on as the car shoots down the hill. Hopefully, it wouldn't snag. And I could remove it from the scene. That's what I'd think about doing. The cigarette lighter was missing from the dash."

"Why not just go down the hill and light it with a match or toss down a cigarette or a lighted cigarette lighter?" asked Einar.

"He could have. Local residents didn't hear any boom or whoosh from the fire, but there was a witness two houses down who heard the crash of the car. By the time he got to the top of the hill to investigate, the car was on fire, and no sign of anyone around."

Alton fumbled through the file until he found a photograph and laid it in front of Paul.

"This was on the hillside looking down on the car. If he followed the car down the hill and somehow lit the gas around the tank and the front seat, he could have gone west through the taco stand on Twentieth."

"The neighbor who heard the crash was Mr. Sutter," said Einar from the corner. "He did not get there before the fire started. But he heard it as he was getting dressed. Said it didn't boom, it sort of whooshed. Nobody else heard anything. The people south of the embankment were gone. They were at their cabin on Orcas Island."

Andros looked at Einar quizzically.

"Isn't it convenient that our crime scene is up on Queen Anne at a remote location where the nearest neighbor is gone? Where does our friend live?"

"Northeast from there. I haven't counted, but I'd say twenty or so blocks away."

Alton Williams looked at Andros skeptically. "You guys got Mr. Invisible in sight?"

"No, no," Andros demurred. "We're just going to check the whereabouts of a few people."

"Yeah. Right. OK," said Alton. "Whatever."

Priming the protein pump

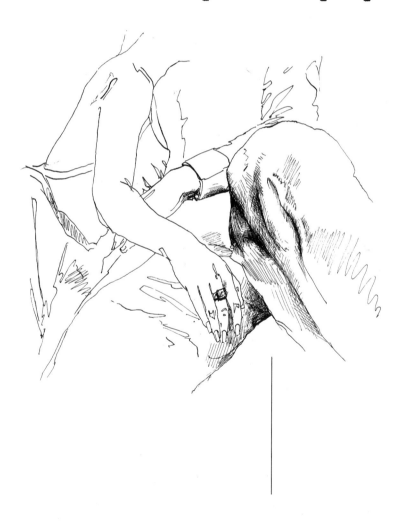

FOURTEEN

AUNT STEFF HAD BABIED THE OLD BUICK. Just a few dents and the need for a paint job, but the car purred healthily as it moved on I-90 toward the Eastern Washington desert.

Terry kept the speedometer at just under sixty-five. Cars and trucks regularly swept past him, but he didn't want an overeager trooper to pull him over for speeding.

The young girl, Mavis, sat beside him with her back against the passenger door, hugging her knees, her bare toes kneading Terry's leg. She watched him closely. She was cat-like, lithe and quick in her movements. Her light brown hair was thick and grew close to her forehead. The short haircut didn't really flatter her, but it was fashionable.

Mavis was the third girl Terry had picked up cruising around Sea-Tac. The first was an attractive thin blonde. She was so hyper that Terry thought she was on drugs. He just stopped the car, gave her $5.00 and told her to catch the bus. The second was not particularly attractive, too experienced, and asked too many questions. Terry had picked Mavis up on South Airport Way where she waited to jump into cars with any willing passerby. When she had agreed to Terry's proposal that they team up, she had taken great care to make Terry take her to her girlfriend so that she could assure her that she had not been done in by some crazy. They had spent the day shopping. After a $200 trip to a Bellevue second-hand clothes shop, Terry had taken all her clothes away. He transformed her wardrobe from high school teeny bopper—boots and jean skirt—to college sophomore—a pleated skirt, two cotton sweaters, a white cotton dress, a flower printed jumper, and a khaki shirt dress to which he had added a red neck scarf.

She was not resentful. Terry fascinated her. He had even brought back shampoo and conditioner. He would like her to have a better haircut, but it was really too short to do much with. He had pronounced her makeup a bit heavy, but the colors fine.

Terry reached under her skirt and stroked her bare calves. He stopped and put his hand palm up in front of her mouth.

"Gum," he said. "Spit out your gum."

She did so.

Terry threw it out the window.

"Never chew gum when you're working a trick."

He went back to stroking her calf. "I think we should talk a little bit about what's ahead. What we're gonna need on this trip is production. You're gonna have to hump your ass. You gotta get your mind on getting them in and getting them out.

"Working hotels and conventions is a different kind of operation. Forget that pretend-ride stuff like when you're working the streets. That's the pits, Mavis. Fifty bucks, whatever, and you're out of commission for what, forty-five minutes? An hour? What, Mavis?"

"I don't know, Bill." Terry had told her his name was Bill Dempsy.

"I suppose it makes no difference if it's that or sling burgers, huh? But time is gonna make a hell of a difference now. What do you do on the streets— guy a night? Three?"

She looked away from him and stared at the mountain landscape. They were past Snoqualmie Pass, starting the slow descent through the sparse vegetation of the easterly Cascades.

"Hey, look, honey. We gotta have bread. You do your job. I do mine. After expenses, we split the take. I've never had a beautiful young girl like you to work with. We're gonna do great ..."

"Let's do something else, Bill. Let's get jobs and get a place together."

Reeney, Reeney, Terry thought. Where are you when I need you?

"Baby, baby," he cooed, reaching up her skirt to stroke her hip. "We will. But we're broke, Baby. We gotta get some money."

"I got money," she said.

"You've only got a couple of hundred bucks. That won't do it, honey. We'll just hit a few towns on our way to Reno and we'll pick up enough to get set up. Then it'll be just like you want it, baby.

"Now listen, babe. Here's your story. You're stranded. See? You're on your way to your cousin's in Montana. Near Missoula."

"Missoula," she said the word as if she was learning a foreign language.

"Missoula," he repeated.

"Your name is Mary . . ."

"No, Susan. My name is Susan."

"Okay, Susan. Susan, this is my friend, Frank—or whatever. He wants to meet you and talk about helping you out."

Terry changed his voice. "Hi, Susan."

After a pause, she said, "Come in, Frank."

"Take his hand. Softly."

He put his hand in front of her. She took it into both of hers.

"That's good, that's good. You want to touch him as soon as you can. Get him into the room. Get me out and get the door closed."

"Mmmm," she said, holding Terry's hand. Terry took his eyes from the road and studied her.

"Control, Susan. Be in control. I've screened the guy. He should be ready. He's not a weirdo. All he wants is to get his rocks off with a pretty girl. Now get his money."

She thought for a moment. "Frank, I hope you can help me. I hate to ask, but could you loan me two hundred dollars? I'd be so grateful."

She gently pulled Terry's hand to her breast.

"Good, baby. Now let go and take a step back. You gotta let him get to his money and you gotta let him see something. Like if you wear that jumper without a blouse or a bra you can let a strap come down. Or just button up the waist and let the skirt come open at the leg."

"I know *that*," she said.

"Production, babe. By the time you've got him on the bed, he's gotta be ready to pump protein. Like what do you do if he gets started but you can't get him off?"

"Go faster?"

"You can do that if you want to be all night. No. Get off him, or get him off, whatever. Then, get up. Do something. Go to the bathroom. Adjust the blinds. Get where he can see you. Go back. Fondle him, then get on top. That'll spark him."

"Mmmm." She moved her breast under Frank's hand.

"Two hundred dollars you said. It's one hundred fifty. Look, if the guy gives you something more after, that's okay. But it's one hundred fifty. We gotta have our story straight. My story is gonna be that I gave you one hundred fifty. The guy is going to feel ripped off if you ask for more from him. Got it?"

"Okay. I thought we could go for more. It's just going to take so long to make any money at one hundred fifty."

"Hey. This is when we work, baby. Whoever said the easy life is easy never tried it. We gotta at least make a grand a night, and we got two hundred in expenses.

"Now one other thing. The rubber. You gotta get a rubber on him or you ain't gonna last the night. Do it last thing. Tell him what a stud he is."

"Where will you be, Bill?"

"I'll be working another guy."

"What happens if something goes wrong?"

"What do you do in a car if something goes wrong?"

"Kick. Scream. Jump out, I guess. I never had anything go too wrong."

"Well? Why will it happen here, then? The room will be on the ground floor. You'll bring in a small piece of luggage, but except for that the room is empty. If there's a problem, just get out. Get to the other room."

"We have another room?"

"Yeah. In another motel. But just keep your mind on your business and nothing will go wrong. Then we'll have plenty of time to unwind. It'll be okay."

Again he reached his hand under her skirt and caressed the notch under her folded left knee. "It'll be okay," he repeated, barely moving his lips.

The oracle of
the Delphi Cafe

FIFTEEN

THE DOORS OF THE DELPHI CAFE were seldom locked—Christmas Eve, Christmas Day and Easter Sunday, and, perhaps, on other solemn occasions decreed by Helen Andros. As he pushed open the heavy doors with their stained glass grape and grape leaf patterns, Paul was sure Jimmie Smith's funeral would be such an occasion.

One of Paul's afternoon conferences with Einar and Scott had been interrupted by a call from his mother to tell him that Jimmie was dead. It was not unusual for him to be asleep in his chair, tilted against the kitchen wall, but Michelle, one of the new waitresses, had observed that it was unusual to see his book spilled onto the floor. Being a "new" waitress meant that Michelle had served at the Delphi for at least five years. During that time, she had seen Jimmie Smith asleep but always with his current book pressed against his stomach, embraced in his folded arms. She checked to see if he was all right. Whether Jimmie Smith was "all right" had become a teleological issue. He was no longer alive, no longer a living member of the Delphi Cafe's close family.

Helen Andros had always felt strongly that Paul should have his own life. She had pushed him into the outside world. As a result, Paul had worked very little at the Delphi. But he always remained an honorary member of the Delphi family. He knew Jimmie Smith well and he loved him.

Paul did not believe, nor did anyone else, that his real name was Jimmie Smith. Nor did anyone believe, when he came to the Delphi over thirty years ago, shortly after Paul's father died, that Jimmie Smith was forty years old, as he claimed. Mid-fifties was more likely. He would be well past eighty when he went into his permanent sleep beside the dishwasher.

Helen Andros appeared to treat Jimmie Smith with the same distant tolerance that she treated everyone, customers and help alike. And, over the years, it had been Jimmie Smith who had quietly become the heart and soul of the Delphi. He set the pace for the others. He worked rhythmically. Never hurried. When his "65th" year came, he did not retire nor did he claim Social Security. He said that, if he did not have some work to do, he would simply sit in his room and read until his body "stove up like a post."

Jimmie Smith's reading was omnivorous. He read the *National Geographic* from cover to cover and he loved *Mad* magazine, to which Paul had introduced him when he was in high school. Jimmie usually had with him in the kitchen some worn books of poetry. He liked Emily Dickinson "cause it rhymes," he liked Walt Whitman "cause it don't rhyme." The book that he died with was a selected collection of poems by William Butler Yeats.

Paul had always been close to Jimmie Smith. Before his marriage to Jane, Paul would often come into the Delphi for early morning or late night meals. Jimmie Smith would sit with Paul while he ate, getting him to talk about what was going on in his life. Their discussions were like friends. Unlike Paul's mother, Jimmie's depth of knowledge and experience spanned any generation gap. Helen Andros was incapable of any non-judgmental view on Paul's life, or for that matter, anything else. But when Paul and Jimmie were deep in conversation she would let them alone. Once, back when Paul was an undergraduate college student, Jimmie Smith had picked up one of Paul's college texts, a world literature anthology, and thumbed through it.

"Looka heah," he said, one of his fingers between the early pages of the thick book while he opened the book to the rear.

"Heah's a po'm by Miss Emily Dickinson." He flipped to the front of the book. "Heah's a po'm by Sappho. Two women centuries apart. How do those two works compare, Pauley?"

"Geez, Jimmie. We're still on the *Iliad* and the *Odyssey*. We haven't gotten there yet."

"Well, it's somethin' to start thinking about. How about comparing the point of view of the storyteller in the *Odyssey* to Sappho? I'm trying to help you here, Pauley."

"I appreciate that, Jimmie. You maybe been down this road before?"

"Now. Now. I just read a little bit, and I like to think about what I read"

Paul grasped at the possibility of using Jimmie as a crib sheet to make his work load easier in literature while he concentrated on his other classes. But Jimmie's tutelage was so stimulating that his A in world literature came at the cost of B's in Early American History and Post World War II Economics which were subjects of much greater value for his career preparations.

Helen Andros seldom discussed Jimmie Smith, or, for that matter, any of the other staff. She had once explained to Jane, when the topic of Jimmie Smith came up, that this is Jimmie Smith's second life and that it is probably best that we not inquire into his first.

Helen Andros had two offices in the Delphi. One was a neon-lighted work area off the kitchen where money was counted, supplies ordered, checks made out, and other paperwork tended. The other "office" was the rear booth next to the swinging kitchen door where conferences were held. She guided Paul to the conference booth.

"I was not ready for Jimmie Smith to die," she pronounced in the throaty, hoarse voice she used for business.

"None of us were, Mom."

"No. I mean I was not ready for Jimmie Smith to die," she said significantly.

Paul said nothing, waiting for a clarification that she was gathering herself to issue.

"You don't know what it has been like waiting for someone to come through the door and take Jimmie Smith away. I loved

Jimmie Smith," she said, tears quietly running down her cheek. "Oh, I hate this. The grief-show. I won't do the grief-show. But, you have to understand, Pauley. Jimmie and I have been ... together."

"Together?" Paul said dumbly.

"Paul," his mother hissed. "Do not be an idiot!"

Paul fell back in the booth, comprehending at last.

"I was a young woman when your father died. I am still a young woman," she said, preening herself in that eyes-half-closed way she had as if she were putting her self on the outside to check herself out.

"Of course," Paul managed to get out.

"Of course!" she mimicked. "You whelp. What do you know about me? When do you even think about me? You ..."

"Mother," Paul said, calming her outburst. "I understand how life has dealt with you harshly. You have pointed this out to me countless times. You have also pointed out, as I have acknowledged, that I am neither the author nor the source of your problems. I am here to help. I will always be here. When you need me, I am there."

Helen Andros reached across the table and pulled Paul's hand to her cheek. "My Paul. My Pauley. I do not deserve you."

"Oh, stop it, mother," Paul said withdrawing his hand. "Are you going to do the grief-show or are you going to get on with it?"

She sat back stiffly, affronted. "If only I had had another child ... A child to honor and respect his mother. If you had had a brother, he would have kept you in your place ..."

"Will you stop please with the brother. You started to tell me something about you and Jimmie Smith and now you're chickening out."

"You are a snip. A snippy son."

Paul sat back and waited. Anything more said by him would simply provoke another personal rebuke. When Paul was a child, his mother was very steady, tolerant, and wise with him. Since Paul had become an adult with a rewarding profession and a wife and family, Helen had developed the habit of being erratic and childish with him. He sometimes wondered if she were indulging herself by going through an adolescence she never had.

Finally, she spoke. Quietly. "I was pretty enough as a girl, but I lived in two worlds. Who knows if a Greek girl is pretty? Covered head to foot."

"Mother. I've seen pictures of your high school class. You dressed no different. Besides, boys know."

"Well, I did not feel pretty. None of the attractive boys would have anything to do with me. There was always Michael. Your father was just one of the family ... A nice Greek boy. Nice!" she hissed.

Paul appeared to listen impassively, but he was shocked at the first indication in his life that Helen Andros thought of her husband in less than a perfect reflection.

"He killed himself being 'nice'. How much money would this place make catering to Greek trade? Huh? Old men drinking fifty-cent coffee, irritating the other customers. Hanging around all day. Talk. Talk. Talk. Greek man talk."

"We've agreed on this, Mom. This restaurant is ideally suited to serve medical offices and hospital staff as an ethnic variation from tasteless food prepared by 'nutritionists'."

Helen's dark eyes blazed. "Will you just listen to me, Mr. Know-It-All-Lawyer?"

Paul started to argue, but held his tongue.

"Where was I?" she asked.

"Changing the image of the restaurant after my father died."

"That was the first thing I did after your father died. Chased out the old men. I picked on one of them and the rest got the message. Ever after, I was the sharp-tongued widow of Michael Andros. The reputation grew and I relished it. I did not want some ne'er-do-well-coffee-house-loudmouth thinking he could take charge of me. Come in here. Marry into a restaurant. Stand around. Let the little wife do all the work. I would not have it."

"Uncle Stavros never helped you?"

"Stavros carries his share. I could not keep the restaurant open twenty-four hours without Stavros. But, Stavros was never the man his brother was. Michael Andros was a decent, hardworking man. But, you must understand, Paul, he was perhaps too decent. I don't think he wanted to take over the restaurant, but with his father ill and his mother gone, what could he do? The decent thing. He did the decent thing and I am tied here for a lifetime."

"What could he do?" Paul agreed, wanting to get on with it.

"Just like my little waitresses—trapped until the next pay day. How to pull oneself out? You did, but at what cost? Did you ever sleep in college?"

She reached across the table and lovingly brushed Paul's hand with her fingers.

Paul risked another outburst. "This isn't about me, Mom! This is something about Jimmie Smith."

Helen sat back in a most unusual submissive pose. As she spoke, tears began to drop down her cheeks.

"Jimmie Smith," she whispered. "He was such a beautiful man. His large hands felt so good when he touched me. His touch was like a blessing . . ."

She broke off unable to speak.

"You and Jimmie Smith were . . . intimate?" Paul offered.

She shook her head affirmatively. "I am no fool. I am sure Jimmie has known many women, but these last few years we drifted together. We never even discussed marriage. He was already married, and his wife had collected life insurance on his death. . . ."

Paul could only ask himself, how had her relationship with Jimmie Smith gone on without his knowing? He said nothing, hoping his mother would continue.

"He had been an English professor at Ohio University in Columbus."

"Ohio *State*?"

"He said it was big."

"Ohio State."

"He was from the South. Alabama. He had gone north when he was sixteen. New York. But he always wanted to go back South and teach black students, like himself, in a state school. He said personal choices on the basis of race are a personal right, but the public schools should be open to all."

"That issue seems to be settled," Paul observed.

"It wasn't settled in his day. But Jimmie Smith ... his real name was John Frederick ... Jimmie Smith had ... weaknesses."

"Women?"

She nodded. "He had affairs with students, fellow teachers, graduate students ... He left his wife and son once to live with a graduate music student. Another time he left to live with a young girl who had dropped out of school to write a novel. But he always went back to his family. He did not feel he should abandon them."

"Strange marriage, with him coming and going."

"He once said that in his day when a man got a woman pregnant he married her. Remember? He said that over and over when Madeleine got pregnant."

Paul remembered Madeleine, a guileless little blonde waitress whom everyone at the restaurant had adored. She had been living with her boyfriend, a business student at the University of Washington. When she became pregnant, he moved out, left her brokenhearted. Paul was in the prosecutor's office at the time and had personally handled a filiation action against him, but the boyfriend, determined, refused to have anything more to do with the girl or the child than the bare minimum legal requirements. Eventually, Madeleine moved back to Astoria, Oregon, her hometown, her whereabouts became lost in the coastal fogs.

"Why was Jimmie Smith here? Why was he hiding his identity?"

"He said the reason he settled in here was that this was the first place where he was with white people that he lost his sense of being black …" Helen Andros choked. She buried her face in a napkin.

Paul waited for her to collect herself. He felt a wave of grief himself for his own loss. Had he ever told Jimmie how much he enjoyed his friendship—the quiet counsel from the depth of Jimmie's life experience passed on?

"Why did he run away?" he asked after a while.

"It was about a student. A white girl. A tragedy really. She had been in one of his classes. A bright girl, he said. He watched her as she went from being a cheerful bubbly girl, a cheerleader type, to a depressed drudge. He was concerned that she was being overwhelmed by her schoolwork. He went out of his way to talk to her. It turned out that she loved her schoolwork. Her eyes were opening to a larger world. But her boyfriend was driving her crazy. All he did was follow her around. She could never talk to any of the male students. He would just walk in and haul her away."

"Obsessive," Paul observed.

"Some men are like that, like their existence depends on their woman. She tried talking with the boy about slowing down. They had known each other since high school. Maybe they should both date other people before making a permanent commitment. He went wild and told her if she left him he would kill himself. She was afraid for him. For herself.

"Jimmie told her that it was too bad but that it was obvious they were growing up in different directions. If he was not the man for her then she would have to make a break. Her boyfriend could not hold her in bondage by threats of suicide."

"Did he do it?" Paul asked.

"Worse. Worse. The girl became dependent on Jimmie. She would walk with him to his office after class. They would talk. Jimmie never saw the boy, but he sensed he was there. He didn't put any moves on her, but she gave him signals that she was … receptive. Despite his nature, he said, in this case, he just counseled her. Talked.

"One day she said she had told her boyfriend that she would be busy the next day and not to meet her. Lunch? No. Break? No. This will just be a day we will not see each other.

"She and Jimmie Smith were in his office when the boy opened the door and walked in. He had a gun. He was in a rage. He said one word, 'busy,' and then he shot her dead right in front of Jimmie's eyes."

"Jesus, Mom! What did Jimmie do? Was there a struggle?"

"Froze. He said he was frozen. He watched the boy without moving. The boy looked toward Jimmie as if he were not there. Then he did point the gun at Jimmie, and Jimmie told me he died in those twenty or thirty seconds that boy pointed that gun at him. Finally, the boy just smiled and said, "Dr. Frederick goes from nigger heaven to nigger hell. . . .

"But he did not shoot Jimmie. He put the barrel in his mouth and blew the back of his head off."

"Mother . . ." Paul gasped, incredulous this tale had never come to him before.

Helen's eyes were distant as she remembered Jimmie Smith's story.

"Jimmie Smith said he looked around the blood-soaked room and just walked away. He remembered there were people there, outside the office, but no one stopped him. He never went home. He sent a letter eventually to his wife saying not to look for him. That he was for all intents and purposes dead."

Paul thought it all over. "No life insurance company's going to pay on that," he finally commented.

"After so many years?"

"Maybe. I don't know."

"Well, they should. Because the man Jimmie Smith was—whoever he was—*was* dead."

"OK—where did he go? What did he do?"

"He floated around. On the road. In the streets. Wasn't that the Love Generation? I was so busy then I don't remember what was going on in the world. Anyway he somehow arrived here. He was a good worker and he stayed."

"When did you get ... together?" Paul asked hesitantly.

"It was after you graduated from college. Those long talks you and Jimmie Smith had. I knew, you knew, Jimmie Smith was not a busboy, a dishwasher. When you sold back the fish bar and started law school, it was the first time in years that I could stand back and sort of look around me."

Shortly after he had graduated college, Paul had managed to talk Charles Knowles, the longtime owner of Charlie's Fish House on the Seattle waterfront, into a contract allowing Paul to open a small Charlie's Fish House take-out in Capitol Hill. Paul did it on a fast-food format—food only—but the fish was genuine Charlie's. Paul had talked his mother into a mortgage on the Delphi to finance the deal, which he had financially wired together as a junior executive at Seattle-World Bank. Less than two years later, Charlie Knowles was in the process of selling out his business when his lawyers and the buyer's lawyers discovered that Paul had buried in the paperwork a clause that, arguably, assigned him the franchise rights to Charlie's Fish House. The buyer wanted Paul out as a condition of purchase. Paul and his mother sold out the entire business, splitting between them a $95,000 profit.

"That was when I quit my job and plunged into law school," Paul recalled. "I guess that's how I lost track."

Helen Andros reached across the table and to hold Paul's face in her hand. "You did not lose track, Pauley. You were living your life."

Paul grasped her hand softly. "And you were living yours, mother—quite so, as it turns out!. Here I am sad, but glad that you found someone. But now he's gone."

"No. Jimmie Smith is here," she pointed to her heart. "Just like your father is here. That is life."

Paul sat trying to understand Jimmie Smith. He had always been good-humored quiet, intelligent. Gave no hint of personal agony.

"There is something. More. I promised to do some things for Jimmie Smith if he died."

"What things?"

"You see, Pauley. I owe him."

"Owe him."

"Yes. Jimmie Smith hasn't been on the payroll for over five years. We made an arrangement. I bought the apartment house next door where he had been living for so long."

"'The Norseman? But it's been fixed up. Remodeled."

"I know. I own it. Years ago. I took the Fish House money and my savings and mortgaged this place and bought it. Five years ago, I borrowed the money to fix it up. We contracted for part of the fix-up but we did a lot ourselves. That's why he wasn't on the payroll. It increased profits and no social security or benefits. I had more money for payments and expenses on the Norseman."

"What if he got hurt?" Paul asked.

She shrugged.

"Did Jimmie Smith own it too?"

"No. It was not in his name. But I promised that if he died, for each year he worked without wages I would give five thousand dollars to Columbia University and ten thousand to his son. In round numbers, I guess I owe twenty-five thousand to Columbia University and fifty thousand to his son."

"Whew," Paul sat back.

"It will take me a while to get it together, but when I do, I want you to take care of it for me. It will prey on my mind until it is paid off."

"Do you want me to help? I'd be glad to help."

"No. I can do it. I might sell the apartment building."

"Do you want me to see if I can find a buyer? I'll talk to Scott. We can probably find someone. *If* you're willing to be reasonable."

"Huh!" his mother said noncommittally.

"Don't worry about this, Mom. We'll get it done. Don't worry."

Paul put his hands over his mother's limp hands folded in front of her. She was quite spent from telling her story. Her eyes were still welling with tears. For the first time in his life Andros felt, with a heart-clenching jolt, that his mother was not indomitable.

She withdrew her hands and straightened herself up.

"Thank you, Pauley. It's late. You'd better get home to your family. This will stay just between us."

It was half question and half statement.

"Our secret, mother. To my grave."

"Do not make a promise you do not intend to keep," she hissed, theatrically but with meaning. Her spirits were recovering.

"It is a promise I do intend to keep."

"Go home, Pauley. Go on home."

Paul rose from the booth to do as his mother directed. He was tired. He looked down at his mother. She flipped her wrist toward the door.

Dismissed.

Foal play

SIXTEEN

ANDROS THOUGHT ABOUT RETURNING to the office after the emotional conference with his mother, but when his hands gripped the steering wheel of his car, all he could think about was Jimmie Smith. Gone. It was the first death of anyone close to him that he had faced in his adult life. With his mother's revelation of their relationship, Andros felt his mother's sorrow as well as his own. Automatically, his car found the Cherry St. on-ramp to I-5 and he was heading home.

When Andros turned off Turner Road into the narrow gravel driveway leading to his house, he thought about how he had been spending his days immersed in office details. That entire morning had been spent at a county council meeting supporting Herb McAuliffe in gaining the council's approval of a settlement of a road contractor's claim for unanticipated soil conditions. Such commitments occupied his time day after day. He had not been home before 7:00 P.M. since becoming the county prosecuting attorney, except for one or two Saturdays and Sundays when no one else was willing to continue working. He thought about Jimmie Smith's prediction that the job was going to eat away at his personal life.

The area between his house and the road was thickly wooded. Andros maintained only a small grass yard around the front of the house. The west and north acreage was in woods. To the south and east, away from Turner Road was a grazing meadow for his wife and daughter's horses.

He drove around a red VW Cabriolet convertible in the wide driveway and parked his Volvo in the carport to the east of the house.

"Marvin," he sputtered to himself. It was only 6:15, still light, but the thick cloud cover and light rain made it seem as if night was falling.

He could see two figures in the corral. Beatrice's horse, Mona, was laying on the ground. She was foaling.

He ran over to where the two figures were standing. Jane and Marvin. They were engrossed in the purposeful grunting of the horse.

"Should we try to get her into the barn?" Andros asked quietly.

"We talked about it, but I didn't want to try to move her. I think she's OK here," Jane said.

"My vet told me it was healthier just to let them foal in the field, but, my God, in the rain?" Marvin added.

The horse started to push the ground with her front legs.

"She's going to get up," Jane said. But the horse dropped back down on her side.

"Doc Trainer?" Andros asked.

"He's supposedly on his way, but he had an emergency at the clinic," Jane said.

"This is not an emergency?" Paul asked.

Neither responded.

Andros stood helplessly for a moment. His business suit was slowly absorbing the light rain. Marvin and Jane were in boots and rain clothes.

Paul ran to the kitchen, substituted a raincoat for his suit coat, and grabbed the keys to the pickup, a '72 Chevy 402 with high wooden sides around the bed for hauling hay. It was neatly backed in next to the barn on the opposite side from the corral. It started up faithfully. Paul put it in four wheel drive and drove around to the corral. He entered at the gate and drove slowly to the opposite side of the horse. He backed up the truck beside the horse so the driver side of the bed was about five feet away.

He jumped out of the cab and dashed to the barn. He tore open the packaging on a big 10' by 18' plastic tarp stored in the tool room, located hammer and nails, and rushed back towards Jane and Marvin.

"Get this sucker unfolded and we'll hang it between the pickup and the Volvo," he said, handing them the tarp.

He ran over to the Volvo and backed it slowly into the corral, parallel to the pickup, on the other side of the horse.

Jane and Marvin held the tarp high on the wooden side of the truck bed while Paul tacked up one side. He and Marvin walked the tarp on opposite sides of the horse and secured it to the trunk and the front door of the Volvo. Mona's head was still in the rain, but her flanks were under the cover of the tarp.

Jane, Marvin and Paul lined up against the truck fender and watched the horse.

"At least we're in the dry," Paul said.

"It's kinda cozy," Marvin said.

Jane concentrated on the horse. She knelt and stroked the horse's head.

"Come on, baby girl. You've got to push," she said softly.

Earlier in the month on day 330 of Mona's pregnancy, Jane had wrapped her tail with an elastic leg bandage. Several weeks before that, the vet had come by and opened up her Caslick's closure. Her vulva was now open and dilated almost the full length of her flanks. She had broken water and the membrane that surrounded the foal during gestation was protruding through her cervix. A miniature hoof was just visible through the milky white membrane that blanketed the foal.

"Feet first, that's good," said Marvin.

"Do we need to help? Pull or something?" Paul asked. He wanted to do something.

Jane shook her head. "The vet said, whatever you do, don't pull on the foal. There's not much we can do unless there's a problem. And I hope there's not a problem."

Suddenly, Mona started to rise up. She contracted and the miniature hoof moved further from the birth canal. A second hoof could be seen.

The horse began to stand up. Marvin and Paul went to opposite sides of the tarp and released it from the vehicles to get it out of her way.

Paul ran back to the barn and came slipping back across the yard with an armload of hay. He spread this around the rear of the horse.

Marvin said quietly, "I can see the muzzle of the colt."

Suddenly, the mare contracted, and the foal's head was visible between its two front legs. The foal's neck emerged. The white membrane ripped open as the foal's shoulders worked free from the mare. Jane cleared away the sticky tissue from the foal's nose and eyes. Several contractions later, the foal was lying on the bed of straw behind Mona with only its rear legs still within the birth canal.

"What should we do with the umbilical cord?" Paul asked.

"Just leave it alone and keep quiet. She should rest a few minutes," Jane whispered.

The three fell silent, Jane at the horse's head and Paul and Marvin behind, watching the foal. The foal wriggled its legs, and broke entirely away from the mare's womb.

"You can help the foal move on its stomach. Carefully," Jane said.

Paul gingerly rolled the foal onto its stomach. Mucous dripped from its nostrils. The foal attempted to stand up and fell hard against the ground.

"OK. I'm sorry," said Paul, reaching to help the foal.

Jane laughed quietly. "That's all right. Don't worry. Helps open the lungs."

The umbilical cord broke during the foal's fall.

"Marvin," Jane whispered. "Go into the barn. Just inside the door on the right there's a shelf with a bottle of iodine . . ."

Marvin stepped away quietly.

Meanwhile, the foal was starting to stand up again.

"Look at that," Paul said. "He's a scrappy little guy."

"Maybe he's a scrappy little gal."

Paul looked. "How are you supposed to tell? Uh oh, I see it. It *is* a guy."

Dr. Trainer arrived soon after. He examined both animals and pronounced them healthy. He administered a tetanus shot and with Jane's help gave the foal an enema to assure that its colon was functioning properly.

The foal greedily sucked his first meal, then collapsed for a nap.

"Didn't you tell me that foal is out of Blue-Ribbon-Boy at Chesterton Farms?" Dr. Trainer asked Jane.

"Yes," she said smiling.

Dr. Trainer smiled back, shaking his head. "Your fortune is made if he grows out as good as he looks right now."

Jane turned to Marvin. There were tears in her eyes. "Thank you, Marvin," she said.

"What are friends for if not to exploit and cast aside. Just remember us little people," he said.

Paul looked quizzically at his wife and his seemingly ne'er-do-well neighbor.

Jane looked over at Paul. "The Chestertons are friends of Marvin. They let me send Lisa over for siring with their prize stallion. You're in the horse business, Mr. Andros."

"Just what I wanted. More stalls to clean."

Dr. Trainer hurried off and Marvin headed off to a dinner to which "no one dares to be late."

Paul went inside to fix some dinner, microwaved enchiladas and a salad. As he washed lettuce, chopped onions and tomatoes, and sliced an avocado, he realized that the evening's events had cleared away office concerns and thoughts of Jimmie Smith. He outlined in his mind an edited version of his mother's relationship with Jimmie that he would tell Jane. If his mother wanted to share the whole story with Jane, which sooner or later she would probably do, Paul would let that happen in its own time. He called to Jane when dinner was ready.

"Young Blue Ribbon Boy woke up and pooped mightily," Jane said, helping herself to a handful of corn chips.

"Hooray," said Paul. He reached over and kissed Jane on the check. "I'm happy it went well. I'm sorry I haven't been much help lately."

Jane smiled. "It's my thing, Paul. But I'm glad you were here."

"What an experience. That was my first time. You were like a veteran."

"I was at Thelma's when her mare foaled, but she was so skittish I just stayed in the distance. Lisa's such a doll. She didn't even get jumpy when you brought in the pickup. I thought about stopping you but she didn't seem to notice."

"I never thought about making her jumpy. I had to do something."

"I know, dear. I know," she said, chomping on a jalapeno. "And you did do something. It's taken me a few years, but I think I understand that's how you express your love and commitment."

"Huh?"

"I don't care what you do out there." She waved her arms toward the world outside their home and acreage. "When you're here, and I wish you were here more with Bea and me, and you make a hay run in winter or help Bea clean the barn or when you try to help like tonight, you are the man I love."

"Even when I don't come up with a thoroughbred sire for your little thoroughbred mare?"

"Well, Marvin has his points too, but I'm not sure you compare to any disadvantage to a gay man."

"Gay?"

"Oh, Paul, you are such fun to tease."

"That's really why you keep me around."

"That . . . and other things."

"Marvin," Paul muttered to himself. "I don't believe it. He's just faking it."

"What's that?"

"Humpf. More salad?"

After Hours, Inc.

SEVENTEEN

JAKE SATELLO PAUSED AT THE OPEN DOOR to the prosecutor's conference room like a bear impassively catching the scent of the next direction in which he would choose to move.

Paul rose from the conference table and motioned for him to come in.

It was the beginning of the fifth week of the investigation. Einar had assembled sufficient documentary background surrounding Sherman Falkes' apartment house investment that they felt they were now ready to interrogate Sherm's business partner.

"Thank you for coming over today, Jake. I haven't seen you for a long time. Since I previously left the prosecutor's office, I think. This is Einar Torgeson."

Jake and Einar nodded toward each other.

"So how can I help you guys?" Jake sat down, heavily. "Papers said it turns out Sherm got done by somebody. Sherm and I were good friends."

"That's why we wanted to talk with you, Jake. We want to learn more about his personal life and people he knew outside the office. You and Sherm were also business associates, weren't you?"

"Yeah." Pause. Jake did not volunteer to forward the discussion.

Paul filled in. "You were landlords together? How did that come about?"

"I ran into a deal on an apartment building on Capitol Hill. Couldn't handle it on my own. Is that what you guys want to talk about? I can get my records, but Sherm kept the current rent and expense records."

"Actually, I have some records from Sherm's effects. Did you do any of the bookkeeping?"

"Sherm had been doing the books. We were just gonna trade off at the time he died. I told you that on the phone, I was just planning to pick up the records so I could start my turn managing the apartment and sort out what our deadbeat tenants owe."

"And you planned the change how long before he died?"

"Maybe a week or so."

Paul reached over to the pile of papers beside Einar and picked up a fat mailing envelope.

"Well, we found some checks made out to After Hours, Inc. That was you and Sherm, I guess."

"Yeah. When can I have them?"

"Soon. Einar is just checking out a few things. We made copies of everything we have regarding the apartment. I believe you know that Sherm's former wife, Mrs. Bennett, will be the executrix of his estate. Just keep her informed of what you're doing. Her address and telephone number are in the packet."

"Is the apartment building gonna be tied up in court or anything?"

"Not particularly, except Sherm's children are your new partners, and you have to account to the estate for the income and expenses."

"Great. I'm partners with a couple of kids. I hope they got more sense than mine. Sherm and I had to feed it, you know. The apartment."

"That's funny," Paul said slowly. "I've looked at the past few months of the bank account and it looked like it was doing all right to me."

"Well, we had to feed it to start with, but maybe it had been running about even the last year or so. But I'm not sure. Sherm kept the books."

"But he hadn't hit you up for a while, had he?"

"It had been a while, maybe. I didn't keep track."

"In fact, the After Hours, Inc. bank account showed a surplus of around fifteen grand."

Andros had wondered if this would come as a surprise, but Satello did not react.

"Our monthly payment is maybe three thousand, plus taxes and insurance. And we owe for some repairs and remodeling. We've been doing a lot of remodeling and we've got more coming up. And a roof."

"Do you have all the units rented?"

"Yeah. We're working on a couple of units, but those that are ready are rented."

"What's the rental income?"

"Generally, one bedrooms now are two ninety-five. Two bedrooms three ninety-five. They aren't very modern, but bigger than what you get in newer units."

"How many ones and how many twos?"

"Some of them are laid out funny, because they were originally large apartments that got broken up. I think there's thirteen two bedrooms, and eleven or twelve one bedrooms. So we say twenty-four units."

Paul mulled over his notes. "So that's what? Eighty-five hundred a month versus what? Five to six grand per month expenses?"

"Well, of course, you got vacancies and we're just now getting the units into shape so we can get those kind of rents."

"Vacancies," said Paul. "That's curious. Deposits I saw showed ten thousand and fifty dollars per month, regular as clockwork. You've spent fifty grand on remodeling expenses to Ventures Seven, Inc. and still have a fifteen grand surplus. I didn't find Ventures Seven, Inc. as a building contractor. Tell me about that firm."

Satello sat up and put both of his large hands on the table. "It's a group of moonlighting police officers. Guys that wanted to do something besides work after hours at security jobs."

"Do you know their names?" Paul asked.

Satello looked out the window pensively. "Art Newson sort of heads up the group. He's the guy I deal with."

Pause.

"Anyone else?" Paul asked.

"No. He's the one I dealt with."

"I mean anyone else in the group?"

"Oh, Milt Patterson ... Tom Flagg ..."

"Anyone else?"

"Gee, I'd have to check with Art. I forget everyone. Like the name says, I guess there's seven."

"I'll check with you later then," Andros said. He set his pen on the table and pushed his chair back. "Maybe you can tell me when you first got to know Sherm?"

"I'm not sure I can. Sherm and I go way back. I guess it would have to be when he started here at the prosecutor's office."

"Before he got married, then."

"Oh yeah."

"Did you socialize?"

"You mean did we go out and boff little girls together? Naw. Only coffee after court. I didn't see him in the evenings or anything."

"That's right. You're a veteran family man."

"Four kids. I do my duty for the Vatican."

"Four kids. That's great, Jake. How old are they?"

"David is nineteen. He's at Seattle U. Samuel is seventeen. Tammy is just sixteen. Virginia is thirteen."

"Ties you down to spread them out like that, doesn't it?"

"Makes you have to keep moving. I've always worked two jobs."

"What other work do you do?"

"Used to be a fisherman. Then that Boldt deal came along. The resource was dwindling and the Indians were gonna get first crack. I could see the handwriting. So I got into real estate."

"Selling?"

"No, no. Buy a place. Fix it up. Rent it. Maybe sell it."

"Like you did with Sherm."

"Sure."

"Do you have other partners?"

"Not exactly. My dad and I were into a couple of duplexes. Since he died, I manage them for my mom. She gets the income. She just socks it away, waiting for a rainy day. She gets sick, it's gone in no time."

"Gee," Paul said admiringly. "How many places do you own?"

"A few here and there. But the Argo was the only place I had with Sherm."

"Argo?"

"Yeah. Argo Lane Apartments. That's the name of it."

"Do you have any idea whether Sherm had any other outside ventures like the Argo?"

"If he did, he didn't mention it to me. Fact he was the one pushing to find a deal like the Argo, 'cause he was always moaning that he didn't have nothing going for him except his pension."

"I noted that you and Sherm bought it five years ago. How did you run into it? Three hundred thousand for twenty-four units. That's a little over thirteen thousand per unit. Well located. Even for nineteen seventy-four that was a pretty good deal. How did you manage to find a place like that?"

"You got all that from Sherm's papers?"

"What?" Andros asked.

"All that information on the Argo."

"Yeah. It's all there but it doesn't tell the story."

"Well," Satello spoke hesitantly, "it only had sixteen units when we bought it. We redivided the units and got eight more."

"How did you find the building? Was it listed?"

"No. Apartment owner's association. I knew the guy. A dentist."

"Any idea why he wanted to sell?"

"Said he wanted to take things a little easier. I don't know. Maybe the maintenance was driving him crazy. Vacancies. Slow pay. Who knows why a guy wants out?"

"What was his name?"

"Rossierre." He spelled it out. "I don't at this point remember his first name."

"How long had he held it?"

"Huh?"

"How long had he owned the property before he sold?"

Satello pushed himself away from the conference table. "You guys just asking a lot of questions 'cause you don't have nothing else to do? What's this got to do with who killed Sherm?"

Einar shifted in his chair wordlessly.

"Take it easy, Jake," Andros said. "It turns out that you know a lot more than most people about Sherm. We're just trying to get the picture of what was going on in Sherm's life . . ."

He paused to understand Satello's mood. He didn't seem angry or contemptuous. He sat impassively. Paul concluded that Jake Satello was a pro. He wouldn't start babbling just to fill a silence. He tried again.

"How long'd he held it, Jake?"

"How should I fucking know?" Satello asked slowly, almost in a singsong cadence. "You got the records. You got the deeds. Look it up yourself, Mr. Andros"

Andros remained calm.

"Well," he replied, mock amiably. "It does seem an awfully good deal. Even five years ago."

"Maybe you should talk to Rossierre. Maybe you should try managing property, dealing with sixteen rentals and leaky plumbing and trying to satisfy the goddamn building inspectors every time you do a little work on the place," Satello said.

"Or maybe I should talk to Dr. Rossierre about a nineteen-year-old son whose apartment got busted with two kilos of grass and several baggies of what appeared to be cocaine that got lost in evidence so that the prosecutor's office charged misdemeanor possession of marijuana."

After a pause: "I'll check on that," Jake said.

"Do that, Jake. The boy's name was Michael Rossierre. I checked with Norton. He said he recalled the bust and that his people told him there was cocaine. I checked our file and he copped only to marijuana. He is now out of the system. As far as we know, a successful rehabilitation. But, you know it's really not our job to guess who will rehabilitate and who will keep on selling drugs. Is it?"

"I don't know nothing about any drug charge."

"Tell me how you got together with Rossierre."

"We were sitting together, I guess, and they were talking about some new sprinkler law, I think. Some dumb thing the city came up with. And he said he'd like to pull out."

"Nothing about a drug charge?"

"I'd have remembered. No."

"Do you have anything to do with the Evidence Room at Seattle PD?"

Satello took a minute to think about it. He knew that Paul knew that the chief clerk of the evidence room reported to him. "I don't think we're having a friendly discussion here about Sherm, Mr. Andros. I'm just a dumb cop, but I haven't been advised of my rights and all we do is keep talking about me."

"Should I be advising you of your rights, Jake?"

"You're the prosecutor."

"Well, I haven't advised you, have I? I want to know about Sherm. Let's forget about Rossierre for a moment. Did it come as a surprise to you when it came out that Sherm was with a female minor at the Majestic Motel?"

"You never know about people, Mr. Andros. I've always thought I understood fish better than people." Satello paused and looked out the window of the conference room. "I always looked for their brains, fish, when I cleaned 'em. Trying to understand them. Fish brains are hard to find but fish do all right. They don't need to build houses. Drive cars. Make boat payments. They live wherever they are. Pick off a piece of food that comes by ..."

"That's very philosophical, Jake. But what was your reaction when you heard about Falkes and this girl?"

"I was just trying to tell you, counsel. I thought about fish. I thought about the dark deep waters I used to take fish from and how fishing's always better on cloudy days. I thought about dark days and dark waters when you only stayed out on the Sound 'cause the fishing's good. I thought about how people I knew, people my father knew, how they got swallowed up by the water. Gone. I guess when I think about death I see dark, heavy water that swallows up people."

Andros waited for more.

"I don't know what you're trying to tell me, Jake," he prodded finally.

Satello, hunched in his chair, lifted his eyes towards the mute Torgeson.

"I was shook up. That's what I'm fucking *telling* you, Mr. Andros. This guy is my business partner. He's got big political problems. He's ten or fifteen years away from retirement. As a kiddie boffer, he won't get re-elected to dogcatcher. Does he lose his license? Beats me. Even if he keeps his license, what does he do? Court appointments for indigent jaywalkers?"

"Where did all this come from?"

"Huh?"

"You're describing your reactions to a living Sherm Falkes. Near as the pathologist can tell, Sherm died between two and three in the morning. So he was dead by the time word of the bust got out in the newspapers. Were you on duty that night?"

"Naw, I was home. Somebody called me."

"Who called you?"

"Forget it, counsel. I'm not dragging anybody else in this."

"Could be important, Jake."

"Why so?"

"Why do you think?"

"You wanta know whether Sherm or somebody else told me about the bust. I'm thinking you oughtta be advising me of my rights, cause your finger is trying to point at me for something, counsel. Yours truly."

"I'm not advising you of your rights, Jake. For one reason. I want to know what happened. It's important to put together a case, but it's more important that the case be put together against whoever killed Sherm. There's a difference, Jake. I'm here because of a political compromise, but while I'm here I don't have to make decisions based on politics or public relations. Before I charge, win or lose, I want to know in my mind and heart that I've charged the guilty party! That's even more important to me than whether we charge a winnable case."

"So whatta you talking to me? I didn't murder Sherm. Why the hell would I want Sherm dead?"

"I'm talking to you because ..."

"I know, I know. You're talking to me 'cause I knew Sherm. But all I hear is 'where were you on the night Sherm died' stuff. Whyn't you talk to that fuck they busted at the Majestic? Terry what's-his-name? If he'd been providing Sherm twat he sure as hell knows a lot more about him than I ever knew..."

"The city dicks tell me they're following that lead, but nobody knows where he is."

Jake's tone grew slightly conciliatory. "Any ideas where he might be?"

"Not that I've heard," Andros continued, conversationally. "Detective Bailey is leading the investigation. He tells me that, except for the girls, Terry is kind of a loner. There were three girls that we know of. Might have been girls in other rooms but all Seattle PD could bring into the bust was Irene Johnson, Shirley Miller, and Margaret Cross, the kid who was with Sherm. Irene Johnson is still 'failure-to-appear' after she and Barnes bailed out. Shirley's a pro. Talks to nobody. She couldn't make bail. She pled guilty as soon as she could get to court and is doing six months.

At least we know where she is while she's in jail, but good luck to anybody trying to get anything out of her."

"What about the kid?"

"Same story: no story. That leaves us with the question you haven't answered, Jake. Where were you on the night Sherm died? And who called you to tell you that Sherm was involved in the Majestic Motel bust?"

"Look, Mr. Andros, like I told you. This is a real messy deal. Now you're asking me to drag family and friends into a matter that ought to be left alone. You're a well-connected guy. Why not put together a task force from the King County sheriff's office, and let them investigate this mess while you run for the office here?"

Andros waved his hand dismissively. "Jake. I'm not filing for the prosecutor's office. I'm out of here as soon as I can get out."

Jake shrugged and looked at Andros and then across the room at Einar. "Well, I wish you guys a lot of luck. If you don't have any more questions, I got work to do."

He leaned on the table as he rose.

"That's it, then? Any thoughts of your own on Sherm's death? Any avenues that should be investigated?"

"Sure. You find that Terry guy who ran that herd of girls and I think you can get your answers."

"We're looking. Oh, Jake. One more thing. We found eleven thousand eight hundred dollars in Sherm's apartment. There was also fifty-three hundred in checks to After Hours. If Sherm had collected cash from the other renters for the June rent, that would only be about thirty-five hundred. Any idea where the other seventy-five hundred came from?"

"Maybe he was stealing from somebody," Jake said impulsively.

"Maybe he was. Was he stealing from you?"

Jake's wily eyes indicated that he immediately perceived the implication. "Naw, counsel. Sherm was always straight as an arrow with me, we'd go over the receipts together, decide what to do about any deadbeats. Sherm was a good business partner. Maybe he just liked to keep cash around."

"So you'd say the money was his, then?"

Without a flicker of remorse at surrendering any interest he might have in the cash, Jake said. "Sure. Except for the rent receipts. And as for the cash renters, I'll check when I collect the July rent. But I imagine After Hours is entitled like you say to only thirty-five hundred of it."

"Right. Anything else that might assist us in the investigation?"

Jake looked over at Einar, quietly taking notes on the meeting. "Yeah, whyn't you fuckheads turn it over to somebody knows what the hell they're doing?"

Einar looked up from his notes and asked, "Is 'fuckheads' one word or two?"

It was his only participation in the discussion.

Andros smiled, rose and opened the door. The conference room was connected to one of the secretarial areas. Five women and one man were busy with the prosecutors' voluminous paperwork. Two desks were near a large copier and were piled with papers and file folders for copying and assembly.

Mary Lynn Pierce's office overlooked the scene from a glassed-in work area between the secretarial work area and the prosecuting attorney's office beyond. Two other women sat on the other side of her desk.

"He's coming out now. Just look to your right, Margie, over Mrs. Jensen's shoulder."

The auburn haired girl was screened from the men coming out of the conference room. She looked around the woman seated next to her. Immediately, she sat back behind the woman like a child playing peek-a-boo.

"Is that the man?" Mrs. Pierce asked.

Jake Satello ambled out of the conference room. Margie Cross glanced at him again and then turned back to stare at Mrs. Pierce wordlessly.

Einar Torgeson and Andros followed him out. Then they turned and walked past the secretarial area and Mary Lynn's office into the prosecutor's office.

"Call Art Newson, Milt Patterson, and Tom Flagg right away," said Andros. "Ask if they were on duty on June eighth and if they talked to Jake Satello that night or early on the ninth. Then check with the secretary of state and see if there are any other names associated with the incorporation papers for Ventures Seven, Inc. If you find other names, check with them, too. Quick. Before Jake gets to them and coaches them. It's not much, but we might catch them up in something."

"What about Margie?" Einar asked quietly.

"Oh, OK, OK. You've got the rapport with her. I'll make the calls, and you talk to her in the conference room."

Einar left the office and stepped into Mary Lynn's doorway.

"Margie?" he said. "Would you come into the conference room with me?"

Margie followed Einar and seated herself quietly.

"That's a nice outfit. Very nice sweater," he said. "Are those clothes Reeney and Terry bought you?"

"Mrs. Jensen picked them up for me at the motel. They had packed it and put it away. They didn't pack things neatly."

"Margie, was that the man?"

"That was the man I saw with John, or Mr. Falkes, at the market."

"What about the car, Margie? Is that the man you saw in the car that followed Terry?"

"I think so, but I couldn't see his face too well. It was just that he put his arm out the car window when Terry walked toward his van."

"Did Terry talk with him?"

"He might have said something. All I could see was that it looked like they left together. Terry got into his van and he and the other car just pulled out and left together."

"Do you recall what floor you were on?"

"Third."

"And the man who looked like the man you just saw, Mr. Satello, spoke to Terry and they each left in their own cars at the same time?"

"Yes. But from upstairs I just saw part of his face. I'm trying to help as much as I can, Mr. Torgeson."

"Einar."

"Einar."

"Okay," Einar said. "Margie, Mrs. Jensen says your aunt will take you if the judge will let you go to Wichita. Are you sure you can get along with your aunt?"

"I think so. She's nice."

"Remember, you'll have to be nice too. Anyway, we'd like you to stay around here just a little while longer."

"When I get to Wichita I can call you if I have a problem?"

"Sure," Einar said. "Let's go get Mrs. Jensen."

Meanwhile, Andros had called Newson, Patterson, and Flagg. All three unavailable. Patterson was in Oregon to pick up a prisoner on extradition. Newson and Flagg were off duty. Andros had to go through Chief Hellman to get their home telephone numbers. He tried Newson's number. No answer. He tried Flagg. Line busy. Several minutes later, he rang again. No answer. Ten rings. No answer.

Andros shook his head. He knew that the next time he asked the question of how Jake knew about Sherm's death, he would be given the name of a policeman who would verify that he called Jake and told him.

"A slow-moving man who gets things done fast," he said to himself.

Reeney
leaves an
impression

EIGHTEEN

THE NEXT MORNING EINAR TORGESON parked the State's venerable Dodge Dart on Potter Street less than a block away from
the Argo Apartments. He felt lucky to park that close. This
mid-summer morning was his third try at finding Martine
Rodriguez at home. On his other visits, in the late afternoon,
the heavy traffic of non-residents visiting the bars, restaurants,
and shops and the residents returning to their homes off and on
Broadway had forced him to park several blocks away.

According to the inscription on the southeast cornerstone
of the building. the Argo had been built in 1923. It was gracious,
inviting, and well maintained. The front door, constructed of
heavy oak and thick glass panes, was at street level. The door
was protected from the weather by a glass canopy supported by
a heavy oak frame, faded, but in some distant past, matching the
oak doors. The tarnished brass door handle worked well as Einar
entered the oak paneled foyer. There was a buzzer system connected to the mailboxes that was out of order. A block had been
placed on the floor to keep the inner door open. The mailboxes
had previously informed Einar that Miss Rodriguez lived on the
third floor. Einar trudged up the wide stairs and knocked lightly
on the door of #304.

Einar was surprised to hear a feminine voice answer immediately, "Yes?"

"Miss Rodriguez, I'm from the county prosecutor's office. I'd
like to talk to you about Sherm Falkes."

The door opened almost immediately.

"Einar Torgeson," Einar said, extending his right hand and
holding up his ID in the other.

Her hair was strikingly brunette, which contrasted with her unusually light skin. She wore light red lipstick, but no makeup around her dark brown eyes and long dark eyelashes. Her slim figure was clothed in tight jeans and a denim shirt with bright, multi-colored embroidering just below the shoulders.

"Yes, yes," she said. "You look authentic, even though I can't read that card you're waving around there."

"Einar handed her his worn clear-plastic ID wallet.

"Human Rights Commission?"

"I'm on loan to the prosecutor's office."

"Well, Mr. Torgeson. I shed tears when I learned that Sherm Falkes had died, but I can tell you it was probably fortunate for me that he is out of my life." She turned her head to show him where her hair was short just above her right ear.

"It's growing back. Under there is a three inch slice the surgeons made to drain a cranial edema. I'm lucky to be alive. It was that whore girlfriend of his, but like I told the police I can't testify to that. Didn't see her."

"Did you give a statement to the police? All I have is an incident report we found among Sherm's things."

"He had a copy of the report?"

"At his condo."

"I'm touched."

"Did you make a statement?"

"Seems like somebody came by when I was in rehab, but I don't remember writing anything out or signing anything. Sherm also came to the hospital. He died when I was in rehab."

"Tell me about rehab?"

"It's where they get your stupid brain to working again. Oh, yeah. I've got deficits. I was in the hospital for I think seven days and ten days in rehab. My parents took me to their cabin at Priest Lake for a month. I just got back ... a few days ago. It's coming back. Real fast. Come in. Sit down."

"Am I keeping you?"

"Yeah. I'm auditing a class at UW. Ten o'clock. I can be late."
She smiled. "I've been playing it for all it's worth."

"What are you studying?"

"Art history. I'm sort of established as an artist. At least
people buy my work. I share studio space with Travis Carter and
he pushes my stuff."

Einar didn't know who Travis Carter was, but he assumed
he should.

"He made me enroll in Henry Jones' art history class. If
you're a reasonably attractive woman with artistic talent, you
sort of get into a network of established artists, dealers, and con-
noisseurs. It's not *all* sexual, but ... I know some unattractive
women artists who have had to pound on more doors than I did.
But ... you know, I have to tell you that one of the effects of my
concussion is that I go on and on. I tell people that if I get boring or repetitive or off the subject, just turn me off. I won't be
hurt. It's all sort of clinical."

"Have you been able to work again?"

"Try and stop me, Mr. ...."

"Torgeson. Einar, actually,"

"Einar, Einar. Dog-gone it, Einar. I'll forget that before
you're out of here, but I'll try to remember."

"May I see what you've done since the ... a ... attack?"

"At the studio. I've been into sculpture. Travis thought clay
would be therapeutic. I used to throw. A lot. But I couldn't do
it after. Travis cleared my space in the studio of canvases and
gave me a hundred pounds of clay and said, make something. So
I'm hand building. Heads. I'm pre-occupied with heads. My
head. Now your head. Travis. Irene's head."

"Irene?"

"The woman who attacked me. I can't identify the person
who attacked me but I know it was Irene."

"Why is that?"

" 'Cause I was getting too close to Sherm."

"What can you tell me about why you think that?"

"I don't know. Whoops, I said it. After I got out of rehab I said 'I don't know' so often I vowed to stop saying it. So, you asked?"

"You feel it was Irene Johnson who attacked you in the Fred Meyers restroom. Why?"

"Irene was the building hooker. It was fun for the rest of us women. I think the men in the building were a little embarrassed. Everyone knew it. She never brought anyone here, but once in a while I'd see her go out in her little outfits with Blondie, that's what we called her boyfriend, and I would say to myself 'Hi ho, hi ho, it's off to work we go.' I'd discuss her outfits with the other girls in the building. I suppose it was like gossiping. For me she was fascinating. I'd never been around anyone like that who was so determinedly ... professional at enticing men."

"Did you ever see her with Sherm?"

"I don't.... Was she with Sherm? Well, he was the landlord, but I'm busy. I don't see much of anyone here. I saw her. I saw her with Blondie. But I can't recall seeing her with Sherm."

"How often was Sherm here?"

"It seemed like he was here quite a bit. I moved in here in January and, of course, met Sherm. I had a sale fall through in late January and when Sherm came around, I was short the February rent. I explained the situation to Sherm and told him I could get a loan from my folks, but he said for me to pay him what I could and we would go out to coffee and discuss a payment schedule. I knew he was coming on, but I was short the rent and he was cute. Did you know him?"

"You know, I dealt with people in the office, but I never met him. What was he like?"

"Well, of course, he was older. A little gray on the temples and in his hair. He was tall and thin and had a lean face and blue eyes. His lips were just right, not too full and not too thin. I study lips. He sort of looked a little like that actor—William Holden. And he always looked so cute in his little lawyer suits.

"I never thought of him as a prosecutor person or anything important like that until he died. When he smiled and said let's have coffee, I was smitten."

"So you started seeing each other?"

"We did. I even met his kids. Nice kids. Sherm was nervous about it. He asked me not to mention the Argo. He didn't like his ex-wife to know his business. So, I was just a friend."

"What did you do on that occasion?"

"Oh, we picked them up Saturday morning. Went to lunch and a movie. Then we went back to Sherm's condo and sat around and he took me home. They were old enough to be there by themselves, but Sherm dropped me off and went back home right away."

"What about Irene? Why did you have the feeling it was Irene? The police report said your purse was taken. Could have been a random robbery?"

"Yeah, yeah. It was taken." Suddenly, her eyes flashed. "I remember what it was that made me think of Irene. Sherm and I were coming back from an early dinner one weekday evening. Irene was leaving the apartment building. She was carrying that huge purse, her toolbox I called it. I was coming in ahead of Sherm as she came around the bottom of the stairs. She stood there to let us by. She didn't acknowledge me. She just looked at him. I would like to capture that look on her face as he passed by. It was half contempt. Half caring.

"As Sherm and I started up the stairs, she was still standing there. All she said was 'Hi, Sharm; Y'all have a nice dinner?' Sherm said, 'Yes we did, Miss Johnson; very nice.' 'That's good,' she said. She didn't look at me at all. But I felt ... menaced. I've been over on this side of the mountains for four years. I get around, a lot, uh ..."

"Einar."

"Einar. There are lots of artists and actors and wannabes up here in this neighborhood and mostly it's safe. At least I try to tell my mom that. But there's also a rough crowd on the edges. Lots of guys with too much testosterone. Girls that are ...

aggressive. I'm usually watchful. That girl was somebody you wanted to watch.

"When I was coming out of that toilet stall and I heard the steps behind me and the rush of . . . the rush of . . . energy. I said to myself, 'uh oh; she's got me.' And I was out."

"Was the assailant strong? One police office I talked to speculated it might have been a transvestite."

"Oh, yes," she said. "Wouldn't the cops love to start rounding up transvestites in Capitol Hill?"

"I don't know."

"Well, I don't have any idea and I'm not about to suggest anything of that sort. I have a vague impression of coming out of the stall and then the rush . . . like an airlock closing."

"Sort of a whoosh?"

"And even that is a sort of subconscious impression. I'm not sure my impression is conscious or subconscious. Maybe its subconscious raised to consciousness."

"Did you see your assailant's legs when you fell?"

She pointed at her head. "If it's in there, I can't bring it out."

"Are you safe here? Could someone be stalking you?"

"Well, I suppose there are other menaces but I'm not going to let it stop my life. Sherm's dead. Irene's gone. My friends June and Nadia on the second floor. They saw Irene a day or so after Sherm died. But Monday night she was gone. Long gone."

"Where's their apartment?"

"It's 208. You'll have to catch them in the evening."

"What did they tell you?"

"They said that Irene was beat up. She gave them some story about her boyfriend beating her up and needing a place to hide. They're good-hearted women. They didn't care. They took her in. She took some clothes when she left, but they'd give you the shirt off their back if they thought you were a victim of male aggression."

"Did Irene Johnson ever *say* anything to you? Threaten you?"

"No."

"How did you learn her name?"

"I don't ... Probably from June or Nadia. They sort of befriend everybody. June loved Irene's fetching outfits. If you saw Irene in a miniskirt with those long, slim legs ... her light brown skin. She had a sort of arch in her eyebrow. She made an impression. You'd say who the hell is that."

"Where was her apartment?"

"Second floor. I don't know which one."

"Did Sherm ever discuss her with you?"

"No. Wait. Yeah, he did. We were talking about the different tenants—there are some other characters as well—and I asked him teasingly how Irene was as a tenant. He said, 'always prompt; always cash'. I remember that."

"Have you met Sherm's partner, Mr. Satello?"

"Who?"

"Jake Satello. He's a Seattle policeman. Heavyset guy. Usually wears a suit. Not a uniform."

"I don't think so. I certainly don't remember that name or any person like that."

"Anything you can remember that I haven't asked?"

"No. I haven't helped very much. You've got more out of me than I thought I knew."

"Where were you on the night Sherm died?"

"Rehab. Providence Center, probably relearning how to use a fork. Everybody goes through the same program. Then they take you individually over stuff you don't get back right away."

"How did you learn about his death?"

"My mother told me. She was over from Spokane during my rehab. I had mentioned to her that I was seeing him. It wasn't disturbing at first, but after a while as my memory came back it really hit me. Hard."

"I'm sorry for your loss."

"You know, I thought Sherm and I were hitting it off pretty good. I guess I have a hard time understanding what he was doing with the under age girl. I mean I was in rehab and all, but ... I don't know."

"Do you recall if you went up to school the day of your attack?"

"That was in May. The class I'm taking didn't start until mid-June. So no. I was at the studio with Travis. I went out to pick up some stuff for our lunch."

"Ah. So you didn't go there directly from the apartment."

"Oh, no. I'm usually at the studio by nine, or earlier depending on what I'm working on."

"So, if it was Irene, she would have had to spot you in the store."

"Well, yeah. But I don't remember seeing her in the store. Maybe I did and that's how my subconscious is making the connection. But I'm not putting that in any kind of statement. In fact, my statement would have to be I don't remember seeing her. Look, Einar, I don't think I've been much use here. Maybe I should head on to class."

"Are you driving?"

"I'm bussing it."

"I'll give you a lift. It's not a police car or anything."

Einar made small talk on the way to the UW campus while he tried to outline a statement that Martine Rodriguez might sign. But how could he explain a revelation from her subconscious? He would write up a brief report, mentioning her prior contact with Irene and her suspicions, but he would emphasize that she could not identify her assailant. The subconscious had meaning for Einar, but he doubted it would play any evidentiary role in Andros' investigation.

Drones for the
Talbot queens

NINETEEN

LATE THAT SAME NIGHT, Jane and Paul Andros ate a light supper and listened intently to Bea's stories of hiking ordeals in the North Cascades. Normally, the girl was quiet and retiring, like her mother and her grandmother Turnbull. But on this night, her brown eyes glowed with the volubility and determination of Paul's own mother. Some gene from Mama Andros must have been kindled in the higher elevations to help Beatrice complete the ten- and, sometimes, fourteen-mile-a-day trudges. But then, he reflected, only Jane and Grandmother Turnbull's aesthetic genes would have enjoyed being out in nature. To the Andros clan, nature was cold, hard, and unforgiving. A sheltering fire, good food, and a warm bed were the only worthwhile objectives of travail. What a mongrelization of personality each generation begets!

The phone ringing interrupted them. He answered, gesturing to Bea and Jane for momentary pardon.

"Hello."

"Paul, this is Alice." An uncomfortable quaver in her voice.

"Beatrice is back. She was just telling us about her trip," Paul volunteered.

"Scott is off the wagon. I don't know what it is that takes possession of that man . . ."

"Alice. 'Recovering' means recovering. Maybe the tensions of covering for me at the office. Too much pride to say it's too much. I don't know."

"I'm sorry to bother you, but I don't want to see him get arrested on a drunk driving charge. Enos called and said Scott just left the Rainier Club and was walking downhill toward the water. You know Enos vowed never to get in the middle of Scott's drunken escapades. Where should I go to look for him?"

"Alice, I thought *you* made the same vow as Enos! Don't sweat it, I know where he went and I'll get him home."

She did not quibble. "I would be so grateful if you would do that. Could I talk with Bea?"

"Sure." He lowered the phone and called to his daughter, whose exhaustion evaporated at the opportunity to tell her stories to fresh, and even more doting, ears.

Paul went back into town and parked under the Alaska Way Viaduct. He didn't have to walk far along the waterfront to find Turnbull. He was seated at a small table window for two at Salty's overlooking the ferry dock. It was a tourist trap but Scott's favorite place to go if he was staying downtown for the evening.

"Well, well, Northwest Mounted Police to the rescue," he said as Paul seated himself. A wilted plate of fish and chips sat before him, only a few bites gone. Scott picked up the water pitcher and refilled his half-empty highball glass. He held up the pitcher for Paul to see, giving it a sneering shake.

"Look. Remorse. Second thoughts. I had a couple of drinks at the Club, but on the way here I decided it was not a good time for a binge. Enos or Alice send you?"

"Alice."

"Alice. Alice, my love. My woman. My woman? I query that. The truth of it is, Paul, that she is *not* my woman. No indeed. You see, Paul, I'm her man.

"No, you won't see her swanning around the Showboat whining about 'her man' and her helplessness in the power of my masculine appeal. No, I am her man because I am her possession, like a goddamn sheep set out to graze in her pasture. Like her house is her possession. Her garden is her possession. Her wealth is her possession. Her goddamn breeding is her possession."

"I like Alice," Paul said quietly.

"Of course you like Alice. Everyone likes Alice. She was bred and trained and educated for everyone to like her. To accept her. To respect her. The great myth perpetrated by the American oligarchy is that rich people are just like everyone else."

He looked out the window at an embarking ferry. "You know, I met her in forty-five," he said slowly. "I was back from the war and just starting in law school. She was an undergraduate at Reed College. That was when anybody could go to the University of Washington. So people in Alice's circle went to private colleges.

"There she was. At a tavern in the University District. It was Thanksgiving holidays. She was with a group. I was with a group. But I was never shy. Have a lot of faults. Shyness? No.

"I'm sure I said something incredibly clever. I was a great mimic of Robert Benchley. A great talker, and she, a great listener. We were married that June. Honeymooned at Banff, Lake Louise, McKenna Resort. You know, we still go there."

Turnbull focused on Paul intently. "But you know, Paul, Alice never finished college. She had no interest. She's a very smart person. Smarter than me by far. But she has no interest to compete. Except maybe competitive gardening.

"When I got a job clerking for Judge Walker in U.S. District Court, we got a little house, surrounded by . . . mud. By summer, our house was a showplace—Stanton Talbot's little pampered girl knew how to work, work hard I mean. I couldn't keep up with her then. Can't now.

"What I'm saying is that you and me, Paul, we're drones. Drones to the Talbot queens. We go off to the office every day. We outmaneuver this guy and that guy. Clients break down the doors for us to pull them outta jams. The county council looks to you to straighten out this Sherm Falkes mess. And who are we but a couple of drones? We make the big decisions, like how to bring home money. They quietly make the little decisions like where and how we will live, who will be our friends, what society we will move in, who will claim our intimacy, who will be politely rebuffed . . ."

"You sound like you have regrets, Scott."

He laughed. "Me? I found my niche in the world. I'm a capable lawyer. Always have been. I just wonder sometimes if I'm anything besides that. Even the best hunting dog is still a dog . . . Likes to roll around in the dirt."

"Why didn't you go with one of the larger firms, Scott? I always wondered that."

"Funny about that. Stanton Talbot, Alice's father, was the reason. Was he alive when you met Jane?"

"No. I never met him."

"Small man. Looked frail, but he was . . . bold. An adventurer. Made his money in real estate and insurance. He didn't go to law school, but he was a better lawyer than most lawyers. I respected him. He asked me one day when I was studying for the bar how a Democrat, an idiotic New Deal Democrat at that, thought he was going to get along in Marvell and Zinde or the Peterson firm or one of the other established Seattle firms? Established law firms make their money by protecting people who have money. How did that fit with my misguided ideology? I told him I could do the work. He said skills were secondary. Social status and values were primary. He said that, even in the unlikely event that I were hired as an associate, I would not last. He said that I would, not should, go into practice on my own."

He sipped his water reflectively. "Talbot believed and acted on the premise that this country was an oligarchy. Gold and silver ruled. Pure and simple. He believed that banks and bankers ran this country, particularly at the local level. He said that if I had a healthy bank account, I would be an established lawyer. Bankers blab. To everyone. If you have money, you're successful. You have status. He suggested that I establish accounts in more than one bank—that would spread banker gossip about my instant success. Then he told me that he was retaining me as his lawyer and that the retainer would be a thousand dollars per month for one year. That was a ton of money in nineteen-forty-eight, even for him. I was directed to take no more than five hundred per month to live on. I should build up and maintain a firm bank account of fifty thousand or better. And it should always be such. . . .

"He directed me to comfortable, not exorbitant, offices. The retainer was to be conserved. He wrote me a fifty-thousand-dollar check for my trust account and thereafter he ran all of his real estate deals through me."

"But, Scott, why do we keep such a large general account?" Andros asked. "The banks get the float. Our general account is hardly ever under a hundred grand today. We don't get a dime's worth of interest. It's stupid."

H. Scott Turnbull spoke softly. "But the bank loves it. It's the formula for business success as a legal practitioner according to Stanton Talbot. I'm a better lawyer than Stanton, not a better businessman. His business advice always served me well."

"Learn something new every day."

"I should hope so. Well, are you ready to charge this Satello fellow for Sherm's death and come back to work?"

Over the years, Paul had become accustomed to Scott's sudden changes of topics. If you could not keep up with him, that was your problem.

"Not that easy," Paul started. He recounted the conference with Satello the previous day. Turnbull labeled it "one of the great performances in the history of knavery" and they agreed upon some avenues for further investigation.

Both Bea and Jane were asleep when Paul finally returned home. Since he had entered private practice, late meetings and long hours had intruded into his private life. A successful private practice was built on long hours and a sense of recognizing and grasping opportunities. As he undressed, an old feeling returned to him from his prior years in public service. Not resentment; more a feeling of pointlessness. One never quite gained a sense of personal achievement from lawyering in public service. One became a sort of insensitive technician, without empathy for person or cause. He reflected that Sherman Falkes had never been in private practice, had always worked in the prosecutor's office. He'd never had the elation of winning a favorable jury verdict for an individual who needed redress for personal grievances or losses. He'd never suffered a shattering loss that wrecked a life or a business. Paul wondered if the long hours and years had worn Sherm down until the system he helped administer had lost its meaning and value.

Andros checked the alarm and fell into bed. He pressed his body against Jane's back and stroked her leg.

"How bad was it?" she asked sleepily.

"Your father decided this was not a good time for a binge and went home," Paul said.

She absorbed this astonishing news thoughtfully. "Well," she concluded. "It didn't seem like him to fall apart when everyone needs him to keep going."

"He also said that he and I are drones for the Talbot women," he said.

Jane turned over and put her arms around his neck. "I should have thought you would have figured that out for yourself," she said, moving to kiss him.

The Pasco
Oasis

TWENTY

IT WENT OKAY FOR TERRY IN YAKIMA; it went okay on an extended side trip to Wenatchee where they ran into a week long restaurateurs convention; and it might have been okay in Pasco if Travis Smith had not impulsively fallen in love.

It started off textbook. They had rented a room on the first floor of the Pasco-Oasis Motor Inn. There was a travel agents association meeting and a real estate seminar on the hotel events calendar. The first three marks had been recruited at the travel agents' no-host cocktail party, to which Terry had freely invited himself. Travis was the fourth guy Terry brought to Mavis' door.

Terry had spotted Travis at the bar of the cocktail lounge, seated by himself after the party had broken up. He did not look like one of the stop-by-for-a-drink-after-work crowd. He was clean-shaven, washed and combed, wearing a crisply laundered aqua sport shirt and washed-light blue jeans. He wore cowboy boots—a new pair, polished and shiny. He appeared to be look-ing for action, and, fortunately for Terry, there were no unat-tached females in the bar.

"Carta Blanca," Terry said, pointing to the bottle in front of the mark and seating himself. "I haven't had a Mexican beer in ages. Sounds good."

"Give me one of those and beer nuts," Terry said, as the bar-tender approached. "You ready for another?"

The mark shook his head. "No," he said quietly.

"My name's Bill," Terry said, extending his hand.

"Travis Smith," said the mark.

Travis gripped Terry's hand lightly and removed it. Travis was obviously not a greeter.

"You with the travel convention?" Terry asked.

"No. I'm just having a beer and watching the game." Travis motioned his head toward the baseball game in progress on TV.

"You from around here? I'd sure like to line up a few good restaurants to tell my travel clients about."

"No, no. I'm from Spokane. Just finishing up a refrigeration unit. Fruit shed."

"Did you find any good restaurants around here?"

Travis sipped on his beer. "Mister, I put in twelve-hour days. I wolf down a big breakfast wherever. If I'm lucky I break for soup and a sandwich. By nighttime I go back to my room and have a couple of beers and some chips by the TV and I'm out."

"You must be ready for a break, man."

Terry looked down the empty bar. Across the room in the corner were three women and five men at a large table who appeared to be conducting a raucous post-work drinkathon. There were two other tables occupied by men earnestly using the hotel lounge as a business meeting place.

"Nothing going on around here," he observed.

He took down a large gulp of beer and threw some nuts into his mouth. "Man," he chewed. "I really scored this afternoon."

His change to a low confidential tone caused Travis to look away from the TV and look at him quizzically.

Terry washed down the nuts with a quick sip of the beer. This time he judiciously picked a single nut from the pack and chewed it deliberately.

"We checked in at the same time. This young chick. Good looker. She's stuck here. Car problem. She was asking the room clerk where to take it. I said I'd check it out. Had to take it to a garage. Valve job. We're on the way back to the hotel. She puts her hand on my leg and says, 'Bill, I don't have enough money to pay for the car repair. I'd be so grateful if you could help …' Man, was she grateful!"

Travis sipped his beer quietly and watched the TV.

Terry took another nut and chewed on it.

Travis shook his head. "I hear about that stuff. I never seem to run into it."

Terry laughed. "Well, she's still here and still being grateful. She says she's gotta raise a thousand dollars and she only got a hundred and fifty out of me. Hey, I don't mind paying if the stuff is good."

"I don't know if that's for me."

Terry shrugged and settled onto the stool, picking another nut from the pack and watching the TV.

Finally, Travis swivelled his stool away from the bar.

"Maybe I'll just see if I can help her out," he grinned. "Where is she?"

"Thank you mmm thank you," Travis called out as his final thrust jetted the last of his sexual juices.

Despite her youth, Mavis by this time was tiring. She collapsed on top of Travis, and, as his organ shrank, fell off to his side and cozied into his left shoulder.

They did not speak. Travis' hand rested on her firm buttock and he began to stroke her.

"Mmm," she hummed sleepily.

"So, Missoula, Susan. What's in Missoula?"

No response.

He wiggled gently. "So, what's in Missoula?"

"Oh, you know, family. A cousin."

"Well, I've been to Missoula. All it's got is smokestacks and horny cowboys."

She rubbed his stomach. "Maybe I like horny cowboys."

"That's me, then!"

Travis felt a sudden impulse. He was a lonely man. His craft as a refrigeration technician paid him well, but two broken marriages had been the price of the long hours and travel to remote work sites.

"Tell you what," he said. "I'll take you to Missoula. I'm paid tomorrow on my job. I'll bail out your car. Park my truck, and we'll just go. We can see a little of the country. 'Jelly-stone,' maybe."

She lifted her head and looked at him as if it were the first time she was seeing him. She saw a craggy-faced 35- to 40-year-old man with bristly receding brown hair.

"You'd do that for me?" she asked.

"I've got nothing else to do. Look, it ain't a proposal of marriage. You gotta get to Missoula. I got nothing else to do. We'll just go along down the road together. If I've had enough, I'll split. If you don't like me, just tell me to git and I'll git . . . 'sides, I need some time off. I work too fucking hard."

Mavis laid back on his shoulder. Her mind was racing to its full capability. Men were never to be trusted. Never. Not even Bill, even though he was fun and he made her feel so good.

"I don't want to belong to you," she said. "I don't want to belong to nobody."

She sat up and put her legs over the side of the bed. She pulled her shoulders back and lifted both her arms to brush her hands through her hair. Travis could see the unconscious movement of her left breast. Her motions to shake off his offer of dependency only attracted him more. He put his hand on her hip and gently pulled her to him.

She broke away and stood up, turning to face him, hands on hips. "If you want to go again, John, it'll be another hundred-fifty."

Travis refused to be put down by her contempt. He only laughed and sat on the side of the bed. "Travis. The other guys may be John, but I'm Travis, and you know it. You ain't so tough, little lady. Whatta you want to act like some two-bit whore for?"

She took a step back and grabbed for her dress on a chair beside the bed.

"Relax," he said softly. "I'm just making a reasonable suggestion. If the time to git is now, like I said, I'll just git."

He swung his legs over the side of the bed, sat up and looked around for his clothes. Mavis went into the bathroom and closed the door wordlessly.

Travis slipped on his underwear and jeans. He had just pulled on his boots when there a soft knock sounded at the door.

"Susan?"

It was the voice of the guy from the bar. Bill. What the hell was he doing here? Probably dragging another guy in to "help out" the little gal. So young. Such a babe. Firm and willowy.

The adrenaline rose and smothered Travis's usual matter-of-fact, quiet manner.

Five swift strides and he flung open the door.

"Whyn't you give the little gal a rest!" Travis said. "Whadda you, some kinda pimp?"

Terry did, in fact, have another "helper" in tow, a plumpish middle-aged man whose amiable grin was frozen on his face as he took an unsteady step back from the shirtless, obviously fit, and obviously hostile man barring the doorway.

Although he had recently suffered a long string of misfortunes, Terry Barnes was not a man without personal resources. Over his life, he had taken a gift of raw sexual attractiveness and developed an ability to study and evaluate females and to select those who would serve him unquestioningly. Women were the tools of his craft. He had also figured out that his craft required that he would often have to deal with men under the most primordial of circumstances. He had thus found it necessary to learn to fight. After several false starts in aikido and judo, he had settled on karate, which met his need to defend himself in hit-and-run skirmishes quite adequately.

He smiled disarmingly, open palms forward and up. Left foot as base, he brought his right foot forward. Travis watched him questioningly, not ready to fight but angry and frustrated. Terry put his left and right hands on Travis's right forearm and pushed down to right. Travis resisted and pulled up hard. Terry let go and shifted weight to right foot. Travis slightly lost his balance to Terry's left. Left foot to right foot shift, left foot to right foot shift again, and now Terry was behind Travis grasping Travis' left arm and pulling it up behind Travis's back.

Here misfortune struck Terry again. The contagion of Travis Smith's adrenaline had passed to Terry. It was also mixed with resentment at the loss of the plump and amiable Mr. Harley Middlefort, who had scurried off down the hall, obviously having no taste for whorehouse brawling.

"Shit," said Terry, and, mindless of the defenseless position in which he held Travis, anger flooded his awareness and he jerked Travis arm up and back.

There was a meaningful pop and Travis screamed loudly. Painfully.

The door to the bathroom cracked open and Mavis peeked out.

"Get your stuff," Terry said to her, menacingly.

Travis finally got his breath sufficiently to emit an anguished, frightened wail.

"Quiet," he said to Travis, holding his loose arm. "Lay down on the bed, and I'll get you some help."

Travis continued moaning loudly. Terry helped him to the bed. Mavis whirled around the room, picking up her scattered things.

"Do you have the money?"

"Yes," she said.

A face appeared at the door, an older man, his hair tousled, slippers, shirt unbuttoned. Looking. Deciding whether or not to get involved.

"Mister," Terry called to him. "Could you call the desk and tell them this guy needs a doctor? Room 139."

"Sure," he said huskily and trotted back down the hall to his room. Not asking why Terry or the girl could not use the phone in their own room.

Mavis was ready to go. Travis moaned uncomprehendingly. Terry grabbed her and they hurried away from the room.

Mavis then stopped. "He didn't pay me."

"Whadda ya mean he didn't pay you? Were you waiting for him to get a bank loan?"

"I trusted him," she said.

Terry reached across Travis and pulled his billfold out of his jeans. There were three 50s, several 20s, some 1s. He removed the three 50s and dumped the billfold on the bed.

"I paid her," Travis murmured.

Terry did not hear him. Or did not care to. "Let's go," he said to the girl.

They had rented a room and left their car at a small motel four blocks away that advertised "commercial rates." Terry hustled the girl down the corridor to the rear exit. They would have to walk. Because Terry had dressed her for that wholesome look, the girl was wearing low-heeled pumps and kept up pretty well with his long strides.

They stepped over a low barrier between the east side of the hotel and a shopping center next door and walked southeast across the shopping center parking lot. An aid car was pulling up in front of the Oasis; no lights, no siren. Their motel was south, but Terry wanted to get as far away from the Pasco Oasis as he quickly could.

They made it to their room as Mavis was finishing her explanation of how she had lost control of the situation with Travis.

Terry listened without sympathy or apparent interest. "We should leave tonight," he said, almost to himself.

"I'm bushed," she said simply and fell on the bed.

Terry measured the risks. Would Travis go to the police? Would the police get involved in his injuries? Even if they do, he thought, they won't have his correct name, and he was registered here as Bill Dunbar.

Maybe it was better to leave town in the morning traffic.

But Terry was wrong. Travis had not been shy about talking to the police. A patient and unusually concerned police officer had showed up at the Emergency Room. Travis outlined exactly what had happened. Before he went too far, the officer warned him that Pasco had a "John law." In other words, a person agreeing to prostitution could be charged the same as the person who offered.

Travis explained that there may have been or may not have been prostitution. He was complaining about how the man, Bill something, took his money after he dislocated his shoulder.

Robbery and felony assault, then, the officer had agreed and had written on the incident report: Robbery complaint; Victim Travis Smith, 105 Avalon Ave., Spokane, WA; Suspect Bill "Doe," address unknown, 5'10" to 6', 180 pounds, dark hair, color of eyes unknown.

The officer was polite and professional but not optimistic about Travis' chances for retribution.

Early in the morning at his motel room, Travis rose from bed, took another pain pill. The doctor at the ER had warned him that, although his shoulder was not actually broken, in terms of incapacity, it might just as well have been. The ligaments and tendons around his left shoulder were torn and stretched. The doctor had immobilized it with a wrapping and a shoulder sling, given him codeine pain pills and told him to rest a couple of days because it was going to hurt "if you blink your eyes."

The doctor was right.

It was starting to get light and Travis had only dozed once or twice. The painkillers had produced a sort of fog in which he temporarily lost touch with himself, but any body movement put him quickly back in touch with his pain.

A shard of sunlight—dawn—cut through the crack in the curtains. He peered through the windows to peek at the sun. He saw movement in the lower wing of the building to his left. He opened the curtain a bit wider, looked again.

"My God. It's them," he said to himself

It was the man, Bill, and the girl. They had stopped at the same motel and now they were getting into an old blue Buick.

He went back to the bed and sat down. He put his hand on the phone to call the police. Bill and Susan No-Name, he thought. What the hell would the police do?

He put his feet through the pile of pants on the floor by the bed. He stood up and somehow wiggled them on. He crammed his right foot into his right boot, reaching down to pull the inside strap.

Uh. A flash of pain.

He sat and repeated the procedure for the left boot.

He patted the truck keys in his pocket and, shirtless, he hurried from the room.

From the balcony he could see the Buick turn north from the motel driveway. Travis' truck was behind the motel, parked against the building. He felt dizzy as he went down the steps. He avoided the pop and ice machines that loomed in the corridor.

He grabbed the railing and moved as steadily and smoothly as he could. He tried not to bounce.

An exit at the bottom of the stairs opened from the building onto a row of off-alley parking. His truck was a one-ton Jimmy with metal tool and equipment cabinets built into the back of the cab and on both sides of the bed. It had an overhead rack for carrying pipe and tubing. It was an awkward and clumsy pursuit vehicle.

He fitted and turned the key in one habit-trained motion. Reaching with his right hand to pull himself up with the steering wheel, a flash of pain in his left shoulder reminded him of what he had just learned through the long night: that shoulders worked in reciprocity.

He knew he had to catch up before they got on the highway. If they were going to Missoula, they were probably on the way to Spokane. He had seen them turn north from the motel. They could go east or west at Highway 395, which ran through the business district. If they backtracked and went west, he would lose them.

He got to the corner and turned north. Suppose she lied about where she was headed, just like they lied about everything else? Even so, Spokane was their most likely destination, but, if they were headed southeast, Highway 395 ran parallel with Highway 12 through town.

He turned east on 395. Bill hadn't gone far: there he was, at a gas station, fueling the Buick at the self-service pump. Travis didn't see the girl. Maybe she was inside the mini-mart.

Travis checked the cab to make sure that both doors were locked. Slowly, to avoid jarring his shoulder any more than he had to, he pulled in the driveway. Bill was parked at the inside aisle on the forward pump so that his car extended from the pump island. Travis could see three twelve-inch concrete-filled steel pipe stanchions at the end of the island, guarding the pumps. He pulled the full length of his truck to the front of the old Buick so that the back of his truck was angled off its right front fender. The rear of Travis' truck was fitted with a heavy-duty, cast-iron bumper, mounted by the previous owner. But Travis knew it was there.

Travis began to back up his truck. Not fast, because he did not wish to jar his shoulder. When he felt the thump of contact, he hit the accelerator hard. He watched in the side view mirror as the heavy truck pushed the Buick into the stanchion guarding the pump island. Crunch. More acceleration. Spinning of the truck's tires against the slick surface of the service station.

Bill ran to the window of the truck, his hand on the door handle. Locked. Bill and Travis locked eyes in recognition. Then, Bill disappeared from Travis' view.

Terry knew he was screwed. The right front fender of his Buick was collapsed against the right wheel. Gas nozzle still in hand, he felt an urge to douse Travis' truck in gas and set fire to it. Instead, the urge to run won out.

He grabbed his gym bag that contained his extra clothes from the back seat. Fortunately, Mavis had given him the money, except for the extra hundred and fifty from Travis that she was holding out on him.

He began walking briskly east toward the downtown area. He needed alleys, people, traffic.

"Bill!" He heard Mavis calling. She was running behind him. He started running himself. He got to a wire fence surrounding a vacated equipment yard. He vaulted the fence and ran to the back of the lot without looking back.

"Bill!" He could still hear her voice as he went through an opening in the back of the lot and continued northward through a small apartment complex.

Mavis would probably be at the next corner. He found a vacant lot mid-block and continued northward, avoiding streets. He reached in his bag and took out a white shirt and changed from the blue polo shirt he was wearing.

He was three blocks north before he decided to double back east and continue north along a side street. Somebody was going to report a prowler if he didn't stop cutting through people's yards.

It was a mistake. A police car pulled up beside him and slowed to his walking pace. He cursed to himself. He should have tossed the fucking gym bag he was carrying.

He could hear the crackly sound of the police radio. He had to look over at the car. It was an old guy. Gray hair. Gaunt-looking. He wore gold-rimmed glasses. He removed these and placed them on the dashboard. He had brown no-nonsense eyes that took in all of Terry like a net cast over a school of fish.

He motioned Terry to the car.

"Some guy back at the filling station seems to have a beef with you," he said.

"Me?" Terry started toward the car window.

"That will do right there, son. Just stand right there beside the fender. Put down the bag. Keep your hands where I can see them."

"Hey, what is this?" Terry said. Indignant.

"That's just what I want to know. Some doped-up character backs his truck into a man's car, and the injured party runs for it. Makes me think you don't want to talk to the police."

"I don't know what you're talking about."

The policeman's brown eyes widened.

"Don't piss me off, son. You comin' here to little ol' Pasco to piss off a Pasco cop? I'm going to give you another chance. Let's try it again. Before we do, should I tell you the consequences of our failure to reach rapport? Should I tell you that the guy in the truck claims you broke his shoulder last night and took his money? That's a felony. I can arrest you for a felony. But all I want to do at this point is to investigate. Okay?"

"Okay, okay, but I don't know what you're talking about," said Terry. He could outrun this guy, he guessed, but where would he go? He should have spent more time scoping out the town. Spot some hidey holes. As far as he could tell, these ticky-tacky little houses in northeast Pasco just went on forever.

"Why did you run?"

"We had a fight over the woman. I didn't want to fight again. It's not worth it."

"Turn around, please. Slowly, and lift your shirt tail."

Terry did so. He could hear the car door open. He looked over his shoulder as the policeman came out of the vehicle with a thin, black baton in hand. His chances to run were diminishing.

"Now, I want you to turn back and face the car and spread your legs apart."

The policeman was behind him now.

"Now lean forward on the hood," he said, his baton in the small of Terry's back.

Terry did so. The policeman patted down the small of his back, all around his waist, pockets, under the crotch, down each leg.

"Let me see some ID, son," he said at last.

"I've got a billfold, but there's nothing in it. I got my ID stolen last week."

"Where?"

"Portland," he said.

"What's your name?"

"Bill Darby," he said.

"Okay, Bill. We're gonna go back to the station and sort this out. So I'm not gonna put you under arrest. I'm just gonna give you a little ride, for free, at the expense of the good citizens of

Pasco. We'll just compare everybody's statements and see if we can make any sense out of this deal."

Luckily for Terry Barnes, the Franklin County prosecuting attorney's office rejected felonious assault cases unless a firearm or weapon inflicted the wound. Knowing this from his experience in dealing with the county prosecutor, the Pasco city attorney reviewed the statements and the police reports, both from the service station incident and Travis' statement from the night before, and, equitably, charged Travis Smith with malicious destruction to property, "Bill Darby" with third degree assault, and Mavis Jackson (under police questioning she had dropped "Susan") with prostitution.

At noon they were taken before the Municipal Court for arraignment and bail setting. Since the city did not have its own jail and wanted to avoid booking and jail expenses at the county facility, the city attorney recommended two hundred fifty dollar bail on Mavis, five hundred on Travis, and five hundred on "Bill Darby."

Mavis sat wordlessly through the proceedings.

Travis went over to her and said, "Don't worry, little lady, I'll do your bail."

Mavis looked over at Terry, who sat without any emotion or evidence of concern. He had not spoken to her once in the police station or in court.

She shrugged and looked at Travis with a smile of resignation. "I guess we're on our way to Yellowstone," she said.

Mavis Jackson and Travis Smith were leaving the courtroom while Terry was still being arraigned. "Your honor," the city attorney said. "I'm sorry. The police officer has brought to my attention that Mr. Darby has apparently lost his driver's license and other identifying documents. I propose that we run Mr. Darby through booking and verify his identity, and check for outstanding warrants. Could you make his bail subject to verification of identity? If there's a problem, we'll bring him back for tomorrow's arraignment."

Terry jumped forward.

"What's that? What's he saying, your honor?"

The judge, a black man with soft wisps of gray hair and round cheeks, who exuded an aura of good will and tolerance, smiled soothingly.

"It appears the city prosecutor wants to hold you without bail, Mr. Darby, because there is a question of who you say you are."

"I don't see why they can walk out of here and I've got to go to jail." He motioned toward Mavis and Travis, exiting together past the clerk's counter.

"What was your father's name, Mr. Darby?" the judge asked.

"Uh, Martin. Martin Darby."

"Is he living?"

"No, sir, he is dead."

"Mother dead also." More a statement than a question. The judge had been down this road before.

"Yes."

"Well, can you give me the names of anyone who can verify your identity? Wouldn't we look a bit foolish here in Pasco if we let some kind of public enemy number one slip through our fingers? You are not a dangerous, wanted criminal, are you, Mr. Darby?" said the judge, smiling with reassurance.

"I don't have anyone. Mavis, the girl?"

He pointed toward the door where Travis and Mavis parted.

The judge smiled. "I hardly think so, Mr. Darby. School-teachers, neighbors, uncles, cousins. We need someone whose verification of your identity is indisputable."

Terry continued to argue. "Your honor, this is not fair. I'm ready to post bail right now."

"Now, now, Mr. Darby, don't get excited. You indeed may feel that this is unfair. You've lost your identification documents. Can't think of anyone to verify your identity and we appear to be treating that as if it were a crime. I can understand that. You seem to be a remarkably composed young man. I appreciate that . . ."

The judge paused. His kindly look faded. Terry said nothing. "But I am disappointed that you cannot make a better account of your identity."

The judge picked up the paperwork and began to recite. "William Darby, you have been charged by the City of Pasco with a crime of third-degree assault. You are before this court for the purpose of dealing with this crime. And as a preliminary matter we are now dealing with the issue of your identity. Now, let me assure you that we will go no further with this matter before your identity is verified. If you are not who you say you are, you are obstructing justice and, further, I will not set bail or proceed further on anything else until this matter is cleared up."

He now looked Terry in the eye. No smile, lips compressed.

"I'm a very tolerant man, Mr. Darby. But one thing you will not lie to me about in my court is who you are. Can you imagine the tangled web we would create for the criminal justice system if we allowed people to use false names in criminal proceedings? It will be the order of the court that you will be booked and held in the county jail until your identity is verified to the satisfaction of the city prosecutor or until tomorrow's arraignment, whichever occurs sooner. Sooner or later, the FBI fingerprint check will come back and tell us who you are. Subject to proper identification, bail is set at five hundred dollars on assault three. Any questions, Mr. Darby?"

"Yeah. Is there such a thing as a public defender around here?" Terry said disgustedly.

The judge was not at all affronted. He smiled broadly. "Yes, indeed. The man slumped in the back row there, trying to appear inconspicuous, is hereby appointed as your attorney."

"Mr. Tolliver," he said looking to the back of the room. "We have added another person to your flock of misunderstood miscreants."

All smiled, except Terry, at the judge's return to his natural demeanor of tolerance and goodwill.

The Alki bust

TWENTY-ONE

SHORTLY AFTER THEIR ARRIVAL IN PASCO, Andros went alone to meet Terry Barnes' attorney, leaving Turnbull and Torgeson at the Pasco-Oasis Motor Inn. Scott had been in the office when a call came through from Lee Tolliver, an attorney in Pasco representing Barnes. When he learned that this might be the first opportunity to find out something from the elusive Barnes, Scott could not be restrained from riding over to Pasco with Andros and Torgeson. Tolliver had asked Andros to meet him that night, as soon as Andros arrived in Pasco.

Tolliver's office was a small storefront office a block off the city square in downtown Pasco. Andros was waiting at the front door when Tolliver rolled up in an old Datsun pickup. He wore a dark blue T-shirt, faded blue jeans, and dirty white Nikes. He had bushy dark hair and brown eyes that penetrated through round, horn-rimmed glasses. He was light on his feet and seemed to get from the truck to the office door in one movement.

"Welcome to Pasco," he said, extending his hand. "Thanks for taking my call this afternoon."

Andros smiled and shook hands. "I had an inkling it might be interesting."

"I'm sorry I had to browbeat your secretary. I hate that."

"She was so elated to have a break in the case she forgot all about it."

"You told her?"

Andros put out his hand reassuringly. "I had to tell her, and the chief deputy, where I was going."

Tolliver looked at him doubtfully and headed into the office. Andros followed.

"As you requested, I didn't tell anyone from Seattle PD."

They went through a waiting room with a secretarial front area to a back office. A large Navajo rug hung on a brick outer wall. In the office were arranged ancient oak chairs around an oak dining table that served as Tolliver's desk. Tolliver sat down heavily in an old leather chair behind the table. Andros selected one of the sturdier side chairs.

"All I want to do is get this guy out of my life as fast as I can. But I did ask you to tell no one," Tolliver said.

"You also asked me to figure out how to get your client safely back to Seattle. I used my best judgment, Mr. Tolliver. Frankly, isn't his identification inevitable? Isn't it just a matter of time?"

"I argued time to Judge Farrell. I said it would take at least five days for identification. I said he couldn't hold the man for five days without bail."

Tolliver laughed. "Of course Judge Farrell didn't want any part of this Barnes. I was in court when he showed up. I spotted him for trouble that first day. So did the judge. He held him without bail the first day and he appointed me. He knew he was on thin ice. I came in the next day and beat my chest about bail. He smiled, as he always does, and said that yes, bail should be set. He asked the prosecutor did he not feel, under the circumstances, that he had probable cause for an obstructing charge? The prosecutor went along and said he did. So he sets five thousand on the assault charge, five on obstructing and five for contempt of court.

"I say contempt of court—what's that? He says the defendant's adamancy in refusing to identify himself and his disrespectful attitude in refusing to do so amounts to contempt of court, from which he may purge himself by providing information that would determine his true identity."

Andros laughed. "Belt and suspenders," he said.

"Yeah. Barnes didn't think it was funny. He made a desperate attempt to get a bondsman, but there was no way. So, finally, this morning he tells me I can put out the word to you that he wants to talk about certain persons in the Seattle PD. But he wants a signed waiver of prosecution and witness protection."

"Witness protection! I haven't got any witness protection program. You know that," Andros said.

"Well, I was thinking you can hand it over to the feds. Racketeering or something. Conspiracy to fart. You know the feds. They always got some charge."

Andros mused. "You know, Mr. Tolliver, I thought early on about going to the feds. Particularly, when ... Well, I thought about it. I concluded that it's our mess. We will have to clean it up as best we can. Just filing charges is going to ruin lives. I've seen it before."

"What about my guy? He talks about police corruption and he's a pariah to cops wherever he goes. No one in officialdom will help him no matter what outrages are committed against him. And how deep does it go? Somebody walks. That's the guy who does in my client. They get probation or a short sentence—they're out looking for my guy. Your predecessor didn't make out too well when the shit hit the fan. My guy doesn't think he'll do much better."

Andros raised his hand dismissively. "I don't know what you're talking about. I'm glad to see you're conscientious about your client. But the fact is that you told me yourself that his prints went back to Washington yesterday and in a few days the FBI is going to come back with your guy's identity. Shortly thereafter, a whole flock of Seattle PD are going to be over here to take him back anyway. Your Judge Farrell has put paid and *fini* to your client's wanderings. I *would* like to get a statement from him, and I will consider waiving the soliciting charges. But I want to look at the goods before I buy."

Tolliver stretched out his legs and stared at the ceiling.

"What have we got here?" Andros asked.

"Here?"

"Here in Pasco. What's gotta be done to cut him loose?"

"No problem. You say the word and they'll happily cut him loose. The prosecutor will defer to the King County charges. Pandering?"

"Felony. Living off the wages of prostitution. He'll do time."

"Oh, that's good. They'll defer to a felony. You say the word and I can get the prosecutor to reduce the bail and take a small forfeiture. The obstructing stuff is just bullshit."

Andros decided not to mention that, as far as Seattle PD was concerned, Barnes was a suspect in Sherm Falkes' death.

"So our problem is a waiver of King County charges to get his story?"

"Yeah," said Tolliver.

"And your problem is 'beat the clock' on the Seattle PD before they come trooping over here wanting to get your guy alone in a dark room."

No answer.

"Look, I'm a reasonable guy," said Andros. "If there's any value in your client's goods, I'll be reasonable. Let's meet tomorrow. Court reporter. Recorder. You stop him whenever you want."

"Naw," said Tolliver. "He's considering just saying nothing and doing the time. He figures there's a chance the cops will leave him alone if he doesn't nark. I was the good citizen suggesting he talk and walk. But I gotta deliver some protection."

"How about the woman, Irene Johnson? If he could tell us where to find her, maybe she'll testify."

"I don't know who she is, but I can ask him."

Neither spoke as they considered their options.

Finally, Andros said, "Tell me this. Does he know anything about Sherm Falkes's death?"

"Look, Mr. Andros, you probably *are* an okay guy, but I don't want to screw things up for my client. Also, I'm scared. For him and for me, because he talked to me. I want to tell you what he told me in the worst way."

Tolliver stood up and stretched. It was a nervous movement that caused cartilage to scrape and pop audibly.

"Let's say I don't tell you what Terry Barnes would say. Suppose we just talk. Two attorneys talking. Telling tall tales. Speculation."

"Understood," said Andros. "Does he know anything about Sherm Falkes' death?"

"If I am called as a witness I will deny this conversation. Are you wired?"

Andros stood up and walked around the desk in front of Tolliver. "Check for yourself," he smiled. "So long as you don't get fresh."

Tolliver did check around his shirt and felt his pants pockets, and his legs and ankles.

"God almighty. I'll be glad to get this over. Look at me," Tolliver said nervously.

Andros sat down. "OK. Our fictitious guy we're discussing. What does he know about Falkes' death?"

"Nothing. He got himself bailed out. Floated around. On the move. Went back to his apartment."

"Apartment?"

"Huh?"

"What apartment?"

"I didn't ask. I didn't take his deposition. I just got a general picture. We're talking about a theoretical guy in a theoretical situation. Anyway, this guy and his girls have just been picked up for prostitution when he thought he was protected from police intervention. He's pissed. He's trying to figure out what went wrong. Where did the cops come from? Who narked? Who were these cops? Goes out to breakfast and finds out Sherm Falkes has gone out in a blaze of glory.

"He knows Falkes has a small apartment in the same apartment building where this guy has his 'hidey hole'—his words, sounds like he OD'd on Peter Rabbit.

"Anyway, the newspaper says probable suicide. But this guy is worried. Here's the deal, Mr. Andros. Here's the scary part. I even sent my wife and kids to her folks' place in Spokane. We were all going, but I sent them on without me.

"This guy claims that some guys from Seattle PD have been protecting his girls and his prostitution operation. He claims girls are his business. But in return he's been fencing narcotics for them. He fronts sales to certain dealers. Not huge sales. Maybe five or six ounces of cocaine in a baggie he'd wholesale for a couple thousand dollars. Lots of marijuana. Pills. Heroin. His police guy would give him the stuff and tell him how much to charge. No percent for him. Just run his girls. His police contact was a big guy. Maybe a vice dick. This guy knows who he is but he wouldn't tell me and I didn't want to know."

"How'd he meet this cop?" Andros asked.

"I did ask that. He says one night a big guy in a black raincoat just sat down beside him in a bar. Told him that he and several others had watched him operate. Complimented him on being discrete. This guy—my theoretical guy—liked that. Anyway, the cop said he was either out of business or he was going to do some favors for the cop to stay in business."

"Where did Sherm Falkes figure in all this?"

"It seems that this theoretical guy had set Falkes up with girls. The prosecutor was a fucking customer of his. He figures that's how the dick got onto him. The dick and Falkes knew each other, but he only dealt drugs for the dick."

"What about the apartment?"

"That came later. Falkes had a small apartment where the guy would bring girls. This guy, my guy, asked if he could rent a place there and Falkes set it up."

"That comes together for me," Andros remarked abstractedly. "I never thought Sherm's condo looked all that lived in."

Both men sat quietly, revolving their own thoughts.

Finally Tolliver said, "That's what my theoretical guy can testify to, a cop fencing dope. He says he doesn't know anything about Falkes' death. But if the cops did in Sherm, which he suspects they did, they won't think twice about wasting him."

"Might be a red-letter day for law enforcement if your client does get done in," Andros mused. "Parties unknown dispose of leading suspect in Sherm Falkes murder. A small-time pimp. A dope pusher, albeit avocationally. No great loss. Books closed. All questions answered."

Andros stood and strode over to the bookshelf in Tolliver's office. Volumes of poetry and literature. No law books, but a battered set of classics, *Ulysses*, and a set of Shakespeare's plays bound in blue paperback.

"Problem is, Mr. Tolliver, where does it stop. Obviously, we can deduce from what your client would say that there are certain parties in the Seattle Police Department who are helping themselves to small quantities of the great quantities of narcotics they confiscate. Probably it is done before the stuff enters the property room. Before it gets into the system. That is the real worry in police procedures. Do all of the narcotics collected at a dope bust make it to the evidence room?

"Unfortunately, all your client can give us is some life-wrecking allegations about one bad police officer whose existence, like a single cancer cell, probably indicates the existence of a number of others . . ."

Tolliver put his feet on the table, rested his head on the back of the chair, and stared at the ceiling. He put his glasses on the desk and closed his eyes.

Andros sat down again in the simple, armless side chair, straight and alert.

"I've been down the informant road before as a prosecutor. You end up nurturing and promoting and extolling the nonexistent virtues of one worthless scum in order to try to make a case against another worthless scum. The question I always ask myself, Mr. Tolliver, is which worthless scum shall I pick? And, invariably, when I have decided to go down that road, I always feel like I picked the wrong scum."

"How else do you make your case, Mr. Andros?"

"What kind of case does your guy make, Mr. Tolliver? 'A Seattle police officer who I can identify—gave me dope to sell— I sold it and gave the money to him.' 'What dope, Mr. Barnes?'

'All kinds, Mr. Prosecutor.' Do you have any to show the court?'
'No.' 'Do you have any money to show the court?' 'No.'"

"Move to dismiss," Tolliver said quietly.

"Damn close to granted if we can't come up with more," said
Andros.

"Maybe the feds, racketeering . . . RICO ?"

"I'm determined to clean this up in-house if I possibly can."

Tolliver removed his feet from the desk, stood up. He looked
at his watch. "Four fucking hours on this case today," he said.
"You know what I get paid by the generous City of Pasco for a
municipal court appointment? Ninety-five dollars. Flat. No
wonder you left criminal law for a lucrative civil practice."

Andros looked at him inquiringly.

"Oh, yeah. We get the news in Pasco, Mr. Andros. Bizarre.
Teeny-boffing-prosecutor-ends-it-all-in-a-blaze-of-glory. In steps
squeaky-clean-former-deputy-prosecutor to clean house and set
all in order."

"I suppose that's a scenario," said Andros.

"So how's it playing out?"

"So I suggest we talk to the sheriff about taking your guy to
Seattle before a select cadre of Seattle cops come over to pick
him up themselves."

"No deal?"

"Greeks love to bargain, Mr. Tolliver. Greeks love to bargain more than buying the goods. But at this time it appears
your goods are shoddy and the price is too high. My offer is to
take your client's statement and see where we go"

Tolliver stood up. "No! I won't do that. You don't get a whiff
from me without immunity and some kind of protection. You
can bargain with some wheeler-dealer over in Seattle, Mr.
Andros. 'Cause once my guy is safely out of here I'm gonna forget about this whole thing."

"I wish I could do that," Paul Andros said quietly. "Look, I
know how we can get your guy out of your hair. *And* he'll live to
bargain another day."

Once the FBI identified the fingerprints of Terry Clayton
Barnes, also known as Bill Darby, also known as Bill Dempsey,
also known as Bill Dunbar, an FBI rap sheet went to Franklin
County sheriff's office, where Barnes was actually being held,
showing his prior arrests, convictions, and an outstanding warrant from Seattle District Court on charges of promoting prostitution, first degree (a felony) and failure to appear (a
misdemeanor). Upon receiving this information, the Franklin
county sheriff's office notified the King County sheriff's office,
who notified Seattle police that a suspect in one of their arrests
was in Pasco.

City and county budgetary constraints often decide the
future of fleeing criminal suspects. The jurisdiction that holds
the suspect, in this case Franklin County by virtue of a jail contract with the City of Pasco, has no duty to return the suspect
to the place where he is charged. But, like Franklin County,
King County Criminal Investigations had no hand in the
Majestic Motel bust. Standard operating procedure is to turn it
over to the department that has the case. If they want him, they
can go get him.

Copies of such reports were also dispatched by the King
County police to the county prosecutor's office. The reason was
that sometimes the prosecutor could light a fire under somebody
to go pick up the suspect.

The report from Franklin County drifted into the King
County sheriff's office attached to the morning jail list—the list
of persons being held in King County jail on various warrants
and charges. An anonymous handwritten note on the teletype
memo from Franklin County reporting the arrest of Terry Barnes
stated simply, "No reports KCS. Please arrange with charging
agency to pick up suspect."

This was not part of the jail calendar. So Mrs. Pickins, the
clerk in the prosecutor's office who assembled the reports for the
jail arraignment calendar, put it aside and did not get back to it
until after lunch. About 1:30 P.M. she found the file on Barnes

and gave it to Lyle Turner, the deputy prosecutor handling the Majestic Motel case. Turner phoned Chief Hellman to make sure he was aware that Terry Barnes had been located. Then he called Mary Lynn Pierce for an appointment with Andros. As directed, Mary Lynn did not tell him that Andros was out of town, but over Turner's objection, she set up an appointment for the following afternoon. Turner hung up and smirked at the thought that Andros' inaccessibility would hold up the Falkes investigation.

Thus it was, following Turner's phone call, that Chief Hellman and his ever-present sidekick, Sergeant Gordon, came to discuss Terry Barnes' future.

"Pasco," said Chief Hellman. "The frigging incompetent didn't make it any further than Pasco? And it took him long enough to get there."

"So who we gonna send to bring him back?" asked Gordon, whose administrative talent was to focus always on the problem at hand.

"You fucking asked me that already," said the Chief.

"So what's the fucking answer?" Gordon asked.

"Whyn't we just send Jake? Maybe he'll have an accident and kill them both."

"I don't think we should send Jake. We don't send captains to pick up small-time crooks," Gordon said.

"Let's think about it," said Hellman, unwilling to discard his off-handed inspiration. "It would be a kind of test. If Jake brings him back safely and then Barnes sings some kind of tale about how Jake was linked up with Sherm Falkes in this prostitution business, we can argue that it's just sour grapes against the guy that brought him back to stand trial."

"Why would we wanna do that?" asked Gordon.

"To keep this fucking department from blowing apart in our face, Gordo. Jake this. Jake that. The guy is everywhere. He's in business with the whoremonger prosecutor. He's got one of the highest civil service positions in the department. He's guild.

The guy is in a perfect spot to know everybody and everything. He's got records, dispatch, court liaison, evidence room. If there's a skimming operation going on, he's the perfect guy to coordinate it."

Gordon thought this over. Finally, he asked, "What's going on, Chief?"

"I don't know. A few months ago I got a call straight through to my extension. My number is not exactly top secret, but interesting that the caller knew my extension. The caller's voice was disguised. He said, 'There were *three* baggies of coke in the Alki bust.' It was the night after we had made a good bust over in Alki ..."

"Including that seventy-seven Jaguar."

"Yeah. So I checked the reports. The evidence listed was two bags of coke—two-hundred-seventy grams in one, two-fifty in the other. Say there's a third bag—what? Two, three thousand dollars?

"It starts to be worth somebody's while to skim the evidence, doesn't it? Think about the times a guy makes a traffic stop. Finds a baggie of marijuana. 'Whose is this?' he asks. 'Not mine,' says the driver. 'Guess it's mine,' says the cop."

"Old story," Gordon confirmed.

"*You* heard anything, Gordo?"

"I hear all kinds of stuff. A PD's worse'n a gaggle of old ladies. Skimming's not a new idea. Guys used to skim booze. Probably still do. Hell, it's a fucking public service. If we put every bottle of beer we took off a juvenile in the evidence room, pretty soon we'd need the Kingdome to store it all."

"What about drugs? What do you hear?"

"Norton-the-Nark and I were having coffee. He just mentioned that he worries whether everything gets to the evidence room."

"He oughta fucking worry. It's his crew ... What would they do with it? Use it?"

"Use it or sell it, I guess."

"Sell it. That gets hairy, Gordo. You gotta keep it someplace. Find a buyer. Do a deal. Keep from getting your ass shot off. Christ."

"Wholesale it?"

"Now you gotta trust somebody. You wanna trust dope dealers? They'll kill you or nark on you at the drop of a hat."

"There's gotta be somebody that you can work with."

"How about the most reliable 'somebody'? Somebody you got something on?" Hellman said, gazing out the window down at the Third Avenue traffic.

"Somebody like a conspicuous white-haired pimp that our vice guys never saw and never heard of?"

"Maybe we need to get this Terry Barnes over here across the mountains and have a little talk?"

"Yeah. Make sure he's deliverable. Pasco may want to hold him for something. In any event, I think you ought to talk to him, whether or not Pasco wants to hold him."

Gordon tapped the paper on which Hellman had scribbled his notes from Turner's call. "Let's give this to the dicks and just see what happens. See where it ends up. I'll bet a lunch Jake gets detailed to this job."

"Tail Jake?"

"Maybe just watch him. Informal."

The Greek
studies the chit

TWENTY-TWO

"JESUS CHRIST, PAUL. You're going to worry this thing raw," Scott Turnbull complained.

Andros' beer, Rainier in the bottle, was untouched. Turnbull was drinking water, Einar Torgeson a Coke. Paul wiped the table in an outward sweeping motion with the palms of his hands. They sat in a quiet corner of the same cocktail lounge at the Pasco Oasis where Terry Barnes had encountered Travis Smith. It was late and the lounge was uncrowded. Paul was oblivious to Scott and Einar's weariness.

"Barnes doesn't give us anything," Paul said for the third time. He was looking at a "time of events table" Einar had put together—a list of significant events related to Sherm Falkes' death and the times, as accurately as possible, that each event occurred. "Barnes bails out at two twenty-nine A.M. The pathologist puts the time of death at between two and four A.M. That makes Barnes a suspect himself. We make a deal with Barnes to testify against Satello, and Jake's defense attorney eats our lunch. How do we know the jail custodian didn't screw up the time and it's earlier or later? 'Two twenty-nine'—where the hell do they get numbers like that?"

"It's stamped on the receipt for their belongings," Einar said.

"How does the pathologist know the time of death from a charred body?" Paul continued. "What about three-thirty to five-thirty? Under any time frame, Barnes himself could have bailed out. Took a cab. Met with Sherm. They argue. Barnes kills him. Now Barnes wants to put the blame on one of Seattle's finest, a twenty-year police officer with a fine record and a commendation for bravery and good judgment."

"Yeah," continued Scott. "And Barnes doesn't know anything about Sherm's death. All he knows is that Sherm and him and Jake were in business together. The prostitution protection can be corroborated maybe by the fact it went on for so long. Maybe a bartender?"

"Oh, they make super witnesses. Scott, believe me, bartenders don't know nothing unless their license is at stake. Then they're a font of knowledge."

"The cash at Sherm's condo gets you motive," Scott continued. "Sherm was holding out on Jake and whoever else was involved. And Barnes' testimony might get you past a motion to dismiss. Then you've got Jake in a box as to whether he testifies. If he does, he's gotta talk about where he was that night, the apartment deal, dealings with Barnes, the missing dope in the Rossierre case. Besides, a Barnes affidavit will get you a search warrant: Satello's desk, locker, his house, car, Sherm's apartment at the Argo ... might turn up something."

The three took a while to collect their thoughts.

"If I sell immunity to Barnes and come up short of a case against Satello, it's all been for nothing," Paul said.

"Wait, wait, wait—what's been for nothing?" Scott asked.

Paul looked at him in amazement. "Taking on the job of prosecutor. Weeks of working day and night to try and unravel Sherm's life. Trying to prove how he was killed. Finding his killer. Restoring credibility to the prosecutor's office. Punishing all those police assholes who sold out their badges and put drugs back on the street ..." He swept more invisible debris from the table.

Scott looked over at Einar. "What the hell's he talking about, Torgeson?"

Einar looked at both Paul and Scott quizzically.

"Keep Einar out of this," Paul said. "If you want to bully somebody, bully me."

Scott laughed. "Bully? Me? Nobody's bullying Einar. I imagine that's been tried. Go ahead, Einar, tell Paul what it's all about. What the hell are we doing here?"

"Our jobs," Einar said.

Paul and Scott waited for more. But nothing more was forthcoming.

"Wouldn't you be disappointed if we didn't convict Sherm's killer?" Andros asked.

"No," Einar said definitively. "I would just like to think I understand. That I know the truth. That people haven't fooled me. People look at me, they think they can fool me. I don't like that. I listen to what people tell me and sort through feelings, language, illiteracy, egos, sympathies, biases, prejudices, until . . . I think I know the truth."

Paul wiped the table furiously. "The truth. The truth is that Jake Satello killed Sherm Falkes. That's it. I know he did. I smell it all over him. I can't let that bastard walk. He's dangerous, he's corrupt. He's gotta be stopped. There's no one else that can do it. *I've* gotta stop him."

The men sat stunned by Paul's outburst.

Scott laid his hand lightly on Paul's table-sweeping forearm. "Listen to me, Paul. Look at me."

Andros faced the older man.

"We are colleagues," Turnbull continued. "We are more than father-in-law and son-in-law. More even than father and son. I have the highest respect for you, and I wish now that I'd told all my politician friends to fuck off.

"But, as usual, Scott Turnbull, Mr. Fix-it, shot off his mouth. Easy. My son-in-law, Paul Andros, can pull all your irons out of the fire. What an egomaniac I am. I'm sorry. You're a friend and you're family. That's more important than any case or any client. This is not your personal problem.

"Look," Scott continued as Paul turned away. "You've got to accept that your job is not to avenge Sherm Falkes. Who cares about Sherm Falkes? Your duty here is to the prosecutorial process. To keep that part of the system going. It's an imperfect world."

"I know that," Paul muttered.

"Then get the system pasted back together and let the next guy decide what to do about the Sherm Falkes case. Just tap dance until November and let the newly elected prosecutor cut his teeth on this jawbreaker."

"Can't wait, Scott. Terry Barnes is looking at a felony prostitution charge involving a minor. He'll do time. Right now, he's looking uphill. If he decides to cop a plea and keep mum about Sherm and Jake and whoever else is involved, he'll be well into his time by November. Then I'm out. The new prosecutor won't bother with Sherm Falkes' death and whatever the hell's going on at Seattle PD. My guess is that Barnes is already scared enough of Jake and Jake's friends that he won't testify against them. Once he starts doing his time it'll be too late. He won't say anything."

"Take him in front of the Grand Jury or the what's it?"

"The inquiry judge? Don't want to do that if I don't know his story. His attorney would love to get him in front of the inquiry judge—instant immunity. I might use it, though, to work on the members of the Ventures Seven Group about their dealings with Jake Satello."

"Maybe you talk with this Barnes like you talked with Jake. Just talk. Get a feeling."

"Jake's a cop. It's easier to talk with him. How does he refuse to talk with me unless I charge him with something? Barnes is a suspect. He's charged with a crime. Minute he walks in the room he asks for an attorney and I'm back where I am right now. Attorney shows up, we're back in barter-city. We're boxed."

Scott looked at Torgeson. "You sure that little bitch can't identify Jake as being with Barnes?"

Torgeson visibly flinched at Scott's profanity. "Margie? Margie Cross. I got her up to identifying Jake twice, but she refused. She had a *feeling* it was Jake and it probably was, but she doesn't really identify him. She can identify Jake as the man with 'John' in the market. That puts Jake with Sherm Falkes, but so what? They're business partners. The time she saw Jake with Terry Barnes she was looking out a third-story window. She won't say whether she saw his face but she says she knew it was him."

"Shit," muttered Scott.

Torgeson sipped his Coke and sat back. "Margie Cross is a kid who has never had a chance in this world. Tying up with Barnes was the first time she ever had new clothes," Torgeson continued. "I would guess that she gave away her virginity, or it was taken, at an early age. Sex has no value to her. She would be disinterested, were it not obvious that it has great value to others."

He sipped again. "You know what?" Einar continued, "I think she wants to be seduced out of the information she knows we want."

Turnbull guffawed. "Shit, Torgeson. You are a piece of work. Seduced ..."

"Maybe he has something, Scott," Paul said. "You know how it is with some witnesses. Question; answer. Question; answer. It is like a seduction. You gain a rapport. Language matches thought. You gradually take over the witness. Intuition leaps."

"That doesn't happen if I'm on the other side," Turnbull said skeptically.

"Go back again, Einar. If Satello was brokering confiscated dope through Barnes, Margie has to have seen Satello and Barnes together."

"Not necessarily," said Scott. "If I was Satello I wouldn't want to advertise social contact with a white-haired, dope-dealer pimp. But then I guess I get more conservative as I get older. More I think about it, I wonder if you got anything against Satello except maybe the narcotics dealings if you can get Terry Barnes to testify. According to Tolliver, the guy knows nothing about Sherm's death."

"But if Margie can put Satello with Barnes, that's at least a start on something," Scott said to Einar. "Margie's our only lead. The Johnson woman has fallen off the face of the earth.

And the other one, what's her-name, the one who copped. Nobody's gonna 'seduce' her out of her name. She's a hard case. What about Sherm's artist girl friend? Did she ever see Jake with Barnes?"

"She's never seen Jake. Her memory's kind of shaky from the concussion when she was attacked. "

"So there we are," continued Paul. "Tomorrow we talk to the Pasco prosecutor about getting Barnes back to Seattle. We talk to Barnes' new attorney and decide whether to make a deal. Einar goes back to talk to Margie. I check the police reports for any useful leads. We're going to put this thing together. We're gonna do it. Jake's going down."

"Are you going to cheerlead this case into a conviction?" Turnbull asked.

"Not cheerlead, visualize, Mr. Turnbull. Visualize." Paul sat back and sipped his Rainier from the bottle. "When I was a kid, before the World's Fair, Seattle was still a small city. I used to wander around downtown and watch guys in business suits hurry here and there. What did they do, I asked myself. Whatever it is, I told myself that's what I want to do. I visualized myself wearing a dark suit and hurry around Seattle talking to people and deciding things.

"Even though we were poor, relatively, I never wanted money. It wasn't important. I knew I could make money. Buy cheap, sell dear. My uncles all made money. My mother always did okay. But money doesn't count in Seattle. Probably not anywhere. It's the men who hurry through their lunches and scribble numbers on napkins and put down their money absentmindedly that have the power."

"Put their money down absentmindedly?" echoed Scott.

"Sure. When a Greek pays for a meal, it is a transaction. Even in America where you pay what's on the chit. The Greek studies the chit. Removes his money from his pocket. No billfold. Then he discusses the state of the world with the moneytaker. Then he makes the preliminary offer to pay. To the true

Greek, this is only a skirmish, a foray. The money is then with-drawn and hands are waved, again in remonstration about the world, the gods, the government. 'Sales tax six percent—what do they do with all that money that you, Mrs. Andros, must col-lect for them—for free?'

"The money-taker must now respond and entice the money. He or she may agree or disagree but the existence of a transac-tion must be signaled. Perhaps a query as to the quality of the food or drink."

"Meanwhile, I'm third in line waitin' to pay my check," grumbled Scott.

"That is because you have scribbled on a napkin and decided how the Kingdome will be financed or how much the stevedores will be paid next year or who the governor should appoint for the next superior court judge opening.

"These are things I watched. Then I decided where I wanted to be."

"Why not money?" asked Scott. "Money buys status."

"I agree. Sure. That's why originally I wanted to be a banker. Perhaps in another world the right bank, the right position, I would still be a banker. But six months as an executive trainee at Seattle-World was all I needed to start studying for my LSATs and enroll in law school."

"Banks aren't very fast-moving," confirmed Scott. "But if status is so important to you, what does convicting Jake Satello do to enhance it? You wouldn't try the case anyway. And even if you indicted him today, it wouldn't go to trial until the new prosecutor is elected. It seems to me your status is best enhanced by cleaning up the office and announcing to the world that Sherm Falkes' questionable private life had no impact on the office. Assure the public that the new prosecutor takes over one of the finest law enforcement operations in the country. That kind of bullshit . . ."

Andros considered Turnbull's suggestion thoughtfully. "My personal feeling about status is ancient history. My accepting this job is not about status. I'm not just a caretaker. This is about my town, Scott. My city. My country. My state. I do not condone corruption, I do something about it."

Scott drank the last of his water and set the glass on the table softly. "I understand. I know," he said. "But you're trying to *kill* the cancer when all you've gotta do is get rid of it. Maybe you need to be a little bit *more* Greek. Inventive. Subtle. Convoluted. *Obtuse.*"

Andros had no reply. He stared at the two men as if about to speak, but he did not. In wordless agreement they stood up, dropped their money on the table, and went off to their separate rooms, their separate thoughts.

TWENTY-THREE

ANDROS AND TURNBULL SAT IN THE FRONT SEAT of the prosecutor's car, a 1978 Dodge. A third man, white-haired, sat by himself in the back seat. The car was backed into a space in the parking lot leading to the overlook of Priest Rapids Dam on the Columbia River, south of Vantage, Washington. The Pasco police had arranged with the Seattle police to bring Terry Barnes there to be picked up and returned to Seattle.

The morning was clear, hot and breezy. Tumbleweeds blew across the parking area. The only other vehicle was a camper, parked inconspicuously in the corner showing no signs of life.

Paul and Scott watched in the distance as a black car turned off SR 243 toward the lot. The car was moving fast, sending up wisps of the sand and dust scattered across the tarmac side road.

As the car approached, it slowed. "The front plates are covered with mud," Scott observed as the car entered the parking lot.

"Are those masks over their faces?" Andros asked.

"I suggest we depart," Scott said tightly.

The Dodge fired up without hesitation. The black car slowed as if to pull up beside them. Suddenly the driver swerved in front of them. A shotgun appeared in the passenger window.

The wheels of the Dodge spun as Andros whirled his car towards the rear of the black car, a full-size Chevrolet Impala. His right front fender scraped the right rear bumper of the black Chevy. The tires caught hold of the hot asphalt and they were heading for the exit.

"Keep down," Paul shouted. No shots had been fired, but the Chevy changed direction, did a quick circle, and moved toward the exit behind them.

The closest inhabited area was toward Vantage. Paul turned left and floored the powerful eight-cylinder engine.

Shortly, about two miles up the road, he saw what he was looking for. A conspicuous white Ford LTD was parked on an access road facing SR 243. It was on a knoll two or three hundred yards off the main road.

"There he is. It's gotta be him," Paul said.

A white head looked up from the back seat of the Dodge.

Andros braked hard, just making the turn leading to the white car. Dust plumed like a small tornado as they sped up the hill.

Andros' car, skidding, stopped diagonally in front of the Ford.

The rear door on the passenger side of the Dodge opened. The white-haired man dived out, headfirst. Andros and Scott ducked down, their heads below the windows. Andros swung open his door and dropped to the road butt first behind the driver's side door.

The large man in the driver's seat of the Ford was opening the door when the white-haired man shouted out, standing at the right rear of his car. "Freeze, Captain," Einar Torgeson said. He held a large .45 revolver in both hands, arms extended in an expert crouch.

"I'm just getting out of the goddamn car," said Jake Satello, holding his empty hands in front of him.

"Okay," said Einar. "Slowly. Please."

He did so. Meanwhile the black Chevy had pulled into the access road and stopped at the bottom of the hill.

Einar Torgeson shifted the revolver to his right hand and removed the wig from his head. He then moved quickly up the hill and stepped to the left at an angle that put Satello between him and the black Chevy.

Slowly the black Chevy backed out onto SR 243, and moved hesitantly north toward Vantage. As if coming awake, the car suddenly accelerated and disappeared up the road.

"Friends of yours from the Police Chaplains Association?" asked Paul, coming up to stand beside Einar and to watch the black Chevy disappear.

"Who?" asked Jake.

"Those two guys in the Chevy. They greeted us with a shotgun in the parking lot where the Pasco police were suppose to meet the Seattle police to pick up Terry Barnes. You know anything about that?"

"Yeah," Jake smiled. "I'm the guy supposed to pick up Terry Barnes."

"Makes sense," said Andros. "You two being old buddies, you could chat away about old times on the drive to Seattle."

"Huh?"

"Buddies. Friends. You know. Or maybe not friends. Just business associates."

"I don't know the guy. Nobody wanted to make the pickup so I said I would."

"Funny. We've got several witnesses who have seen you together."

Jake smiled. "You got shit, counsel. Maybe I've seen this Barnes around. How would I know? Maybe I'll recognize him when I see him."

"You didn't look at the jail photo before you came over? What if Pasco had the wrong man?"

Jake pointed to the car. "Maybe his picture's in the paperwork. I don't know. So where is he? Did you fuck-ups lose him?"

"Change of plan. Barnes is on his way to Seattle by another route. Compliments of AAA Bail Bonds."

"Have the bondsman deliver him. Good idea. The bondsman always gets his man," said Jake. "Anyway, looks like the plan to meet partway got out to the wrong people. I'd say this Terry Barnes is connected to some really bad people."

"Yeah. I wonder how that happened?" Andros pointed to the ground where they stood. "How come you were up here? You wouldn't be able to enjoy the sight of our blood from this distance."

"Whaddaya talking about, counsel? I hadda take a piss. Might not have had another chance while I was escorting the prisoner."

Einar relaxed his arm. Turnbull had gotten out of the car and stood on Einar's left. Andros stood on his right.

"Look, partner, my gun is all holstered up." Satello brushed back his suit coat to show his revolver neatly shoulder holstered under his left armpit. "Let's put all the firearms away and relax."

Andros shuffled angrily toward Satello, his chin jutted. "Relax. You fat, Italian slob. You lying, corrupt son-of-a-bitch. Tell me relax. Your pals pull up to shoot our ass off and you tell me to relax."

Scott had moved around between Andros and Satello, his shoulder facing Andros. Andros pushed Scott aside. Einar stood clear.

Satello backed up. Smiling. "'Italian slob'? What's this, what's this? That a slur of my nationality? Fuckin' human rights is gonna hear about this, counsel."

He looked at Einar. "Right? You work for state human rights. Whaddaya think about your boss slurring my proud national heritage?"

Turnbull regained his balance and once more moved between Andros and Satello.

Andros composed himself. Calmly, patting Turnbull on the shoulder, he said "Einar, I want you and Scott to sit in the car. Jake and I are going to chat."

Scott and Einar backed off, slowly. "We'll just stand over there," said Einar pointing up the road beyond the two cars.

"Dumb move," Andros observed when the other two men were out of earshot. "Nobody would care about Barnes getting knocked off, but some people might get really concerned if Einar and I were killed in the process. What if the Pasco policemen weren't intimidated by the mask and the shotgun and decided to protect the prisoner? There are cops with a sense of duty other than fucking over the system. I guess you didn't know that. What about Scott Turnbull? You didn't know he was along, did you?"

Jake said nothing.

"I would guess there was a Corruption Anonymous committee meeting, and this was the best idea anybody could come up with. Dumb."

Jake remained silent.

"At least your pals had the sense to pull out when they finally figured out that they'd have to take out fellow law enforcement officers to get to Barnes.

" I wonder, Jake. Have you had enough?" Andros continued. "Maybe you're tired of being a master-criminal? You know I'm not gonna let it rest. I'll start an investigation that the next prosecutor will be forced to continue. But there's a way for you to get out. Not a deal, I'm not making you any deals 'cause if I get enough evidence to put a case together, I will charge you. I'll charge your friends. But all I got now is enough to indict and a less than fifty-fifty chance of conviction. I only want to shoot fish in a barrel. A lay down. Otherwise, the wounds you have inflicted on law enforcement will bleed on forever."

Satello started to say something. Stopped.

"You got something to say? Shall I advise you of your fucking rights so you can say something?" asked Andros.

"Stick it up your ass."

"I hope you're listening to me now, Jake. As of your return to Seattle, you are a sick man. Very sick. So sick you will decide to put in for the nice fat disability retirement you so richly deserve after twenty years of fucking over the criminal justice system."

Satello shifted his gaze to study Paul Andros.

"Not only you, Jake. You and all your Venture Seven buddies. I'm shutting down shop."

"You ain't got shit," Jake said, almost to himself.

"I got all I need to charge. I take Terry Barnes before the inquiry judge. That gives me enough to work over every cop in vice and narcotics. By the time I follow-up every lead, I'll have more. Somebody will crack. Somebody will break. Somebody will tell how he scammed a bag of coke or marijuana and brokered it through you and your pals. You've made it so banal that your associates can't comprehend the enormity of your corruption. That will change. The newspapers will change that. The newspapers will love it. It'll be a feeding frenzy."

"Why?" Jake asked simply.

"Why what? Why let you off? To see you out in such a way that the system holds together. Some cops are honest and dedicated. A few are corrupt. Most are just soldiers getting along in a system they learn to adjust to. They're only as good as their leaders. Unfortunately, you're a leader, Jake. Chiefs come and go, but you're the one the rank and file see as one of them. Rookies see your big house, your family, your status on the force, your 'investments'. They ask, how do I get it together like Jake? Someone answers, ask Jake. He'll show you how to do well on a cop's salary."

Andros shook his head despairingly. "Your talent is that you make it all seem okay. You and your friends take just a little bit here and there, and everybody else in the system protects you. The good old boys."

Jake Satello slowly moved over and leaned on the open door of the Ford. He gazed in the distance at the calm water of the Columbia River. Then he peered at Andros. Their eyes locked.

"Sherm said that to me once. I don't understand what the hell you assholes are talking about."

He swung his large body neatly behind the wheel and started the engine in one fluid motion. He closed the car door and released the brake, allowing the car to amble slowly down the hill and around the car in front without raising any dust.

On the other side of the road, about a hundred yards up from the river, on a sandstone hill Sergeant Gordon lowered his binoculars, skidded butt first down the incline and hauled ass to his car. He would have to hurry to catch up with the old black Chevy from the undercover car lot. What the hell was that doing over here? He'd forget about Jake for now and catch up with the Chevy. There would be plenty of opportunity for him and Hellman to talk with Jake back in Seattle.

Sergeant Gordon passed Jake, traveling at a reflective pace, on the Vantage Bridge. He doubted that Jake saw him. He goosed the unmarked Oldsmobile up the five-mile grade from the Columbia River to the Ellensburg Plains. If he could find those guys and separate them from Jake, it would be a piece of cake.

The stark, rocky landscape of dried tumbleweeds and eroded basaltic rock transformed into green fields of alfalfa, stretching from the Yakima Hills on the south to the out-stretched fingers of the Cascade range to the north. Gordon pulled off at the first Ellensburg exit. Sure enough, there was the Chevy Impala parked at the first restaurant north of the exit. Gordon pulled up and parked behind it, his front fender just touching the back fender of the Chevy. He got out of the car and opened his light jacket, unsnapping the leather strap over the .32 holstered to his belt. He removed a small notebook from the front seat. He was ready. Sergeant Gordon never needed much preparation for confrontation.

Gordon entered the Panda Bear Pancake Shop and spotted his prey immediately. They were sitting at a small booth against the south wall. The waitress was taking their order. Gordon slapped his notebook on the table and sat down.

"Artie Newson and young Tom Flagg. Maybe you guys can help me prepare some questions to ask you when I wire you up. Oh, ma'am, I'll have some coffee while I visit with my old pals here."

"Hey, Gordo. What are you doing over here?" asked Newson.

Flagg had gone pale, but Newson maintained his composure.

"Well, for one thing, I'm trying to figure out where the black Impala went that was sitting in the impound yard. I said to myself, I'll bet the old Impala would like to run itself over and catch the view at Priest Rapids Dam. Sure enough, that's where I find it."

"Oh, that. It's just an old drug forfeiture car. Captain Satello said we should use it to follow him to Pasco. He was picking up the prosecutor killer. They caught up with him, you know. Over in Pasco."

"Follow him."

"Yeah. Protection."

"Protection. Yeah, I guess those prisoners that Pasco lets loose are pretty dangerous. No handcuffs or nothin'?"

"No. I think Jake was afraid somebody might want to see that guy dead."

"Well, gee, Artie, that's not what I saw. I saw Jake being held at gunpoint by Paul Andros and the state investigator he brought in. You guys just backed out and headed for home. Fine protection you guys are. Jake's gonna be disappointed in you. Of course, you guys probably figured Jake doesn't need protection from the prosecutor. Anyhow, if he did, I didn't see he got any."

"Yeah, well, we didn't know what that was all about, and we didn't see any prisoner so we got the hell out. Is Jake in some kind of trouble, Gordo?"

"I don't know, Newson, but you guys sure as hell are. You and Tommy here. Neither one of you report to Captain Satello. And I'll bet when I check the duty roster, I'll see that you guys are on days off. A new first. Guys volunteering to pick up prisoners off the clock. Wait. I'm sorry, provide protection from dangerous criminals that might want to *harm* prisoners. Have I got that right? Is that the story?"

Silence.

"But you know when I get you guys wired up, let me see, I think I'm gonna start asking about Ventures Seven, Inc. Oh, that's it. Maybe Ventures Seven is gonna pay your overtime for this little escapade? Seattle PD sure as hell ain't."

"You can't wire us ," Newson offered.

"Oh yeah? The guild contract says 'due cause', officer New-son. Lie detector tests may be given to members only for due cause. Running off with an impound car without following procedure will make it, I think."

Gordon looked over at Tom Flagg. "Eat your nice breakfast there, Tommy. I'm all worn out from keeping up with you guys. I think you're gonna drive me back from here."

"Look it, sarge. It's just a goddamn car. It's going right back. Let it go. Leave it alone. It's not a big deal," Newson wheedled.

Gordon leaned forward in Newson's face. "Look at me, Artie. Do I look like a guy that lets things go? Did you ever see anybody slap me on the back and say what a good guy Sergeant Gordon is? In fact, am I ever happy? Am I ever nice? Am I ever anything but Hellman's hatchet man? Now, do you still want to ask me to leave it alone?"

Silence.

Gordon made another note. "Then, I think I'll ask about the Alki bust. The Chief got a tip there were three bags of cocaine. I checked the evidence room, Artie, and there were only two got turned in. Gee, Artie, weren't you on that bust? Well, actually, I know you were. I checked the reports. You know, Artie, I'm gonna save you for the last. I'm gonna let you consult with Jake and you two can come up some really great story. At least then it will be a challenge."

"Now you, Tommy. You're gonna begin by telling me how a kid that works traffic pals around with an old vice cop like Artie here. You can tell me about riding around on your shiny motorcycle. And how things are going for you and the young wife and the three little bambinos running around the house. Maybe you can tell me about what kind of work you Ventures Seven guys do on your days off. What do you report to the IRS? You be thinking about the answers to those questions and whatever else I might dream up."

He looked over at Newson. Neither was eating breakfast. "You know, Artie, we're a couple of old guys. Tommy's just starting out. Maybe you're right. Maybe you and me should be think-ing about ways to save his ass. Come on, Tommy, eat up. We gotta get started back. Maybe I can figure a way for you to duck outta this mess. We'll just let Artie here finish his breakfast and then he can get the Impala back to Seattle by himself. Here's five bucks. That oughtta cover for my friend Tommy's breakfast and my coffee. Take your time, Artie. I don't want to spoil your digestion. Oh and look, there's a pay phone. You might want to make a few calls."

"I want a lawyer," Tom Flagg said weakly.

"Oh, Tommy, you're so cute. Come on and get in the car and let me explain things to you. See, Tommy, I'm here under direct orders from the Chief. See? An old hand like Artie understands. In fact, by now, he's thinkin' he'd like to get in the car with me for the ride back to Seattle. He'd like to sing his heart out. But I'm not gonna do it that way. I'm thinkin' about Tommy's little rug rats."

Artie Newson sat back in the booth, breakfast untouched. He looked very tired. Finally, he said, "Sergeant Gordon is an asshole, Tom. But he'll stand behind any deal he makes. It's as good as coming from the Chief. Don't *give* nothin' away."

Old wounds,
new blood

TWENTY-FOUR

AFTER THEIR RETURN TO SEATTLE, Andros heard nothing from Terry Barnes or the attorney from the King County public defender's office who was appointed to defend him. No over-tures about testimony regarding certain Seattle police officers in exchange for immunity. It just died. In fact, Terry Barnes wanted to plead guilty at the arraignment, and the only delay in getting him on the felony offenders' bus to Shelton for classification was the lack of a pre-sentence report. Chief Criminal Deputy Casey handled the sentencing, hoping to impart a sense of "we are serious about this one" to the sentencing judge. He was success-ful. Terry Barnes was presented to the Washington State Department of Corrections with no recommendation as to the minimum time to be served on his five-year sentence.

In early November, Lyle Turner was elected prosecuting attorney for King County. Lyle had duly resigned as deputy pros-ecutor and mounted a noisy campaign based on corruption and misconduct in the prosecutor's office. The voters seemed to decide that with all the recent questionable history of the office, his youth and lack of experience were more asset than liability. The question of how much and what kind of experience it takes to guide the county's largest governmental law firm never came up. His Democrat opponent, Chad Bernhart, had only four years' experience but had distinguished himself in the Criminal Division of the City of Seattle's Law Department with a record of community involvement in allocating prosecutorial resources. The youthful appearance of the two candidates caused one rakish reporter to dub the race "the battle of the babies." The voters decided by a narrow margin to support the brash, tough-talking Ivy Leaguer with no connection to how business used to be done in Seattle.

As promised, Paul Andros publicly stayed out of the campaign, but he was not pleased at the outcome. He liked Chad Bernhart, and his feelings about Lyle Turner's self-serving methods of operation and his disloyalty to Sherm had not changed. Andros had tried as best he could to minimize Sherm Falkes's disgrace and any negative reflection it had on the office. Lyle had done the opposite, intimating at every turn that a wholesale cleanup of the office was necessary. Andros did not believe this and tried to protect the long-term staffers as best he could. Nevertheless, when the election was over, he was more than ready to leave office and return to private practice. He resigned effective November 30, and the county council appointed Turner for the one remaining month of Sherm Falkes' term.

In his brief term of office, Andros did not hand down any indictments for the murder of Sherm Falkes. He handed over the lengthy file he and Einar had developed to Lyle Turner who promised only that he would review it himself.

Andros created no file or report concerning the allegations he had heard in Pasco concerning corruption in the Seattle Police Department. Jake Satello retired from the department shortly after the meeting with Andros at Vantage. In addition, after a number of meetings with Chief Hellman and Sergeant Gordon, there were an unusual number of disability retirements: Sergeants Newson and Patterson, and officers Johnson, Fuller, Dickerson, and Bailey. These officers were also shareholders in Ventures Seven, Inc., which was dissolved for nonpayment of fees by the Corporate Division of the Secretary of State. The seventh shareholder, Tom Flagg, stipulated to thirty days off without pay for improper use of an impound vehicle and was allowed to return to work in the traffic division.

Chief Hellman reorganized the department and spent a great deal of time deciding on the persons to be appointed to fill the positions of the recent retirees. Some of the older officers were surprised at the chief's choices: the captain who replaced Jake was a graduate in Police Sciences from UCLA; the sergeants were replaced by relative newcomers to the force with barely the minimum five years required experience. Veterans were rotated to new and different duties. Officers with more than three years in vice and narcotics were transferred to other areas. Veterans of the "War on Drugs" failed to see how a constant influx of rookies could accomplish anything, but Hellman was satisfied that the cross-breeding of newcomers kept procedural cross-checks fresh and avoided lethargy and cynicism. He was partly right. Rotation did avoid lethargy. Cynicism in police officers cannot be excised.

In late April, five months after Paul Andros had turned the office over to Lyle Turner, he was invited to lunch with the new prosecutor and Chief Hellman. Gordon was, of course, in attendance.

The new prosecutor explained the reason for meeting. He and the chief had learned that a certain Irene Johnson was serving time in the Louisiana State Women's Correctional Facility for assaulting a New Orleans police officer who was in the process of arresting her for prostitution. The same Irene Johnson, a.k.a. Reeney and Tangerine, charged with prostitution during the June raid on the Majestic Motel.

"Apparently she did not take kindly to being arrested for prostitution again," Turner said. "She was packed off forthwith to prison. They don't fool around in Louisiana. Quite candidly, I might let sleeping dogs lie, but something's got to go in the file. You spent a great deal of time investigating Sherm Falkes' death. I am considering the idea of appointing you as special prosecutor to go down and talk to her. See what she knows about Sherm Falkes' death."

"I figure she's gonna tell you to take a hike," said Hellman. "But somebody ought to talk to her."

"Expenses?" asked Paul.

"The county will pay your air expenses and a car and room for a couple of days," said Turner. "I'm sure the county council won't mind."

"Maybe I'll take Jane along, make it a little vacation. I'll pay her expenses, of course."

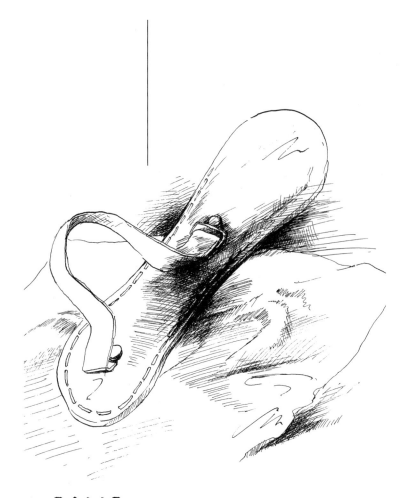

A little

white sap

TWENTY-FIVE

TEN DAYS AFTER HIS MEETING with Lyle Turner, Andros was driving a rented Chrysler LeBaron along Interstate 10 from New Orleans toward Baton Rouge. Jane had stayed behind at their hotel to rest and shop for the day.

Paul enjoyed the drive. Traffic was light and the countryside was green and lush, much more appealing than the narrow streets and urban decay of New Orleans. Dilapidated shacks surrounded by cotton fields seemed more picturesque than the filthy streets of the Latin Quarter.

The Louisiana State Women's Correctional Facility was not too far from the exit that announced its presence. A road sign pointed to a visitors' parking area that was fenced and gated, but the gate was open. A sign at the entrance to the white brick administration building announced that all visitors must check in. The building was new and institutional gray, but the staff was friendly. Official visitors seemed to be a welcome break from routine.

A wiry blonde woman, in a makeshift khaki uniform, sufficient to distinguish her from the inmates, accompanied him to an interview room. She glanced at Paul's gifts—a box of candy and carton of cigarettes—and seated herself beside the door as they waited for Irene Johnson.

"I can leave if you like, but most district attorneys want me to stay for a while. Cops want me to leave. Attorneys want me to stay." She smiled at this apparent irony.

"Are the cigarettes and candy okay?" Paul asked.

"You can open the packages and give them to her while I'm in here. But they need to go through inspection before she gets 'em. We'll consider they're yours for now."

A second door opened across the room from the one they had entered, and Reeney Johnson entered. She was wearing a dark green sweat shirt and black cotton pants. Her fine black hair was tied back in a burgundy and dark green patterned scarf. The dark colors of her shirt and the bright scarf made her caramel-colored skin appear even lighter.

She took in the scene quickly.

"You gonna introduce me to your friend, Miss Dori?" she said. She looked directly at Paul without a glance in the direction of the guard.

"This is Mr. Andros. Come all the way from Seattle, Washington, to see you, Irene. Isn't that somethin'?"

"Seattle. I don't recollect much 'bout Seattle," she said slowly.

Paul stood up and took the carton of cigarettes and the candy over to the guard.

"Could you open that and find us some coffee?"

The guard opened the carton of cigarettes, inspected a pack and gave it to Andros. She took the rest of the stuff and left the room. Andros crossed over to the table and offered Irene Johnson a cigarette.

She took one. "Why not?" she said. "I got nothing else to do."

Andros lit her cigarette and sat down.

"I heard an interesting story from an attorney in Pasco," Paul said, wasting no time while Dori was out. "I heard that you and your friend Terry Barnes were wholesaling drugs you obtained from the Seattle police."

No reaction.

"I heard the prosecutor, Sherm Falkes, was in on it or at least knew about it."

"Who the hell are you? You got a badge?"

"No badge. I'm a lawyer. I took Sherm Falkes' place after his death. A new prosecutor was just elected this year. He sent me down to talk to you, We're still trying to get the pieces together..."

"Where's Terry? Have you seen Terry?" She spoke languidly, as if the question were of only casual interest.

"Terry's in prison. 'Promoting prostitution.' He copped. Last time I saw him he was leaving the courtroom. Couldn't hardly wait to start doing his time. I came down here because we thought you might tell us something about what happened to Sherm Falkes."

"Paper said his car went over a cliff."

"His body went over the cliff. The evidence indicates that he was dead when he went over."

The door opened and Dori bustled in with coffee, three cups.

"Dori," Andros said. "Irene and I seem to be getting along okay. I wonder if we could talk alone?"

"Sure," she said. "I'll be across the hall."

She set down the two coffees and left with hers.

When the door closed, Irene Johnson reached for Andros' note pad and flipped back to a blank page. Andros handed her his pen. She scribbled the words 'Bug—ask for yard' on the pad.

Paul motioned with his hand for her to finish her coffee.

"The jail records show that after the motel bust you bailed out about one-thirty. How is that?"

"What?"

"How come you bailed out before everyone else?"

She leaned back casually. "I had some money."

"You certainly did. A thousand in cash. You didn't want to wait for Terry to bail you out?"

She smiled. "Why should he? Wouldn't you guys use it against him if he did?"

Paul nodded. "Probably. So where did you go at one-thirty in the morning?"

She thought about the question. Finally, she said, "Maybe I spent the night with a trick. That's what I remember."

Andros tossed down his pen.

"Look. I haven't advised you of your rights. Your bail is forfeited and no one's talking about extradition on a simple prostitution charge. But we can sure change that. Let's try a little cooperation here."

Irene Johnson appeared to soften. "Dah'lin'," she said. "Cooperation is my middle name. I've spent a lifetime cooperatin'... and here I am." She opened her arms and looked around the room.

"Maybe we should get some air. Can we do that?" Paul said.

Irene got to her feet gracefully and opened the door back to the office area. Dori was seated just outside.

"Mr. Andros here wants to tour the estate, Miss Dori."

Dori came back into the interview room, and the three of them left through the opposite door from which Irene had entered. There was a dimly lit hallway with a bare cinderblock outer wall on one side and wallboard on the other. They went right, to a steel door, which Dori unlocked. They stepped outside into a barbed-wire fenced area about 20 by 30 feet. They crossed to a second door that was framed into the wire fence. Dori unlocked the second door and walked through first, holding it open for Andros and Irene.

It was aptly described as "the yard." It was large, probably over two or three acres. Picnic benches were scattered in various locations. There was a soccer or football field surrounded by a running track, two basketball courts, and two baseball diamonds. It appeared that a corner of the soccer field had also seen baseball diamond duty.

It was deserted.

"Where is everyone?" Paul asked.

"Lunch," answered Dori. "Just started."

"You're going to miss lunch?" he said to both of them.

"I'll get my lunch," Dori said. "She'll miss hers."

Irene patted her slim hips. "Won't hurt me none."

Dori, aware that her presence was hindering conversation, sat down at a bench near the wire-framed door.

Paul and Irene began strolling along a path worn a few feet from the fence. The inmates paced animal-like as close as they could get to the outside world.

"When's your parole hearing?" Andros asked.

"June. Next year," she said, resigned to her future.

"They're gonna make you sit out a whole year?"

"You kidding? Hit a cop. It's Louisiana. You see the inside of a dark hole for a long time."

Paul thought about doing hard time in a Louisiana prison. "Let's get back to Washington. You saw Sherm Falkes again that night," he said. It was a statement.

She said nothing.

"I've reached the point where I just want to know. Jake Satello is retired and out of the picture, together with his other police friends. If Sherm wasn't involved, he at least knew about it and I'm certain he received part of the income. I just want to know what happened to him and get on with my life."

"Was Sherm a friend of yours?" she asked.

Paul reflected carefully on her casual question. "No. I can't recall that we were close. But I feel like if I don't stay on this, everyone else will want to forget about it. There's no one else but me to push it."

"OK. No note pads, though. All I can talk about are things I *might* have heard from a girl I know."

"Okay."

"What I heard was that Sherm killed himself. OD'd in his apartment."

"Apartment? Argo Apartments?"

"Yeah. He had an apartment there."

"What number?"

"I don't know."

"Where in the building?"

"Second floor. A li'l one-bedroom apartment. Last one on the right. I think it was a big apartment that had been divided in two."

"What did this girl you know actually see?"

"A dead Sherm. Door was unlocked. He was in the bedroom on the bed. Clothes on. Dead. About the time the girl was fixin' to leave, big Jake came in. He looked around and told her to get out. He'd take care of it. Something about insurance. She left."

"Insurance?"

"Tha's what he said."

"Could he have been there before?"

She looked at him quizzically and did not answer.

"What did the body look like?"

"Dead," she said patiently.

"Any blood?"

"No."

"Signs of a struggle?"

"He didn't look all that peaceful. The bedclothes were all messed up. But that don't mean nothing."

"You say Jake came in? How did he know?"

"I don't know. I—the girl—just looked up and there was Jake."

"Had drugs been stored there? In that apartment?"

"Most times. Sometimes Jake would just bring them to us. To the girl, I mean."

"Did Sherm ever bring you any?"

"No. But they were stored in his apartment."

"So he knew. Sherm."

"You kidding?"

"That night. The girl, she left? Did she go back to Sherm's apartment again?"

"No."

"What about Terry Barnes? Did this girl say whether she saw Terry Barnes that night?"

"She didn't say. Actually, I saw him, but it wasn't until early afternoon on Monday. We decided to split in different directions."

"My question was, did the person you know of see Terry Barnes that night?"

She looked at him defiantly. "And I said she didn't say. I also say that the first time I saw Terry after Friday night was early Monday afternoon."

"Was there a note? Did Sherm leave a note?"

She thought about it. "Not by the bed. Coulda been any-thing in that apartment. It was kind of a mess. We used to call it the passion pit. All of Terry's girls at one time or another did time in the passion pit."

"With Jake?"

"No. Just Sherm." She pronounced it 'Sharm'.

"Never Jake?" Andros said, almost to himself.

"Big Jake was all business. And he wasn't around the apart-ment house very much. Terry didn't like to show it, but he was really afraid of Jake. But Terry thought Sharm was a joke. Sharm was odd. He was so ... grateful. A girl could ... It seemed like any girl could take charge of him."

"Pussy whipped?"

"Maybe like that. Only any girl who was outta sight was outta mind. But I liked him. I really liked him." she announced. She looked off into the distance outside the fence. "Terry was a friend. He took me out of a bad situation in LA and we were together for over three years. But Sharm. . . . I think about him."

Andros tried to grasp the dynamics of this handsome black woman with her native street smarts linked to Terry Barnes, her pimp, and to Sherman Falkes, an attractive public figure willing to forfeit his personal life and career to his carnal desires.

"How did it all start? Satello ... Falkes ..."

"I don't know. Terry and me was in Seattle. Just me and Terry. Terry hustled Sharm to my room. I opened the door and there he was. Sharm was a nice man. Easy. I don't know how he ever got to be a persecutor."

"Attrition. A talent for self promotion. Political smarts," suggested Andros, to himself.

"We better get you outta here."

Andros smiled and started back toward the wire-encased door. He stopped and faced the dark, sensual woman whose livelihood was telling lies and creating illusions. Paul Andros believed that human beings never fully told the truth and never fully lied. Truth itself is an illusion, a concept. But people could sometimes be straight with one another, human to human. Paul believed that, for some reason, Irene had been straight with him.

"I really appreciate your talking with me, Irene. I would offer to shake hands, but somebody here might take it wrong."

She shrugged. "I hadda talk to somebody. When you're in a place like this, you got lots a time to think, but, if you're smart, you keeps your thoughts to yourself. If people know what you're thinkin', they own you."

Paul gestured toward the fence. "What're you gonna do when you get out of here, Irene? Back to the life?"

"The life," she said vacantly. "I don't know. Maybe I'll sell something."

Andros laughed. "I won't touch that. Take it easy when you get out, Irene. This place doesn't suit you."

Dori was opening the door as they walked up.

"So what now?" Dori asked. "You want to go back to the interview room?"

"I think we're done." He turned to Reeney. "Are you ready to return to the population?" he asked.

"Just one question. Who was the dude who broke into my room at the Majestic Motel?"

The name 'Beaman' automatically came in Andros' mind from his memory of the police reports, but nothing escaped his lips. "At the motel?" he said, stalling.

"Yeah," she said.

"I don't know," Andros lied. "The raid was led out of the police chief's office. Vice wasn't involved. It was sort of an ad hoc operation."

"Ad hoc?"

"Yeah. You know. Spur of the moment. Outside channels. If it had been vice or narcotics, your friend Jake would have warned you."

"But you don't know his name?"

"No," Paul lied.

She looked at Dori. "I'm ready to go back," she said.

"I'll call," Dori said to Reeney.

Without a word, Reeney Johnson became the compliant prisoner. Her face expressionless, she turned and walked across the yard toward the other women. Dori and Andros walked back to the empty office area, where Dori phoned in a report concerning Irene's whereabouts.

"May I see her file?" Paul asked.

"I can't give it to you, but maybe the warden will," Dori said.

"Could I see the transcript from the court that was sent down? I'd like to see the police reports or find out what happened to get her in here. What happens here is your business."

Dori crossed the room to a desk. She opened a drawer that held several files. She located, removed, and looked through one of them She unclipped a pile of papers stapled together and fastened to the left side of the folder. She handed these papers to Paul.

"I have her file here to make an outside contact report. I guess I can't help it if you looked through it while I wasn't looking. I'll be back in a minute."

The thick pile of papers represented the pleadings, affidavits, and reports from *People* v. *Irene Johnson*. Mixed in with the prosecutor's presentence report was a copy of a New Orleans PD report which named Dexter Hoggins as the victim and Irene "Reeney" Johnson as the suspect. Essentially, Hoggins was an undercover vice cop who had made his deal with Reeney and then proceeded to arrest her. She had seemed resigned and compliant, when suddenly—per Hoggins—all he knew was, he was out. Fortunately for law and order, Hoggins' backup was outside the room and stopped her.

She had struck Hoggins expertly above the ear with a white leather sap; a ladies' sap, which was found in her purse. The weapon was described as about eight inches long and weighing about sixteen ounces. It was shaped like a flexible round tube with a slightly enlarged knob on one end. The core was a spring around which a white leather cover was sewn and into which fine lead shot was poured and sealed off. Paul visualized that it would take very little strength to whip the weapon against an adversary and cause painful injuries. Hoggins had suffered a depressive concussion and was off duty for a week.

Andros could see that under these circumstances, Reeney's imprisonment was a foregone conclusion: an example had to be made of whores who took to carrying saps and beating up on police officers.

Irene Johnson was charged with assault and intent to kill which, through a plea bargain, was reduced to felony assault. The procedure, like Barnes's, had been expeditious. In less than a week Reeney was serving time.

Andros, declining an invitation for a late lunch with the Assistant Warden and Dori in the staff dining room, profusely thanked them, and the other officials at the facility. By 1:30 he was back on Interstate 10 heading for New Orleans. Now to finish—or was it start?—that vacation with Jane....

From New Orleans, Jane and Paul took a side trip to Columbus, Ohio. They rented a car at the airport and headed south to the town of Circleville, twenty miles south of Columbus.

They were going to pay a visit to Barry Frederick, Jimmie Smith's son.

After taking the first exit on the freeway south of Circleville, the directions Mr. Frederick provided Paul over the phone led to a narrow miniature valley. The main road wound along a forested creek at the bottom of the valley. Occasionally, access roads snaked off to the left and right, up to houses just visible on the ridges.

At a mailbox neatly lettered 'Frederick,' Andros turned left and followed the narrow lane across a reinforced concrete bridge. About twenty yards into the property from the bridge one could look up and see the house built into the hill above.

They were pleased to see that, whatever Barry Frederick's calling, he had done quite well. The house was a wide, two-story "prairie" style with a daylight basement built into the hill. The roofline cantilevered outward, providing a wide overhang. Under the overhang, one could see that the facing boards between the heavy roof joists were varnished to a high sheen. Large picture windows overlooked the valley and the creek below.

The driveway ran the full length of the house and turned to rise to the upper level and passed by the entranceway which was at the side of the house. At the top of the hill and beyond the entranceway there was a driveway plaza surrounded by the back of the house, a three car garage, and a workshop and office.

The long entranceway echoed the spine of the house with a twenty foot covered walkway proportioned to match the roof line. The huge wood-carved front door was open, and a handsome black woman with streaks of gray hair walked toward their car.

"That's fine, right there," she waved smiling. "Come on in."

She came around the rear of the car to greet Jane.

"I'm Emily Frederick. Did you have any trouble finding us?"

"None," said Jane. "Once you find the Trellis Creek Estates sign, its easy. I'm Jane Andros. This is my husband, Paul."

Emily Frederick shook hands warmly with both of them.

"Well, come in. Barry is here, but I'm going to apologize for him right now. He just gets in a big pout whenever the subject of his real father comes up. Don't take it personally."

They entered the house and by passed the great hall that overlooked the creek and the access drive. She led them to a comfortable sunroom that overlooked an open brick courtyard separated by a wall of French doors. Several skylights provided a feeling of openness and illumination.

Through a swinging door in the opposite corner of the room, which appeared to lead to a kitchen, came a heavy-set man carrying a tray full of plates, glasses, food and drink. He set the tray down on a large glass table surrounded by comfortable-looking chairs.

He turned and extended his hand to Paul, but his eyes conveyed none of the friendliness of Emily Frederick. "I'm Barry Frederick. You've met my wife. I suggest we just sit down and partake of this good food and drink here that Emily has prepared."

They did so. There was a pot of coffee and a pot of tea. There were soft drinks. Liquor was offered, but Jane and Paul declined. There was a plate of fine cheeses, another of cold meats and sausage. There were pate, crackers, breads, fruit. Paul drank coffee. Jane and Emily drank tea. Barry Frederick drank fruit juice.

When the pleasantries subsided, Barry Frederick asked, "So this visit concerns John Frederick?"

"Do you remember your father?" Paul asked.

"I remember John Frederick, Mr. Andros. My mother remarried to a man named Tobey. I think of *him* as my father. He was a master builder. This development that you drove through was but one of my father's many visions. Everything I am I owe to Mr. Tobey."

"... And to your mother," said Emily Frederick quietly.

Barry Frederick raised his eyebrows toward his wife. "We are speaking of fathers here. The whole man, and woman, is made of many parts."

It was not a condescension. The exchange instantly conveyed to Paul that Emily and Barry Frederick had a relationship that communicated on many levels.

Andros continued. "As I explained on the phone, the man we knew as 'Jimmie Smith' at the restaurant was John Frederick. He had an apartment full of books, which we will be glad to send you, plus I owed him a substantial amount of money for work he did for me for which he accepted no pay, except my promise to see you and to pay you the money I owed him."

Paul reached in his coat pocket, and handed Barry Frederick a check from Paul's trust account for fifty thousand dollars.

Barry Frederick took the check into his hands without looking at it. Slowly he tore it in half, in quarters, in eighths, in sixteenths, in thirty-seconds, and so forth until his stubby fingers could no longer grasp any of the pieces, which fell onto his plate.

Paul was dumbfounded. How would he face his mother and explain the failure of the simple mission she had entrusted to him?

Without saying a word, Jane reached in her pocket-book and took out her wallet. She opened the wallet to a blank check, and rewrote the check. She handed the check to Emily Frederick.

"I predated the check to Monday so that Paul can put the money into our account. I suggest that you hold onto this for a while. It's a gift. You can give it to a charity or a church, a school. Whatever. It's not a huge amount, but you would do us an immense favor if you would clear that check and put it some-where." She faced Barry Frederick. "If your Mr. Tobey had wanted you to do something for him, I'm sure you would want to see it done."

Barry Frederick sat back and folded his arms. He looked at his wife who was holding the check lightly between her fingers. "Well said, Mrs. Andros," he said. "I'm sure Emily will find a good use for the money."

The tension in the room relaxed, and Paul seized the moment to ask, "Where do Mr. and Mrs. Tobey live?"

"Mr. Tobey died three years ago," answered Frederick. "My mother lives with a sister in Florida. Awful place. But she is quite comfortable with her bingo and whatever it is they do down there. I told her that you had called and that it was at last confirmed that John Frederick was dead. I asked her if she had had any premonitions about it. She said no, but I wonder. She loved John Frederick. Never would allow a bad word about him in her presence. I think that John Frederick underestimated the depth of her character and her native intelligence. As I got older and had to deal with where John Frederick fit in my life, I realized that, although his affairs and his absences deeply hurt my mother, she looked on them as just a part of 'Mr. Frederick's

Search for Self-Discovery'. From a very early age I looked upon his actions as self indulgent and malicious."

He looked at his wife. "You know it was the most amazing thing. Before the incident, on the other occasions when Mr. Frederick would leave us, Mama would say 'Daddy will be back.' When he disappeared after the incident, she never said that again. It was only six months later that she met Mr. Tobey and they began to live together. She told everyone that John Frederick was dead. . . . She wouldn't even get a divorce before she married Mr. Tobey. I guess she was a bigamist for the last twenty-five years. . . ."

"Not in her mind," Emily said.

The Androses didn't stay much longer. It was clear to Paul that Barry Frederick did not want to listen to or accept anything good there was to say about Jimmie Smith. Emily was clearly fascinated to hear the story of the Lothario professor from Columbus transforming into a beloved dishwasher in Seattle. But each detail seemed only to inflict pain on Barry Frederick. Paul immediately liked Mr. Frederick and respected his simplistic dislike of his biological father who had abandoned him.

Yet Paul had to admit to himself that he loved Jimmie Smith and that he would forever suffer a feeling of deep loss at his passing, especially knowing that Jimmie would no longer be there at his mother's restaurant to listen to him and to reflect for him the human dimensions of the people and activities in his life. No one in Paul's life, not even Jane or Scott Turnbull, could so adroitly help Paul to reach what was in his heart and stay on track with what was truly important in his life. Paul suddenly realized, sitting at the glass-top table with the Fredericks, that he had taken the place of the son that Jimmie had lost, and Paul had gradually accepted Jimmie as his surrogate father.

Paul, of course, said nothing to the Fredericks about his mother's relationship with Jimmie Smith. (This would have been truly a showstopper for the fascinated Emily!) It was clearer to Paul than ever that John Frederick had indeed died that day on the OSU campus. Barry Frederick really did not care about the insightful shadow-man that Paul had known in Seattle. Barry and his mother had found another life, just as Jimmie Smith had known they would.

And Barry Frederick had found a real father in the apparently solid, dependable and talented man his mother had married. Although Andros had also lost his father, he had taken his loss with defiant independence, denying the need to claim a father or a father figure. As he and Jane drove back to the airport, it became clear to Paul that Scott Turnbull, the overbearing, mercurial, sometimes brilliant sometimes obtuse man who had become his law partner, would always be a close friend and associate, but never a father figure. No, it was Jimmie who was the closest thing he would ever have to a father and he would always hold him in his heart as such.

Maybe my relationship to Scott is like a marriage, Paul thought to himself. For better or worse.

Upon his return to Seattle, Paul met with Turner and Hellman and Gordon. He explained that Irene Johnson had been friendly but unwilling to make a statement or be a witness regarding Sherm Falkes' death. It was his opinion, he told them, that she would rather come back to Seattle and do time on the prostitution charge than be involved in the murder case. It was up to Turner whether he wanted to proceed on that. He told them her unofficial, off-the-record story that Sherm's death was a drug overdose, deliberate or accidental, and that Jake had took over the clean-up duties with talk about wanting Falkes to be able to collect on his insurance. Chief Hellman argued that it would be unfair to involve Satello, a retired police officer after all, in uncorroborated rumor-mongering by a whore who was in jail for attacking a policeman. They all agreed that a case against Satello wouldn't go anywhere without some corroboration—of which there didn't appear to be any. It was decided that the file would note only her unwillingness to testify. Then the file would be turned over to one of the deputy prosecutors for a fresh look at whether there was any kind of case. Against anyone.

To prepare his brief report for the file, Andros asked for access to the entire Falkes file one more time.

Not much had been added since Andros left the office. Two of the older documents were of interest to him though: the inventory of Irene Johnson's belongings the night she was booked into King County jail, and the autopsy.

The inventory included a white leather sap. For some reason, it had not been confiscated.

The autopsy report included no exterior observations of head injury. Paul was not surprised, since the epidermis had been pretty well crisped in the fire. It was likely that, if there had been any hematoma or skin laceration, the fire had obliterated evidence of it. The X-ray reading indicated fissures in the left frontal bone, the left and right temporal bones, and the occipital bone of the skull. The autopsy acknowledged these findings and suggested "skull fissures of unknown source but possibly consistent with heat expansion of brain tissue." The heat from the fire expanded the brain tissue until the skull cracked. There were amphetamines and alcohol in the stomach and blood, suggesting a possible drug reaction, but the pathologist had stated the cause of death as inconclusive. Could one or two of the skull fissures have been caused by blows from a white sap of such excess as to kill Sherm?

It was curious that no one had asked Andros whether he had any conjectures or thoughts about how Sherm Falkes had died. It was as if the unstated policy of Chief Hellman and Prosecutor Turner was: leave it alone. They were quite content to dump the whole sordid mess in Paul's lap and walk away. Sherm Falkes had disgraced himself. Who cared how he died?

Andros' report concluded that Irene "Reeney" Johnson would probably be of no assistance in any legal proceeding regarding the death of Sherman Falkes.

He further conjectured that she would not assist because it was as likely as any other theory that Irene Johnson had killed Falkes herself, by the ardent use of the same or a similar sap that had injured the New Orleans police officer. Certainly, the evidence of her Louisiana conviction would make her testimony useless in the prosecution of any other suspect, such as Terry Barnes or Jake Satello.

The nature of her quarrel with Sherm would perhaps never be known. It may have been related to Sherm's possibly articulating a decision to go to Chief Hellman about the drug-skimming operation or maybe, if one considered the jealousy angle Einar developed from his interview of Martine Rodriguez, Irene is some kind of borderline psychopath who uses her sexuality to disguise a deeply aggressive personality.

Even if Irene killed Sherm, Andros didn't see how she could pull off the burn-up-the-body-in-a-ravine trick. Her story—that Jake Satello disposed of the body—seemed likely enough. It was possible that Jake bought her drug-overdose story without further investigation. Jake certainly would not want the homicide squad going over the apartment building with a fine-toothed comb. All Jake wanted to do was divert attention from the Argo Apartments and the drug-skimming operation.

Once you saw both Jake and Irene with motive, opportunity, and means to kill Sherman Falkes, then it was a standoff. The prosecutor could require one to testify against the other by granting immunity to the one who testified, but the defense would simply assert that the immunized witness was the real killer. The prosecutor's burden of proof beyond a reasonable doubt meant that the benefit of doubt went to the defendant.

Andros sent Lyle Turner his report but received no acknowledgement of response. He never heard from any deputy thinking about putting a case together. No wonder that the new prosecutor wanted to see the Sherm Falkes file dead. And buried.

Specter

TWENTY-SIX

IT WAS LIKE WAKING to a threatening day, waiting for a rainstorm that never comes. Scott Turnbull became more and more irascible, but he refused to go off on the drunken bender that, in the past, had seemed to result from his inner tensions.

Paul returned to private practice with renewed vigor. The office was doing well. Young Parsons had kept the support staff and the other attorneys happy. Paul had asked him to put together a partnership proposal that would be fair to everyone and create an incentive for the firm to grow. The plan he had presented exceeded expectations. He even made a limited-overhead provision for Enos, so that he could take home most of the fees from the few hours of work he was down to. Scott was, of course, a full partner whose persona created the firm image. The name was changed from Turnbull, Padgett, and Andros to The Turnbull Firm.

All these changes, Andros thought, ought to trigger a drunk. But it did not come.

One evening Paul and Scott sat at Salty's. Scott drank water, Paul his beloved Rainier—in a bottle.

"Okay, Scott, I gotta know. When the hell are you going to fall off the wagon?"

H. Scott Turnbull considered the question judiciously. "Who knows? Once a drunk always a drunk."

"That's true for a lot of people, but you're too cagey about your drinking. You never quite use it as a means to screw up your life. It's like a specter out on the edge trying to get control. Do you enjoy sparring with it? 'Come on, old specter, let's see what you got.'"

Turnbull considered Paul's words with no change of expression. Finally, he said, "I don't know about any specter. It's quite real. Drinking to excess is a direction some people take in life. Who knows why some people get fat? Some get addicted to nicotine and can't stop smoking. Drugs. So who knows why we drunks decide to keep drinking until our minds and bodies are soaked in booze and the booze takes over. It's a line you just cross and you go from human being to alcohol in human form. It's like the booze wants to pour out of the bottle and take another form . . ."

"Is it over?" Paul asked.

"It's never over. It's never over, but every time I think about a drink I think about the last time I had to go to detox. It's too much of a price to pay to return to the land of the living. Another thing that goes through my mind is that the effect of alcohol really isn't all that good. At least a dope fiend feels a brief euphoria. All a drunk feels is that he has to keep going . . ."

To Paul, Turnbull appeared calm discussing his inner anguish. His manner was businesslike, as if they were dissecting a case. Paul wondered, would he ever be close to this man? Or would the differences in their ages and backgrounds and personalities forever bar intimacy?

Scott smiled at Paul's apparent concern. "What about you, you Greek ass-hole? You never seem to have any specters to fight. Business, business, everyday."

"I've got a few ghosts. Sherm's death is still in my mind. My failure to do anything about it. I was sure it was Terry Barnes. Then, I thought it had to be Jake. In the end I had nothing. What was I thinking?"

"Suppose Sherm did kill himself," Scott said. "Where's the failure?"

"I don't believe he killed himself. People accept that story because they want to. I believe that Jake found him dead and bought Irene's story about an overdose without checking it out. He certainly didn't want the body found in the Argo Apartment, or the Argo Apartments linked to Sherm's death. He said something to Irene about no insurance for suicide and went out to create an 'accident'. We never got to search Sherm's apartment. Didn't even know about it until Reeney let it slip. My guess is that Jake shoveled out the apartment, removed all traces of Sherm and the drugs that were apparently stored there and had it rented by the end of the weekend. The new tenant's occupancy cutting off any trace of Sherm's presence."

"How would the prosecutor get evidence to establish a Irene-Sherm relationship let alone a case that she killed him?"

"Maybe through Terry Barnes? But his exit from the scene to the welcoming arms of the joint leads me to believe that he would have no memory of any events prior to Pasco. Listening to her, I think Irene had a thing for Falkes. And Martine Rodriguez thought Irene not only had a thing for Sherm, she was also possessive about him. And that's the female viewpoint. Shouldn't disregard that. Irene was able to attach herself to Sherm and held onto him by bringing him herself and the other girls he had a taste for. With his small apartment at the Argo, she made it all safe and easy for him. She satisfied his fantasies. He would even show up at places like the Majestic when they were working like a regular john. Must have been like owning a candy store. Even when he was developing a relationship with the Rodriguez woman, he couldn't stay away. But finding the police report of Rodriguez's assault at his condo suggests to me that he was developing concerns about Irene. I think that the Majestic Motel bust was an epiphany for Sherm and that he had a confrontation with Irene about the Rodriguez assault."

"Boy oh boy, counsel. How the hell do you get there?"

"The sap. I know the autopsy is ambiguous, but why couldn't one or two of Sherm's skull fractures come from the sap—a little white sap. Sudden and unexpected violence from a woman who could see it all coming to an end. She and Terry had built up a pretty good thing: off the street, working a hotel operation ..."

"Soft beds instead of sidewalks and car seats?"

"Yeah. Protected by Seattle's finest. It was hooker heaven. Then the bust comes out of the blue. Irene not only gets busted she gets beat up in the process. Broken lip. From a cop no less. A thousand bucks of her own hard-earned money to bail out. She hooks up with Sherm at the apartment. And he's talking show's over. Candy store closed. No way to spin his way out of this. In comes Irene. No longer the bearer of carnal sweets. She's a beat up, tired hooker. I doubt that he tried to hit her or anything. All he had to do was say the wrong thing or turn his back on her. That was it. Sherm was suddenly the outlet for all of her frustration and pent-up violence. She would love to get back at the guy who busted her lip. Sherm's maybe the next best thing. I don't think you'd want that swarm of hornets on your back. Especially with a sap that's meant to be administered gently. Enough force and that thing could split your skull into two pieces."

"In bustles Jake . . ."

"Look, Mr. Jake, oh, look. He's killed himself. Jake falls for it. Even if he didn't, what's he gonna do? He's gotta buy time to clean up the apartment and get Terry and Irene in the clear so they won't be tempted to talk about their relationship to him and Ventures Seven."

"At one time you liked Jake as a suspect."

"Jake and Sherm were business associates. Just that. Jake's a realist. Even if Sherm was shorting him on the rent or on however they handled the money from the narcotics sales, Jake could fix that without killing Sherm. It was time to shut down shop when he got the call that Sherm had been busted at the Majestic Motel. He and the others were skating too near the edge. Hellman let 'em off, but I'm OK with that. It's one positive thing that came out of this. We got a bunch of bad apples removed from the bushel. But I didn't do anything for Sherm."

Scott turned up his palms in an uncharacteristic gesture of resignation. "It's a tough case, Paul. What does Turner do?"

"Yeah. It's Turner's show. He has the file. It's his job to decide what to do."

"He doesn't have the story Irene Johnson told you."

"Yes he does. I told him, but I didn't write it up because I knew she wouldn't testify to any of it."

"Seems like Jake got off easy. Any chance Turner could prosecute Jake for something? How does that play out?"

"I liked it for a while. Jake's so fucking arrogant, he almost begs you to come after him. I always thought he burned up the body, but I could never make any sense about him killing Sherm. Shutting down Ventures Seven had to happen, but why kill Sherm? Sherm shouldn't be at the Majestic when he was, but does that mean a sentence of death? I mean, I wouldn't put it past Jake, but he's gotta have a good reason. What is it? Thing to do is to shut down shop and keep your mouth shut. And what did Jake do?"

"Shut down shop and kept his mouth shut. But then suppose Turner decided to prosecute Jake by forcing Irene to testify?"

"What kind of a case does he have if Reeney is forced to testify? Sure I told Turner what she said, but what she said wasn't even a statement. Anyway, even discounting what a lousy witness Reeney would be, nobody wants to prosecute Jake, including me. Prosecuting Jake, win or lose, would expose the whole sorry story of drug-skimming within the Seattle police force."

"So what? Maybe that's a story it's time *was* told." Scott's lips compressed. His eyes squinted. Clint Eastwood, ready to take on the world.

"Relax, Scott. Perhaps justice hasn't triumphed, but the problem did get fixed. We've got a better police force than other cities. What's the gain in prosecuting Jake or a few other guys on charges that would taint the whole department? Besides, I never saw a makable corruption case there. Irene won't testify. Neither will Terry Barnes. Barnes is probably already paroled. If one of the other police officers involved in

Ventures Seven had cracked, we might have had something. But old Jake had them marching in lockstep. They wouldn't give Einar the time of day. We finally gave up. Chief Hellman has ways to do better than we could, because he owns their ass. But you know how vigorously Chief Hellman wants to see his own policemen prosecuted."

"Hellman knows more than he lets on," Scott grumbled.

"Hellman is a politician's politician. He'll continue to back up his boys while plugging up the dike wherever the ooze starts to leak out."

"When a tree falls in the forest there is no sound. A crime unproven is not a crime."

"Is that some sort of revelation to you?" Paul asked.

"I'd never articulated it. As a lawyer, I understand it. As a human, I guess I struggle with the concept."

Paul sipped his beer, and looked out at the departing ferry to Winslow. "You aren't a human being. Neither am I. We're just fucking lawyers. We share a warped view of the world."

"Naw," Scott said. "You're not just a fucking warped lawyer. You're a fucking Greek warped lawyer. That's worse."

All

sewn up

TWENTY-SEVEN

THREE MONTHS AFTER PAUL ANDROS turned in the report on his trip to Louisiana, the phone rang for several minutes in a large, comfortable house in Queen Anne Hill. It was 2:45 A.M.

"Yeah," the large man said huskily, picking up the phone beside the bed.

"Mr. Satello?"

"Yeah."

"This is Charles Norris at the Juvenile Court calling. I'm afraid we have your daughter here."

"Huh?"

"Your daughter, Virginia. She's here."

"Virginia's at a girlfriend's," Jake said confidently.

"No. No, Mr. Satello. It's her," Charles Norris stated dryly. "Look. We're awfully crowded. We'd like you to come down and pick her up. Do you know where the juvenile facility is located?"

"Virginia Satello?"

"Yes, sir. Not very many Satellos..."

"What's she charged with?"

"I'm not sure, sir. The point is that we'd like to release her to you..."

"Read the charge sheet to me," Jake Satello said harshly.

Pause. "Okay. Okay. Here it is. 'Prostitution. Possession of a controlled substance.' Now understand, Mr. Satello, that the prosecutors and juvenile court officers haven't reviewed this report. This is just a brief police report that the officers give us at intake. Nobody's saying she's guilty or innocent. But we just don't have the room tonight."

Satello nearly hung up. Then he looked up, toward Maria. His wife of twenty-five years had gotten out of bed and was standing in front of him. Her face was expressionless, poised to react to sudden bad news.

"She's all right, then," he said into the mouthpiece, nodding affirmatively. "Okay, I'll be down."

"Thank you, Mr. Satello. I'm sure this will all be all right."

"Your name?"

Norris's relief was apparent in his voice. "Norris. Charles Norris. But, not the movie actor."

Jake understood Norris's relief. There was no room at the inn for kids unless they killed or maimed someone. Parents who would pick up their adolescent, acting-out daughters in the middle of the night were heroes. Many parents would say, "keep her" and mean it.

Jake set down the phone.

"It's Virginia. Got herself in trouble. She's at the juvy."

"I'll make some tea," Maria said, and walked off to the kitchen.

We have both of us gotten fat, Jake thought. Fat and old. Jake stared at the wall. He saw himself dead. On a stainless steel slab. Naked. His belly a hairy mound.

Prostitution . . . possession of a controlled substance.

Jake slowly went to the closet, somehow got dressed. He stared at himself in the bathroom mirror as he brushed his hair. Well, not dead yet. His body was still executing lifelike motions. He would go down to the Juvenile Hall and deal with the authorities. But what of his daughter? What about dealing with her?

Prostitution . . . possession of a controlled substance.

"All in favor?"

The woman in the light pink suit nodded. The thin, bald man with the thick horn-rimmed glasses raised his hand.

"Me too," said the white-haired man in the blue suit. He looked jovially at the earnest young man in the brown wool sportcoat seated beside him. "That's one more bed for you there, warden. Who's next?"

"Irene Johnson. She's the one whose file Dr. Vernon wanted to review after last month's hearing. Shall I bring her in?"

"I'm not sure that's necessary," said the woman in the light pink suit. She had a fair complexion, but her blonde hair was turning to gray. Her manner of speech was languid, her voice soothing and friendly, as if she were hostess at an afternoon tea.

The earnest young man in the brown sportcoat obviously adored her. "Did you get the copies I sent you of the tests?" he asked the woman.

"I did. Thank you, Randall. I even came early tahday and studied the originals. No erasures. Firm, sure strokes evenly between the lines. All in the correct categories. What does a psychologist do with a subject who tells nothing about herself? I have a test heah that tells me Irene Johnson could nevah strike a man with a li'l white sap, yet I have a court file that says she did. I have a test that says she could nevah sell her body to a man, yet we have a history that says that's all she's evah done in her entire life."

The man in the brown sportcoat diffidently protested. "Perhaps she was not entirely candid, Dr. Vernon. But she has been a model prisoner. We can't continue to hold her just because of a test score. We need beds. We've got really dangerous people that have got to be held . . ."

"Randall," she stopped his argument. "What makes you think Irene Johnson is not dangerous? Did she not strike that policeman with her li'l white sap? A *lady's* sap. I did not know they made lady's saps. Arthur, you are a man of the world, wheah does one shop for a li'l white lady's sap?"

The bald man with the horn-rimmed glasses shifted his weight and folded his arms. He sat with his chair pushed back from the table, as if he refused to be grouped with the three others at the table.

"Jesus Christ, Phoebe," he said. "Stop joking around. You're still worrying about some cop that didn't watch out for himself in a whorehouse bust. We're not here to pander to the police. The courts keep sending 'em in and poor Randall has gotta house 'em. Her prison record and the rules say she goes. She's been a model prisoner. That's the rule. She walks."

"Arthur. Are you sayin' I am not aware of the rules? I helped write the rules. I am sayin' professionally and as a sworn member of this board that I won't vote to let her out of heah on parole. Evah. This is not just a dangerous woman. This is a dangerous and cunnin' woman. I think she diddled this test and I think she doesn't care if we know she diddled it."

"Maybe Washington wants her..." suggested the man in the blue suit.

"No," said Randall. "They sent word. They won't extradite."

"That's another interesting thing," said Dr. Phoebe Vernon. "Randall was thoughtful enough to get police reports on the Seattle charge. She was the madam, if that's the correct word, who procured the little girl that prosecutor was found with. The one who later died in a fiah. Murky doin's, Arthur. Murky doin's in New Orleans. Murky doin's in Seattle. Dark, murky doin's seem to follow this woman."

"Dr. Vernon," the bald man called Arthur said. "Irene Johnson was sentenced to this institution under a Louisiana crime. A rather straightforward crime of getting into a fight with a police officer who was tryin' to arrest her for prostitution. She has paid her debt. Under Louisiana rules she is eligible for parole. And, by God, I move that she be granted parole."

The four officials fell silent.

From the jovial white-haired man in the blue suit: "Is there a second?"

"Cahrter," said Dr. Phoebe Vernon, addressing the chairman of the small group—he in the blue suit. "If that motion is to be seconded, you will have to do so yourself."

Carter turned to Randall. "Let me understand, Randall. Is it staff's recommendation that this woman, Irene Johnson, be paroled?"

Randall looked painfully at the woman he so obviously idolized. "It is. By the rules we believe her to be eligible."

"Then you will so record that in the minutes," said Carter. "I want you to know I appreciate the staff's position. If the board turns her down, you will have to deal not only with Irene Johnson's resentment, but that of the whole population who will feel that we did not play by the rules. It will be further evidence to them of the perfidy of officialdom."

He tugged thoughtfully on his prominent ear lobes.

"On the other hand, I draw my pay from the great state of Louisiana to exercise my conscience and to try to protect folks. And, though I'm sure I don't understand what the hell puttin' little marks on a piece of paper has to do with anything, Doc Vernon here's all hot and bothered 'bout it. I trust my own instincts. I guess I've worked with the ol' doc here long enough, I'm gonna trust hers."

The room fell silent.

"Randall," Carter directed. "You will record in the minutes that Mr. Arthur de Lavier moved that Irene Johnson be granted parole. That motion died for a second. This case will be reviewed again in eighteen months."

"Can't we shorten the time for review?" Randall protested.

"Eighteen more months, Warden," said the man in the blue suit. "I believe that completes our agenda. What do you have for us for lunch, Randall?"

Later that spring, on a bright sunny morning two thousand miles away in Lynnwood, Washington, Terry Barnes walked into Parker's Wide World of Sewing.

To the right of the entrance three rows of sewing machines were lined up like school desks. The sole person in sight was a young man seated at one of the machines, assembling several patches of a heavy material.

"Is Mr. Parker here?" Terry asked.

"Yes." He motioned to the rear of the store intent on his task. The gray-haired, portly man Terry had met in Shelton came out of a glass-partitioned office.

"Terry," he called. "Come on back."

Terry and Mr. Parker went into the office. "I want to thank you again for the job, Mr. Parker. I was sure ready to get out of there."

Parker smiled. "I'm glad you made it here, Terry. I admit it went through my mind that you might jump parole when you hit the streets."

"Well, I didn't," Barnes said soberly. "But the thought that did go through my mind was, what the hell do I know about sewing machines?"

"Nothing. Now. But you're going to learn. You'll button hole, zigzag, hemstitch, oh you'll do it all. Thing you got to understand, Terry, is that you are not gonna be in the sewing machine business. You're gonna be in the business of selling. And I think you know lots about that."

Terry looked dubious.

"Selling. That's what you've been doing all your life, Terry. Selling."

"I thought I'd just be delivering stuff or repairing stuff. What do I know about selling?"

"What were you in Shelton for? Peddling ass. Right?"

Terry said nothing, assuming the reluctance of ex-cons to discuss the actions that sent them to prison.

"Right," Parker affirmed. "Well, you won't be peddling ass here. And sex with the customers is forbidden. Forbidden. But sex *appeal* definitely is *not* forbidden."

Terry's blank look communicated incomprehension.

"Look. Here's my theory. You have some innate sexual attractiveness. Some guys have it. Most don't. The women will feel it, and you will learn to shift that personal appeal to Parker's sewing machines."

Terry shook his head. "To sewing machines?"

"Sure. It'll work. It'll work. First you gotta learn something about sewing machines. Meg will be in about ten o'clock. She'll teach you everything you need to know."

Parker fished in his billfold for a ten-dollar bill. "Go have some breakfast. Be back at ten. Be prepared to work until five or six. Practice, practice, practice."

Terry sat there. Confused.

"Go on. It'll all come clear after while. We'll talk."

Terry got up. Still confused but aware that he was being dismissed.

Parker looked up. Unsmiling. He gave Terry the primordial look of the leader of the pack. "Oh. And Terry," he said steadily. "Don't fuck with me. I've seen it all. I can smell it. Just remember. I *will* take care of you, but you never fuck me in any way. Ever. Don't even think about it."

Parker waved his hand and reached for the phone, turning his attention to other aspects of Parker's Wide World of Sewing.

Subdued, Terry left Parker's office. Sewing machines. Sex appeal. Selling. Thoughts of Reeney Johnson and Mavis Jackson were absent from his mind.

Einar Torgeson had returned to his state job immediately after Turner took office. No one had replaced him, and the Human Rights Commission's workload had reached monumental proportions. By the following spring, over a year and a half after Sherman Falkes death, Einar was finally able to take a vacation. Shortly after his return, an announcement ran in the *Olympia News* under the weekly listing of marriage licenses:

Einar Torgeson, majority, Olympia, Washington, Marjorie Cross, majority, Wichita Kansas....

About the Author

WRITING UNDER THE ASSUMED NAME "Bruce Edwards," the author of *Andros Draws the Line* here presents the first in an unflinching series of semi-autobiographical explorations into the flawed core of the Emerald City. A lifetime observing the inner workings of officialdom has convinced him that the boldest perps hold the highest ranks, and that the badge conceals as much as—if not more than—it reflects. Such insights are unwelcome to say the least in certain powerful circles.

Early in his career, Edwards negotiated research contracts with the Air Force at the now-notorious Hanford Nuclear Facility in Eastern Washington. It was here he began to realize that the true toxins threatening social stability were embedded within the ever-mutating, proliferating government agencies themselves, not in the hellish concrete catacombs of Hanford. It was here his sense of indignation fermented.

In recent years Edwards has kept a low profile, practicing law in the Pacific Northwest and staying under the radar. As a Deputy Prosecuting Attorney in Washington State, Edwards attended endless court arraignments, where he encountered drunks, whores, petty crooks, dopers, dealers, sociopaths, stalkers, and wife beaters. And these were his *colleagues*.

He also recalls legions of unlucky citizens, detained by the police, being paraded past judges who dictated the terms of their release from jail well before they ever went to trial. These encounters revealed to him the active ensnarement of countless members of society, and their resulting rage at—or capitulation to—the scheming forces that determined their destiny.

Bruce Edwards is determined to become the mouthpiece of the marginalized before his own voice is stilled.

About the Illustrator

HEIDELBERG-BORN NICOLE SCHNELL credits her workaholic nature—and subsequent 90 days of compiled vacation—for her decision to hop the Atlantic in the late 1990s. During her nearly 20 years as a graphic designer and art director for agencies throughout Germany, Nicole has worked on international brands such as Mercedes-Benz, IBM and Camel. For those clients she boasts numerous awards, including several from the International Business Branding Network and EFFI. Today, Nicole owns and operates Schnell Creative Group, an integrated marketing services agency that she founded in November 2001. When she's available, Nicole also provides custom illustrations, such as those gracing *Andros Draws the Line*, for a wide variety of projects.

You can reach Nicole at *nschnell@qwest.net*.

About the Cover Artist

FEW ARTISTS HAVE GONE from Astroturf to canvas quite like Peter X O'Brien. After a successful college and professional football career, Peter returned to his lifelong love of drawing and painting. Today, he works from his Lake Oswego, Oregon studio, where he has created recognized commercial works for the likes of Synergy Financial, Lexus, and the University of Wisconsin. In addition, his personal work resides in private collections throughout the United States and Europe. Peter X O'Brien is available for commissioned works—such as the cover art for the book in hand—and he can be reached at (503) 638-6742.